An Innocent Affair

An Innocent Affair

by

Ann Hulme

*Gloria and David,
With my love
                Ann
                    03:XI:03*

Published by:
Wessex Arts
Unit 5
89 West Street
Bere Regis
Wareham
Dorset
BH20 7HH
Tel: 01929 472371

© Copyright 2003
Ann Hulme

The right of Ann Hulme to be identified as the author of this work has been asserted by her in accordance with the Copyright, Designs and Patents Act 1988.

All Rights Reserved
No reproduction, copy or transmission of this publication may be made without written permission.
No paragraph of this publication may be reproduced, copied or transmitted save with the written permission or in accordance with the provisions of the Copyright Act 1956 (as amended). Any person who does any unauthorised act in relation to this publication may be liable to criminal prosecution and civil claims for damage.

First published in 2003

ISBN: 0-9545858-0-1

Printed by:
ProPrint
Riverside Cottages
Old Great North Road
Stibbington
Cambs. PE8 6LR

DEDICATION

For Paul and Tim and the children of Chris whose spirit lives on in those he loved.

ACKNOWLEDGEMENTS

My thanks to Anna Haycraft (Alice Thomas Ellis) and Shelley Weiner for their encouragement; to Glennis Morrey for typing my manuscript and acting as a reader; Kate Pybus for her constructive criticism, and my editor Rachael Rootham who steered me to conclusion.

INTRODUCTION

The opening line 'Faith died at the funeral of a complete stranger' sets the scene for the whole story. It is Charles Jefferson's funeral and he has died from anaphylactic shock following bee stings. Faith Green, from Ludlow, reads his obituary in 'The Telegraph' and attends the funeral on an impulsive whim and a bet decided by two bees. They never met. As the service in Woodstock church begins Faith dies of a heart attack. The Greens and the Jeffersons are thrown together through bizarre circumstances.

The time span of the novel is six months and it is set in the early 1990's. It is a psychological mystery, rather than a who dunnit, which explores and stretches to the limits human emotions and frailties.

'The Truth shall make you free' John 8: verse 32

CONTENTS

Chapter One	1
Chapter Two	17
Chapter Three	28
Chapter Four	35
Chapter Five	45
Chapter Six	63
Chapter Seven	73
Chapter Eight	84
Chapter Nine	103
Chapter Ten	120
Chapter Eleven	131
Chapter Twelve	149
Chapter Thirteen	163
Chapter Fourteen	176
Chapter Fifteen	185

AN INNOCENT AFFAIR

CHAPTER 1

Faith died at the funeral of a complete stranger.

*****

Faith put down the Daily Telegraph with a sigh and took off her reading glasses. The paper was still open at the obituaries. She had just read of the untimely death of a Professor Jefferson. There was a third of a page of academic and medical distinctions beneath his photograph. Like her he was forty-seven; unlike her he was at the peak of a distinguished career, a specialist in tropical diseases.

What had really caught Faith's eye was his unseemly demise. He died from bee stings 'which caused anaphylactic shock from which he could not be resuscitated.' The bees were a swarm from his own hives. Much as he loved bees it did seem an ironic way to die.

She went into the lean-to conservatory, which led off the kitchen, to see how her own bees were faring. She had found two lying inert on the path that day and placed them, by the open window, on dampened sugar lumps. She'd revived scores of bees in this way over the years. She thought again about Professor Jefferson, wondered whether he had been rushed to hospital surrounded by hi-tech equipment. Her limited experience of hospitals came from visiting or watching 'Casualty' on T.V.

Her bee nearer the pink geraniums thrust his long proboscis into the life-giving sugar syrup. The other one was whirring its wings, very gently, as if warming up ready for takeoff. Faith was pleased to think these two little lives might be saved through such little effort on her part.

She made some coffee and returned to the open newspaper reflecting on the transience of life and its slender thread. She read about Professor Jefferson's eminence more carefully this time. From his scholarship to Harrow, up to Cambridge, University College Hospital, to his fellowship of Wadham College, Oxford – a steady ascension. There were lists of honours from well-known hospitals and medical institutes, both at home and abroad, as well as titles of his books on rare tropical diseases. It made impressive reading.

He looked a characterful, kindly man from the photograph upon which Faith had, inadvertently, left a ring of coffee stain: very attractive too. He was evidently a loved family man and a popular lay-preacher at his parish church in Woodstock. Listed among his hobbies was bee keeping.

She put down the paper again, wondering about this fine God-fearing man, who had been in contact with some of the rarest exotic tropical diseases, being wiped out by stings from his own bees. It seemed so unfair, but life wasn't fair was it?

She wondered about his shocked wife and family as she looked in the deaths column and read – 'The funeral service will be held at St Mary Magdalene Church, Woodstock, Oxfordshire, at 11 am on Tuesday, 15th June, 1993. Family flowers only please. If desired, donations in lieu to your nearest Hospice. A service of thanksgiving will be held in London on a date to be announced later.'

Faith suddenly decided, to her own surprise, to go to the funeral service. She had always wanted to see Blenheim Palace, and knew that the church at Woodstock had a Norman south door and a contrasting eighteenth century tower. She wondered why she had this impulsive urge. She, always so predictable, reliable and sensible – she'd heard it said so many times and knew it was true. But who knows what the future holds, best to do things while you can.

She decided to gamble on her decision and let her bees decide. If both of the bees in the conservatory recovered sufficiently to fly away she'd go, if not she wouldn't. What a ridiculous way to opt for anything, but no worse than tossing a coin and more appropriate for bees to be the deciding factor.

Both bees had vanished leaving sticky, sugary puddles on the faded green plant staging. Faith sang with delight – 'I talk to the bees and they have listened to me…' it went well to the tune of 'I Talk to the Trees.'

She felt absurdly excited at the prospect of a unique day out. Usually she painted on Thursdays, and had planned to finish a watercolour riverscape, but that would keep. This Thursday was going to be different, her private indulgence. She must get a film for her camera.

Faith did not think it wise to mention it to her husband. David was a dear, but extremely logical at all times and would think her quite mad. She could imagine him talking her out of such a hare-brained scheme with a diatribe about his ideas of menopausal women. 'Mind over matter, my love, mind over matter' was his stock response to women's problems. She loved him but was frequently irritated by his narrow-mindedness and lack of imagination.

So she finished off a letter to her oldest friend, now living in Melbourne, and left it ready to post on top of a pile of library books.

*****

Faith arrived at the church at eleven minutes to eleven after a most frustrating morning. David normally left for work at precisely 8.15 a.m. Today he seemed to dawdle over the newspaper and take an inordinately long time in the lavatory. She kept looking at her watch and willing him to hurry. She drove him to the station every morning, for the 8.37 train to Hereford, and never before had to worry about the possibility of him missing it.

'Procrastination and unpunctuality are thieves of time' was one of David's favourite sayings. Their son, Alex, used to wince every time it was said in days gone by. Faith smiled as she thought how she and Alex had silent giggles made up entirely from eye contact. She missed Alex's company more and more.

Outside Ludlow station they kissed good-bye and, as always, wished each other a good day. Faith had worried that David might comment on her smart appearance; now she felt rather cross that he hadn't even noticed.

She made good time on the cross-country journey, picking up the A44 at Leominster. It was half past ten when she parked the car in front of The Feathers Hotel so she just had time to tidy herself up and have a quick coffee before walking briskly to the church. She hummed to herself feeling almost as if she was on holiday as she walked along the street admiring its mellow stone houses.

People were walking ahead of her in a steady stream, all well dressed – some elegant and others more country. Faith felt good in her black and white checked, Chanel style suit; she rarely gave it an outing these days and it was ideal for the sunny but cool morning.

As she reached the church porch she panicked realising that names were being taken. She told herself to calm down, after all there's no law against attending a funeral even if you don't know the deceased. She suppressed a giggle and urge to say 'guest of the bridegroom' as she drew level with an officious-looking, tweedy woman with thick tortoise-shell spectacles and huge yellow teeth.

'Name, address, relationship or representation' she said, gnashing the ill-fitting teeth together and waving her pen.

'Faith Green from Ludlow, Shropshire.' A sidesman gave her a printed service sheet and she walked to the back of the left side aisle not wanting to be obtrusive. The pews were angled and contained richly embroidered kneelers in glowing colours. She had difficulty in finding a place to sit until a couple shuffled up and made room for her. The order of service was simple and the organist was playing Elgar's 'Nimrod' rather well.

Faith felt a little faint; her heart was racing. This was the third time recently she'd had palpitations and shortage of breath, for no apparent reason. The packed church suddenly seemed hot and airless.

The congregation rose but she didn't see the cortège pass as waves of nausea swept over her. She tried to stand up but the faintness became worse and she broke out into a cold sweat, feeling very sick. She sank back on to the hard pew. For a second she wondered what people must be thinking and the woman next to her said 'Are you all right?'

Before Faith could reply a crushingly acute pain constricted her chest, squashing the breath out of her, as she collapsed on to the floor. Faces, distant voices, terrible difficulty in breathing, excruciating pain and then nothing...

Two doctors came swiftly to her aid from a nearby pew. The family party of mourners were momentarily disturbed by the commotion but the service continued.

David was tired as he walked out of Ludlow station and irritated when he couldn't see the white Fiesta. As he looked at his watch he was confronted by a uniformed policeman. 'Excuse me sir, but I'm looking for a Mr David Green.'

'Yes officer, I am David Green. How can I help you?'

'I am Sergeant Owen sir, and I've been asked by the Oxford force to…' the sergeant hesitated and started again. 'It is my sad duty to inform you sir, that your wife, Mrs Faith Green, was taken ill with a…' David looked at the officer in disbelief. 'There must be some mistake. Faith's here in Ludlow' he said, uneasily, praying that the car would come down the hill into the station park, 'she'll be here any minute. Never usually late…'

The sergeant waited patiently, watching David's reactions. 'Has there been an accident sergeant, we don't know anyone in Oxfordshire.' Still the sergeant waited quietly; the colour suddenly drained from David's face and he felt his legs shaking.

'I'm afraid sir, the news is bad. No there has not been an accident, but your wife collapsed in a Woodstock church just as the funeral service began.'

'Funeral, what funeral?'

'She had immediate medical attention sir, but…' David interrupted again 'Well where is she now?'

Her body was taken to the John Radcliffe Hospital and they would like you to get over there as soon as possible.' The sergeant exhaled loudly; he never found it easy to break the news of a fatality. 'We tried to reach you earlier sir, but you were out of the office.' He handed David a sheet of paper. 'This is the number of the hospital.'

David leant heavily on the station fence, trying to take in what was being said. 'You don't mean she's dead' he said at last, hearing a voice talking that didn't sound like his at all.

'I regret sir, that is the case. Would you like me to drive you home Mr Green, I have a car waiting. You could ring more easily from there.' In a complete daze David was driven home by the sergeant and a young constable. He didn't have to give them his address as they drove directly to his house in Broad Street.

The house looked as normal, apart from the twitching curtains of the Morgan's next door. Tabitha, their large tabby cat, rubbed against David's legs as he unlocked the front door, surprised at being ignored. She was well loved and used to plenty of attention. The two policemen stroked her and then the constable left on foot.

Sergeant Owen sat reading the paper whilst David rang the John Radcliffe Hospital. When he heard David saying he hadn't the use of a car the sergeant mimed that he would drive him there.

'It can easily be arranged Mr Green. In fact I go off duty at 7 p.m. and will be pleased to drive you there if you've no family car nearby.' David accepted gratefully, and decided not to ring Alex until he'd seen Faith. He still couldn't take in what had happened and hoped there had been some mistake in identity.

It was almost dusk when they reached Oxford. David vaguely recalled endless corridors and unfamiliar faces. He was shown into an office where an attractive young woman offered him a seat and ordered coffee and biscuits. She told him that Faith had been attended by their senior cardiologist and a consultant physician who were at the church.

'She died almost immediately and would have known little about it, I do assure you Mr Green.'

'What was the cause of her death? She hasn't been ill or anything.'

'We shall have to wait for the post-mortem report, but it appears she suffered a massive heart attack.' Mrs Peabody replied.

David shuddered at the talk of a post-mortem and the thought of them mutilating his wife's body. Faith, who'd hardly had a day's illness in her adult life although, he remembered, she'd had rheumatic fever as a child. She was always at the station to meet him – it was like a terrible dream. He realised that Mrs Peabody was holding the door open for him and seemed to be expecting him to say something.

'Would you like your friend to come with you to identify the body Mr Green?'

Friend, what friend, he thought and then understood she meant Sergeant Owen. More corridors and across a sort of courtyard into the mortuary. A white coated boy, who looked no older than Alex, led him to an examination table. He pulled back the sheet and David thought he was going to faint. He swallowed hard several times, although his throat was like cotton wool, and said weakly 'Yes, that is my wife.'

She looked so normal that he was compelled to touch her to be sure she was really dead. He was instantly repelled by the sensation and Sergeant Owen grasped his arm firmly and steered him into another office. David signed two papers, without even reading them, as he was shown where his signature was required.

As they came out into the fresh air, away from those fearful, clinical smells, a clock struck 10 o'clock.

Bryn Owen was more of a friend than an off-duty policeman by the time they reached Ludlow. They had to stop the car several times as David felt sick. It was, for the most part, a silent journey; both men were tired and David was in shock. He felt numb and scarcely noticed the return journey apart from glimpsing an owl, sitting on a telegraph pole, caught in the beam of the headlights near Evesham.

Broad Street was quiet when they arrived home. Tabitha demanded to be fed and David passed Bryn a tin of Katkins and a dish.

'Um. Excuse me, but I will have to get home to the wife now' he said, putting Tabitha's dish on the floor.

'Oh, of course; terribly sorry; I don't seem to be registering properly. You have been most kind Officer, Bryn, I mean. I don't know what I'd have done without you. What do I owe you for the petrol?'

'Think nothing of it. I'm sure you'd do the same for me in an emergency. It was an extension of my duty. We like to give a good service in Ludlow – not like your big cities here, is it?'

He leant out of his car window. 'Better let your family know hadn't you, sir' he said falling back into his official role. With a friendly wave he drove away. David stood watching the car disappear, as if transfixed, under the arch down the Lower Broad Street. How thrilled Faith was when they'd moved to this little Georgian house sandwiched between two much grander ones. Three youths, jostling one another, bounced noisily down the middle of the road and brought him back to reality.

David closed the door, and with it the world, behind him. He had been trying not to think about Alex and the awful business of breaking the news to him. He started to feel angry with Faith. What did she do this for? Why was she at that funeral so far away? She was all right this morning, how could she be dead?

It had come at a bad time for him. He was hoping for promotion at work and they had booked a holiday abroad for the first time since their honeymoon. She had always been too close to Alex and he was aware that he was jealous of his son. Many disjointed thoughts raced through his mind and none of them seemed to make any sense.

Suddenly he was overcome by emotion – a mixture of shame, anger and exhaustion. He poured himself a stiff brandy and dialled Alex's number. It was after midnight and there was no reply. David was furious. 'Never there when you want him; probably out gallivanting with students without a thought for his parents as usual.' He realised, with a start, he was talking to himself. Tabitha had gone to sleep, curled up on Faith's armchair. 'Even you bloody well preferred her' he said to the cat peevishly as he stumbled up the stairs.

The trauma of the day and the brandy were conniving. Not bothering to wash or clean his teeth he tumbled into bed, half dressed, and fell into an immediate deep sleep.

At Oriel Manor Charles' son Sam said goodbye to the last of the peripheral family and they all breathed a sigh of relief. Elizabeth flung off her court shoes and flopped wearily into her favourite chair. She looked especially beautiful, in a fragile sort of way, in her charcoal grey coat-dress over a white Swiss embroidered lawn blouse. Her fair hair was a little ruffled and her navy blue eyes had dark shadows under them. She had a fine bone structure and sensitive, soft skin. Charles had always been proud of her striking figure and natural style. She had done her best today to look good for his last big occasion but the strain was beginning to show. She longed to be on her own.

'How about a G and T Ma?' said her daughter Rachel, and brought her a glass without waiting for an answer. The ice clinked reassuringly. The two aunts sitting bolt upright on the sofa, sniffed disapprovingly and firmly declined Rachel's offer. She passed them a dish of bon-bons upon which they pounced eagerly.

Aunt Eleanor said, with a mauve sugared almond clicking against her teeth, 'Well it all went off very well Elizabeth. It was a lovely service and I'm sure everyone enjoyed it.'

Her sister, Sybil, nudged her so sharply with her elbow that she swallowed the nut and started to choke. Sam tapped her back firmly and she stopped coughing and wiped her eyes. He looked at his mother but she didn't seem upset by Aunt Eleanor's thoughtless comment. She hardly seemed aware of it.

'Yes,' Elizabeth said, 'it was a beautiful service just as Charles would have liked it. The church looked packed, but he had so many friends. It was a pity that woman who fainted made such a commotion. I can't think why an ambulance was called.'

'It wasn't her fault Ma. She didn't just faint.' Sam hesitated, trying to pick his words carefully. 'I'm afraid she died.'

Elizabeth started, spilling her drink. 'Died, oh dear, how dreadful' she mopped up her skirt with a fresh linen hanky. 'Who was she?'

'No one seems to know really, a Mrs Faith Green. She came from Ludlow,' he replied.

The aunts were all a twitter, eyes gleaming with interest.

'Fancy dying at a funeral, what a strange way to carry on,' said Sybil.

'Was she old?' Elizabeth asked.

'No, in her fifties Dr. Inman thought.'

'At least the church was full of doctors' Elizabeth observed wryly.

Rachel came in from the kitchen where she had been supervising the washing up and clearing away of food from the buffet. 'Mrs Tickle and Mary are going now and want to know if they should both come in tomorrow Ma.'

'Whatever you think best dear.' Elizabeth couldn't even think about tomorrow, she hadn't thought past the funeral day at all. She looked at Rachel. She looked pale and drawn but it was such a relief to see her after years of separation from the family. She must be feeling her father's death terribly having not seen him for nearly three years. Where did we go wrong with Rachel? I must spend some time with her tomorrow. I'm so glad that she's come home. Elizabeth had dreaded the thought that she might not. She was sickened by the aunts but at least they'd be gone next day.

'Ive always enjoyed a good funeral,' said Eleanor graunching another sweet, 'far better than weddings nowadays. It's the only time we get together and catch up on all the news. The other family are such a nuisance at weddings and...'

As they wittered on Elizabeth walked out on to the terrace still in her stockinged feet. It was warmer now than it had been all day. The wind had dropped and the air hung still. She leant against the stone wall and the evening scent of honeysuckle and Albertine roses was heady. How often they had stood here together watching the bees make the most of the fading sunlight. Charles loved his bees but at the moment she felt murderous towards them. It was a fleeting anger. Anything was better than listening to Sybil and Eleanor relishing the situation with such gusto. It was them that she hated, not the bees. Through the open french windows she caught the word 'widowhood' and she shuddered. She'd always thought widow an ugly word and now she supposed she was to be saddled with it. She sat on the sun warmed steps and listened to them trying to decide how much money Charles would leave and to whom. Oh God, why is it that with families it always comes back to money?

Eleanor and Sybil thought they were on their own. They didn't realise that Elizabeth could hear from the garden or that Rachel was curled up, with Tobermory purring on her knee, on the window seat in the alcove.

'She hasn't been home for years you know. Used to be a pretty little girl but was always defiant.'

'Is she a hippie or what?'

'New age I think they call it. Never had the boy's nice ways did she?'

Rachel fumed silently, torn between appearing in order to embarrass them, and hearing more. She remembered how every Christmas they used to give her camel coloured knitted gloves, every bloody year the same. Sam always had a huge selection box of chocolates and sweets. Expecting me to be eternally grateful for ghastly, itchy, bloody gloves; the shrivelled up old bags.

They went on gossiping blissfully unaware of the anger they were provoking.

'You'd think Charlotte would be here wouldn't you Sybil? Her only child after all. What sort of mother could do that?'

'She didn't attend Herbert's funeral either.'

'But her own child is even worse. Something very odd about Charlotte isn't there?'

Rachel wondered why Grandma wasn't there and Elizabeth was shocked by her decision not to come. Elizabeth crushed some lavender in her hand savouring the smell which always reminded her of her own grandmother. Suddenly she felt drained and as if she could sleep. She hadn't slept for more than an hour at a time since Charles died. She crept round the house, well away from the windows, and in through the back door. She scribbled a note 'Gone to bed darlings – I feel I can sleep. Forgive me for disappearing.

Goodnight and thank you for everything' and left it propped up on the hall table. She patted and hugged the two black labradors and kissed them goodnight. Their tails thumped rhythmically.

Elizabeth clung to the banister rail as her stockinged feet slipped a little on the polished oak stairs. She closed their bedroom door, flung off her clothes and went quickly into the bathroom. As she slithered into her side of the bed she pulled Charles' pillow lengthways beside her and fell asleep feeling as if her head was on his shoulder.

The clock in the hall struck 9 o'clock.

Rachel hitched a lift to Oxford and caught the last train back to London. She was full of guilt and anger and grief but couldn't stay in the house another minute.

Alex woke up with a start. The telephone was ringing in the hall. He looked blearily at his radio alarm and it was almost 7.00 a.m. He hoped one of the other students would answer it but the bell kept on ringing. He swung out of bed and it stopped as he opened the door.

The sun streamed through the window as he drew back one curtain. The birds were singing and there was hardly a cloud in the post-card blue sky. He ought to get on with an essay but instead he lay back on the bed thinking how he was enjoying his life in Staffordshire. When people thought of the University of Keele they tended to think of the Potteries and grime and industry like it was in Arnold Bennett's time.

Alex liked Stoke-on-Trent, with its six towns merging one into another imperceptibly, because there was plenty going on and the 'Potters' such friendly, warm people. There was none of the reserve of South Shropshire folk, although he loved his roots and the miles of unspoilt countryside. North Staffordshire has some fine scenery and he was out on his mountain bike whenever possible. His day dreams were interrupted by the 'phone and he was quickly out of bed to answer it.

'That you, Alex?'

'Yes, Dad. Was it you that rang before?' Whatever could he want at this hour?

'If you heard it, why the hell didn't you answer it? I've been trying to get you since last night.'

'Oh well we all went to...'

'Never mind all that,' David interrupted, 'this is serious. It's about your mother.' There was a strange urgency in his father's tone as he went on, 'Alex, my boy, I've some bad news for you. I'm afraid your mother died suddenly yesterday. They think it was a heart attack. She didn't suffer.'

The silence that followed was so long that David felt alarmed. "Are you still there, Alex?'

'Yes,' he said in a strangled voice, choked with emotion 'I just can't seem to take it in. What happened? Were you with her?' Alex had slumped onto the floor looking ashen and much older than his twenty years. The knuckles of his left hand glared whitely as he gripped the receiver. Tears coursed hotly down his cheeks although he was shivering violently. Not Mum, not dead, she couldn't be...

'I don't know more than what the police and hospital told me. She died in Woodstock.'

'Where?' Alex gasped, hardly believing what he was hearing.

'Woodstock, in the church, at a funeral.'

'Where is Woodstock and whose funeral was it? Why weren't you there?'

'Woodstock is near Oxford. I don't know why she was at the funeral. Apparently it was some well known doctor professor fellow.'

'I'll come home right away.'

'That would be best. I can't fetch you as I don't know where she left the car. I shall have to get on to the police about it.'

Alex listened, totally bemused and numb.

'I'll be back as soon as I can. I've got my front door key. It'll probably be early afternoon.' He was struggling to make his mind function.

'Right then, son, see you later on' and the 'phone clicked off.

Alex was some minutes before he realised he was still holding the receiver as if paralysed. Mum, dead...he couldn't believe it.

He pulled on his jeans and rummaged in a drawer for a jersey to put over his sweat shirt. He was icy cold and could not stop shivering. He didn't feel anything except this overwhelming coldness. The kettle boiled and he clasped a mug of steaming coffee with both his shaking hands.

The hot drink pulled him together slightly although he kept feeling rather sick. He decided to pack as quickly and quietly as he could. With a bit of luck he wouldn't disturb Ian or Sean. He couldn't face talking to anyone. He'd leave them a note and ask them to notify his course tutors and friends.

Although he walked briskly to the bus station at Newcastle-under-Lyme he was still numb and cold. He waited for the X64 Shrewsbury bus which left at 9.30. Once on the bus he felt a surge of anger towards the other passengers, greeting the driver cheerily and talking and laughing. He was outraged to think his mother was dead and everything was going on as if nothing had happened.

The bus filled up at Ashley and Loggerheads with women going to Market Drayton. Wednesday was evidently market day. They all seemed to know one another and chattered incessantly; fat women in floral frocks. They piled off with their baskets, shopping trolleys and push-chairs in Market Drayton, exchanging familiar banter with the driver. The time dragged horribly, another hour to Shrewsbury but few people got on and Alex reached the station on time at 11.05. The train for Ludlow left ten minutes later and he was soon within sight of his beloved Shropshire hills. The Longmynd stretched away to the right, the clear sunlight highlighting the countless white woolly dots of distant, grazing sheep. The many shades of green only broken by a blaze of furze and broom and laburnum.

Only now did he start to think about his father and the dreadful business of arriving home. The little sprinter train lurched its single coach out of Craven Arms. In minutes he alighted with heavy heart and shaking knees at Ludlow. The sick feeling returned as he walked up the steps from platform 2 to cross over the passenger bridge. The familiar old church tower stood high beyond the livestock market and lower buildings.

He walked fast avoiding the main streets not wanting to meet anyone he knew.

'Hello Alex. What are you doing home? Aren't you speaking to me this morning then?'

'Oh, good morning Mrs Hemmings, I'm sorry I didn't see you there.'

'You was in such a rush, I expect you'd some young lass you was thinkin' about. What it is to be young' she began, easing her heavy basket to her other arm, 'I remember when I was…'

'I'm sorry to interrupt, Mrs Hemmings, but I must dash. I've got an urgent appointment and I'm late.' He couldn't bring himself to explain about his mother and she obviously didn't know.

'On your way, love. I 'ope she's worth it' cackled Mrs Hemmings with a big wink of her watery left eye.

Again Alex felt a surge of revulsion at the normality of everything. He had not experienced close death before and was sickened by the light hearted way life went on as if nothing had happened.

When he reached Broad Street the house was in shadow and managed to look dead somehow. He thought how thrilled Faith was when they first moved into the Georgian elegance of Broad Street. She loved her home. Now it was just a house as Alex turned his key in the lock, ringing the bell simultaneously so as not to startle his father.

The house was empty apart from Tabitha who purred a welcome greeting with her tail held high. Alex hardly noticed her as he reached down and picked up the mail and the Daily Telegraph. Two letters were addressed to Faith and Alex felt sick again. David must have gone out early and so Alex yielded to Tabitha's pleadings for food. He made himself eat a Marmite sandwich, realising he'd eaten nothing since the day before and was feeling light-headed.

He left his bag in the hall, partly so his father would see it as he came in, and also because he couldn't face going upstairs. He crept about the house as if there was someone who mustn't be disturbed. Every sound seemed like an obscenity and time hung heavily.

The back door bell rang but he didn't answer it. From behind the blind he saw it was Doris from next door. She had probably seen him arrive but he couldn't talk to her now. He wished his father would hurry up and yet dreaded meeting him.

There were signs of Faith everywhere and he could distinctly smell her favourite perfume. He'd bought her some for her birthday. Tears prickled his eyes at the memory of her delight.

It was late afternoon when David's key turned in the lock. For the first time in almost a decade they hugged one another spontaneously, each shocked by the haggard look of the other. Alex put the kettle on to boil thankful to have something to do 'Tea or coffee Dad?'

'Coffee please.'

They sat in silence, drinking their coffee, and Alex was surprised to see his father take out a silver hip flask and pour brandy into his coffee. His look was intercepted and David said 'Want some yourself? It's brandy.'

'Er, no thanks. Are you alright?'

It's been one hell of a day. Been to Woodstock to fetch the car. It was at an hotel called 'The Feathers'. Had to go to the hospital to fetch her things.'

'What things?'

'Your mother's clothes, the ones she was wearing.' They both took large gulps of coffee and went silent again. Some petals fell off a deep claret coloured rose, from a vase on the mantlepiece. The silence was such that the sound they made was more like a noise.

Alex picked up the dark velvety petals. 'Mum's favourite – 'Ena Harkness' – and put them carefully into some paper in his wallet.

David didn't seem to notice. He was deep in thought, brows furrowed. 'We shall have to go to Oxford tomorrow to get the death certificate. The post-mortem was today.'

Alex couldn't bear to think about a post-mortem and didn't really want to go with his father tomorrow. He knew he would though. He felt sorry for him – he had suddenly become an old man – but also irritated by his apparent calmness.

The sun was streaming in through the open french window and seemed thoroughly inappropriate for their sombre, grey feelings. The mantlepiece clock ticked noisily, an intrusive reminder that time, like life, moves relentlessly on.

David switched on the T.V. The weather man said tomorrow would be humid and warmer still, with a possibilty of thunder in the afternoon.

'Have you eaten?' asked Alex.

'Yes, I had a very good bar lunch at 'The Feathers',' and went on to describe all he had eaten with obvious relish. 'The Whinchat' Bar opens on to a pleasant, leafy garden. What about you, have you had a meal?'

'I had a Marmite sandwich when I got here mid-day, but don't seem to be hungry somehow.' He was sickened by his father's unaffected appetite.

David took a sideways look at his son and went to examine the contents of the fridge. Tabitha followed hopefully and was rewarded with a saucer of milk. The fridge seemed to be full of milk and he turned the indicator by the front door to zero.

'There's a piece of boiled ham on the bone, two lamb chops, plenty of cheese and an apple crumble' he reported.

Alex had gone past feeling hungry some hours earlier and was nauseated at the prospect of food.

Another rose fell, this time it was a pale pink one. He picked up the petals automatically and they were soon squashed into a transparent, colourless nothingness in his hand – all their texture and beauty gone. Drained of colour and form, all that remained was a delicate smell. Apart from the slight scent it seemed to epitomise his state of mind.

He switched off the television and went into the kitchen where his father passed him a plate of ham, cheese, tomato and granary bread. He ate it hungrily. He could hear his father ringing up the undertaker. Snatches of their conversation reached him, 'arrangements', 'photocopies of the death certificate', 'a green form.' It all seemed so unreal to Alex.

David slumped wearily into his chair. They were both avoiding Faith's chair which Tabitha had thoughfully adopted.

CHAPTER 2

As Sam drove from Leominster into Ludlow he wondered how his father and Faith Green knew one another. It was strange that she had not written to their family or made any contact with the undertaker in Woodstock.

He decided he should represent the Jefferson family at her funeral today to show their respects on behalf of his father. The rest of his family thought it quite unnecessary, although he noticed a sneaking interest by his mother that morning at breakfast. He had telephoned the undertakers in Ludlow, through directory enquiries, as there had been no notice in The Times or Telegraph.

Ludlow was new to him. He had heard about the Shakespearean productions in the Castle grounds in summer from friends who had enjoyed them. He hadn't expected quite such a properous looking little town with obvious attraction for tourists. He could see a church tower, with a hill range behind, but no clear way of how to approach it.

He stopped to ask directions. The first lady was American laden with charm bracelets which were percussive as she waved her arms about. She thought St Lawrence's was the big church they could both see, but she wasn't sure. She suggested he drove into 'The Feathers Hotel' car park and walked from there. The receptionist would be able to help him. 'It's a fine old building, timber framed Tudorbethan. We are staying there until tomorrow.'

She directed him to 'The Feathers'. Five hundred yards later he stopped an old couple, carrying heavy shopping bags, who looked like locals. They suggested he parked his car on a nearby car park as the streets are narrow and difficult round St Lawrence's. They confirmed that it was the big parish church with the tower still visible.

Sam plumped for the hotel and found 'The Feathers' without any difficulty. It was very central and certainly was a splendid example of Tudor architecture. He had plenty of time and ordered coffee to justify using the car park. He started to relax for the first time since his father's death. It was quite a relief to get away from the atmosphere of grief at home, and the endless letter writing, 'phone answering and paperwork sorting. He was curious to discover something of the background of the somewhat bizarre death of Faith Green.

Ludlow was busy with shoppers and tourists as he made his way to the church at 11.45. It must be one of the largest parish churches in England. The only other he'd been into of a similar size was at Lavenham in Suffolk. Sam thought of the weekend house parties he went to in Lavenham with Maria. He would like to get engaged to Maria but she didn't believe in marriage.

Sam sat about six rows back from where pews were reserved for the family. There were cards on the pews asking mourners to write their name and address. He filled his in and represented his mother and sister. He looked at the order of service – not as tasteful in style as that of his father. Interesting mixture of hymns and reading, they seemed to be church goers from the choices. More people were taking their places, arriving mostly in small groups and talking in hushed voices. There were a large number of young people, in jeans and jackets, who seemed to know one another. One of the girls smiled at Sam from the other side of the aisle. She had wispy fair hair and enormous violet coloured eyes, and was wearing a becoming shade of lavender.

Sam looked very like his father; good bone structure, classical features, shiny brown hair, like a well polished conker, and dark brown eyes. He noted the 'violet' girl's neat waist and slim ankles as she stood up.

He was brought up sharply as the coffin passed on the shoulders of four young men. His eyes prickled with suppressed tears, first his father's funeral and now this woman – both in the prime of life, as they say. The family followed and he noticed with interest the tall, rugged good looks of the father and son. The son was supporting a frail old lady. There were not many in the family party – he counted eleven which included the four bearers.

Sam found this carrying on shoulders strangely moving – more so than the wheeled trolley–like biers. The service itself upset him greatly as his grief for his father overwhelmed him. He had been so numbed, and concerned for his mother, at his father's service that he could hardly remember it. Now the weight of it all seemed to descend on him and he felt utterly devastated and terribly tired and lonely. Perhaps it was a mistake to come after all.

The singing was beautiful. The church had excellent acoustics and the congregation knew the hymns well. There was a long address all about Faith's life and how she would be missed in the community. Her talents as a teacher and an artist. Her voluntary work with disabled children. Her tireless fund raising for The Shropshire and Mid Wales Hospice through working in the local charity shop in Ludlow. Her devotion to the church in the six years she had lived in this parish. Faith was described as a model wife and mother and sympathy was offered to David and Alexander in their grief. There was no mention of the circumstances of her death and no clue as to how she knew Charles. All those present were invited to a buffet lunch at the Green's home in Broad Street after the burial.

Suddenly it was all over. The sad cortège passed by and slowly the congregaton followed out into the warmth of the sunlight.

The 'violet' girl smiled at Sam as they waited for the hearse and funeral cars to leave.

'Are you from Keele?' she asked.

'No, I'm from Oxfordshire, from Woodstock.'

'Oh dear, you must know some of her friends there. Alex said he hoped to meet someone from Woodstock because the family still don't know why Faith was at that funeral. Were you there when it happened?'

'Well, er, yes. I'm Sam Jefferson. Actually it was my father's funeral' he said quietly.

She paled visibly. 'Oh heavens, I'm terribly sorry; I'd no idea. How awful for you, first your father and then Faith' she stumbled on with embarrassed sympathy before collecting herself to say 'You are coming to the house for lunch aren't you? Alex and his father will be anxious to meet you.'

'No, I was planning to go straight home' he began.

'Oh please don't, it would help them so much to be able to talk to you. It's been such a shock you see' her voice trailed off and then recovered again 'Look Sam, I'm not going to the cemetery. So why don't we go to 'The Olive Branch' and have a coffee, and then I can show you the way to the house and introduce you to the family. It's only a few minutes walk away.'

Sam found he was only too glad to be led along by this persuasively fascinating girl. Perhaps she could fill in the many puzzling blanks.

'All right then. By the way I still don't know your name.'

'I'm Kate Evans. Lets go to the café.' She thought she must hang on to him and find out as much as possible for Alex.

'The Olive Branch' was an interesting old restaurant cum coffee house in a seventeenth century former inn. It had a welcoming atmosphere and a delicious smell of home baking and fresh coffee. Sam went to the service counter for two coffees. He was amused by a notice on a ceiling beam which he saw as he carried the drinks back to the table where Kate sat. It read 'MIND THE FLOOR BUMP', referring to a slight ramp on the floor. Sam's feet 'read' the gradient at the same time as his head automatically ducked seeing the word bump on a beam.

Kate laughed, 'I was waiting for that. Nearly everyone ducks instead of looking at the floor slope.'

The relaxed friendly atmosphere almost made him forget why they were there. The owners clearly knew Kate well and some witty repartee went back and forth. She seemed to know many of the people having lunch and the smell of cooking made Sam feel hungry.

'I rather wish we were having lunch here, Kate.'

'We nearly shall be. The Greens have ordered their buffet from here so the food will be lovely.' Kate hoped no one would think she had a date with someone new on such a sad occasion.

They both looked at their watches as a clock struck one o'clock and jumped quickly to their feet. They walked a short distance through the old street and turned into Broad Street. Sam was immediately taken with the impressive, elegant layout. The predominantly Georgian town houses, the high stone pavements with steep, cobbled slopes down to the road level. Every so often there were steps for pedestrians to enable them to cross. The imposingly wide street swept downwards to the Broad Gate's fine archway through which the traffic passes. Over the arch of the gate stands a large Georgian house. Beyond are Lower Broad Street and the Ludford Bridge over the river Teme.

Kate explained that the regular layout of the streets dated back to Norman times. She said proudly, 'We think of Ludlow as the capital of The Marches.'

'I'd no idea you were so erudite' Sam teased. He was reluctant to go in and lose Kate's company in a crowd of strangers.

They stopped outside the open door of a small Georgian house sandwiched neatly between two much grander ones.

'Here we are. Come in and I'll introduce you to the Greens.'

She seemed very at home there and introduced him first to David and his mother. Kate explained, carefully and tactfully, Sam's presence and David shook him warmly by the hand and thanked him for coming.

Alex made a bee-line for Kate and they kissed. 'Come and meet Sam Jefferson. He is the son of Professor Jefferson from Woodstock.'

The eyes of the two young men met and then they shook hands and, simultaneously, expressed their mutual condolences. The little house was packed with people and they had overflowed into a walled garden at the back.

Sam found the Green family and their friends extremely friendly. He particularly liked Alex and his paternal grandmother. Kate kept coming over to him making sure he had something to eat, his glass topped up and someone to talk to. He formed the opinion that the local people were uncomplicated and closer to the earth somehow, quite different from the more sophisticated Oxford set that he moved in. Simpler folk and uninhibited with less of the pseudo aristocratic background that he was heartily sick of at home. His family would have scoffed at the paper napkins, referred to as serviettes, and he realised just how artificial and snobbish it all was.

Shortly after 2.30 Sam went in search of David, to say goodbye, and to find the loo. He was directed upstairs to the bathroom but there was such a queue of women squashed along the narrow landing that he decided he would wait until he collected the car from 'The Feathers.'

Coming down the stairs he looked at three water-colour paintings, all riverscapes and clearly by the same artist. His attention was immediately caught by a boat in the second picture. It was a stretch of The Severn he knew well, and the barge was unmistakably his father's. He peered closely in the rather poor light and found he could just read the name 'Oriole' on the bow.

What an extraordinary coincidence. His father bought the 'Oriole' some years ago. It was Charles' relaxing bolt hole away from medics and academics and the ever ringing bells of 'phone and door.

Elizabeth didn't care for boating or fishing and knew her husband needed solitude and change to re-charge his batteries. She understood his needs and encouraged his hobbies.

Whilst Sam was looking at the other paintings Kate came out of the bathroom and the chattering queue moved along.

'Do you like watercolours, Sam?'

'Yes, and I know exactly where the middle one is located.'

'Faith spent most of her free time painting and sold some in the local shops.'

'Do you mean to say that these were painted by Faith?' he asked incredulously.

'Yes, the house is full of them. Don't say anything to David though – it's rather a sore point.'

'Why?'

'Some crazy idea that all arts are a waste of time. He's always been fanatical about the way one spends time. Drives Alex up the wall.'

Sam said his good-byes to the Greens and Kate and walked thoughtfully back to the hotel car park. He no longer noticed the architecture and antique shops. He suddenly felt the loss of Faith. Who was she? Why had she painted the 'Oriole'? How well had she known his father?

David woke up on Sunday morning with a hangover and tried to bury his head in the duvet to dull the resonance of the pealing church bells. Gradually he emerged to discover it was nearly 10 o'clock. Alex was standing by the bed with a steaming mug of tea for him.

'Glad you're having a lie in, Dad. You must be absolutely knackered.'

'A lie in, indeed, I have never had a lie in during my entire life. Time is not for wasting but using profitably.' The effort of this liverish reaction sent a steam-roller crashing through his head. Alex bit his tongue as he put down the mug.

'Thanks for the tea, son,' he added more civily just as Alex accidentally banged the door to.

'Must you always bang doors? What do you think the knobs are for?' followed more characteristically.

Alex went back to the kitchen to his coffee and CD of Whitney Houston. He automatically reduced the volume pre-empting complaints from upstairs. Not a good start, he thought, and wished he was back in Newcastle with his friends.

Tabitha flew down the stairs as David lumbered across to the bathroom tripping over the cat and knocking his head on the door frame.

'Bloody cat – always in the way.'

Alex took this as his cue to go out for a walk by the river before his father appeared. He must try to understand his black mood but didn't relish the prospect of being the whipping boy for the entire day.

He gave Tabitha a saucer of milk in the garden before slipping away quietly as he heard David moving heavily down the stairs. Alex hurried down Broad Street and turned right, out of sight, into Silk Mill Lane where he adjusted his pace. He went left down the cul-de-sac end of Mill Street to the river. He squeezed through the fence and overgrown herbage and shrubs getting thoroughly nettled. He sat on a large stone by the water and rubbed conveniently handy dock leaves on to the nettle stings.

He had always loved this stretch of The Teme with its woody far side of shady and shaded greens. The sunlight came through giving a painterly dappled effect and there were splendid reflections. The air was heady with the strong, sweet smell of elder flowers. He and Faith used to gather them for cooking with gooseberries instead of using sugar. So many happy memories of the times they spent by the river. She didn't feel so far away here as he let his mind wander freely.

The sun was hot and the sound of humming bees murmured over the gently tumbling water. Flies and midges danced over water weeds and reed beds providing swooping swallows with a fast food chain.

Two boys were fishing a hundred yards away reminding him of days gone by when he came down here to catch brownies. He remembered bursting with pride the first time he caught two respectable sized ones, and how delicious they had tasted. No restaurant would ever equal the freshly caught earthy flavour of his prize brownies.

Even David had been pleased. 'Done something useful for once' had been high praise, he recalled. Faith hated gutting fish but had made no fuss and shared his delight.

He noticed he had amassed quite a number of plaited reeds and grasses. As a child he plaited them for his mother who made mats, small baskets and boxes out of them. Without thinking he reached out for three more reeds totally unaware he was doing it. The bulrushes were almost at their best.

For the first time in nearly a fortnight he felt relaxed and able to breathe normally. The tension fell away in the restoring familiarity of the soft countryside dressed overall for mid-summer. He felt close to Faith here but without that dreadful leaden ache of loss.

The sun was beginning to burn his face and arms reminding him it was mid-day and, reluctantly, he started to wend his way home. Home, what did that mean now? He walked back, leaving his plaited reeds to float downstream, through Dinham and Castle Square. The Square was full of visitors to the flea market. Friends greeted him with an awkward mixture of bonhomie and sympathetic restraint.

The sun went in as he reached the door in Broad Street. It was only a passing cloud but Alex felt the gloom as he opened the door.

'Where on earth do you think you've been all morning? There's work to be done, 'phone to be answered, correspondence to deal with, dinner to be cooked...'

'Sorry Dad. I went down to the river below Mill Street and didn't notice the time.'

'Mooning about, wasting time. Don't they teach you anything useful at that University of yours?' He didn't wait for an answer but went on 'There doesn't seem to be anything for lunch apart from potatoes and bacon.'

'We could have a fry up then.'

'A fry up indeed. It may have escaped your notice that today is Sunday, and on Sunday we have a proper dinner not a fry up as you call it.'

'We could have a take-away or I could make an omelette unless you have a better suggestion.'

David agreed readily and realised he didn't know how to make an omelette.

The afternoon was punctuated by a steady stream of callers and the constant making of pots of tea. Alex had to go next door to borrow some milk from the Morgans. He made a note on the kitchen wall slate to get tea-bags, milk, bread, cheese, biscuits and cat food.

David looked at it and said 'I'm surprised your mother wasn't better organised. We never used to run out of stores. I'm beginning to lose faith in everything here.'

Alex winced at his ill chosen words but he didn't seem to notice. Alex didn't like to point out the obvious about no shopping having been done. He'd always been irritated by how hopeless his father was domestically and the way he relied on Faith for everything. She willingly waited on him hand and foot. Whenever Alex commented on it she said she liked looking after the family and anyway it was quicker than having all the fuss.

The 'phone rang and it was Kate. 'Is it all right if I come round tonight? I'll bring some supper and we could have a game of 'Scrabble' or something.'

'That would be great,' he lowered his voice to a whisper, 'It's pretty heavy here with the old man as you can imagine.'

'I thought it might be. Perhaps David needs something to take his mind off things and you, too, of course.' There was a little pause and then she added, rather tentatively, 'Alex?'

'Yes, what's up?'

'The holiday info has arrived. I didn't like to mention it before but we should have sent off our deposits last week.'

'Shit' he said, I'd forgotten all about it. I suppose it'll still be OK for me to go. Don't mention it to Dad until I've had time to broach it myself.'

'We're going to be one short now Max has broken his leg. I was wondering whether your friend, Sam, might like to take his place.'

'Who is my friend Sam?'

'You know, the guy from Oxford who came to the funeral. We talked for a while and he seemed nice. He's interested in France and likes sport generally.'

'Strikes me he's more your friend Sam' Alex said acidly.

'Oh come on, Alex, don't be an air head. He's got a girl called Maria. In any case you've got plenty of girl friends at Keele. Anyway, think about it or suggest someone else. It'll keep the cost down if ten of us go.'

'He did seem a decent sort of chap, but I don't know whether he'd fit in with our lot. I'll ring him shall I?'

'Yes do. I'll come at 7.30 if that's OK. I can usually put your father in a good mood, although the poor man must be devasted.'

'Right on, Kate. See you.'

'Who was that?' asked David.

'Only Kate. She's bringing us some supper round at half past seven.'

'That's very thoughtful of her. Nice girl that, make a good wife. Pity you don't see so much of her now.' David opened the paper and was soon asleep in his chair.

He awoke to sounds of cheerful chatter and clatter in the kitchen and a good smell of onions. Kate came into the living room looking crisply fresh in a sea-green cotton blouse rather spoiled by the inevitable uniform of faded jeans. She was a pretty, vivacious girl, always well mannered and smiling.

'Hello David. I've brought some supper and thought I'd stay and eat with you. At times like this…in a crisis' she faltered trying to find suitable words, 'one seems to nibble bits and pieces and not eat properly.'

'It's most kind of you, Kate, and smells wonderful.'

'French onion soup – hardly seasonal but I know you both like it.'

They sat down to a well-set table and both men discovered they were famished as they floated large islands of croutons melting with cheese. This was followed by tuna with rice and green salads. They finished off a whole treacle tart with cream.

Kate was in her element relishing their obvious enjoyment of the meal and relieved at the release of tension which followed.

Alex helped her to clear away and wash up and they came through to join David with a tray of coffee.

'How about a game of 'Scrabble' or something', Kate suggested.

'Prefer chess or draughts myself' David replied.

'Only two can play those, am I supposed to take a hint?' Kate teased gently.

'No, young lady, I wasn't thinking. Yes, of course I'll join you in a game.'

Alex wished he could humour his father like that. The evening passed quickly and David felt better for making the effort to be pleasant.

It was going dark when Alex walked Kate back home carrying her baskets. He thanked her profusely and they kissed goodnight in the doorway. He felt very close to Kate and began to think about their holiday as he walked home through the quiet streets. He'd give Sam a bell to see if he wanted to come.

CHAPTER 3

Sam's mind kept returning to Faith's painting of his father's boat. How well did they know each other or was it a mere co-incidence? It was a couple of years since Charles' boat had been moored on the Severn for the coarse fishing. It was now at Tewkesbury which was convenient for the Avon and the Severn.

Sam was torn between keeping the boat for sentimental reasons and also as a personal bolt-hole. He wasn't really the boaty sort and wondered whether he could justify the bother and expense. He thought it would be a romantic way of spending a few days with Kate away from prying eyes. She was more and more on his mind and he was looking forward to their holiday in France.

'You seem miles away Sam. Is everything OK?' asked Elizabeth looking up from her crossword.

'Yes I was just thinking about Pa's boat.'
'We might as well sell it. You've never been interested in it, have you?'

'I think I might be.'

'Oh?' Elizabeth looked at him inquiringly. He seemed to have something on his mind.

'I saw a painting of it at the Green's house in Ludlow when I went to Faith's funeral.'

'A painting of the 'Oriole', are you sure?'

'Yes certain. I recognised it at once and the name of the boat is clear on the painting.'

'How peculiar. Why on earth would they want a painting of our boat, are they boating people?'

'No. Faith was an amateur artist and painted riverscapes. Their house is full of them.'

'But why the 'Oriole'?' Elizabeth persisted, now thoroughly curious.

'Just co-incidence I think, but I'll ask Alex.' There followed quite a long silence whilst Elizabeth puzzled over this new information. Sam stared out of the window watching the dogs chasing each other round the garden.

'What's Mr Green like?'

'A boring old fart. You wouldn't like him.'

'You sound very sure dear.'

'I am. He's just not your scene at all.'

'But you seem to get on with them all right. You're going to Ludlow more and more often.'

'That's because of Alex and Kate; they're great.'

Elizabeth thought about this odd business of the boat and whether it might be the key to how Charles knew Faith Green. She'd thought of her as a colleague or ex-student. So she was a painter and knew their boat. She must find out more about Faith.

Sam was teasing Tobermory. He was a patient old cat but couldn't bear his coat stroked the wrong way. Sam was enjoying annoying him and, with a yowl of fury, Tobermory bit his finger.

'You asked for that. Come here to Mama you poor old puss.' Tobermory walked loftily to Elizabeth's chair and jumped on to the back of it into a pool of sunshine. Her mind moved back to Ludlow.

'Why don't you ask Maria for a weekend and invite Alex and Kate? It would do us all good to have some bright company in the house again.'

Sam hesitated and then said 'I think they'd find it all a bit much. They aren't country weekend types, much more casual and informal.'

'Are you suggesting I'm a snob darling?'

'No, but you are used to a different life style.'

'If you can cope, why can't I?'

'It's not you Ma, it's whether they could feel OK here.'

'Well it's up to us to see that they do.' Elizabeth decided it was time she found out a bit more about the Green family.

Sam rang Kate first and was thrilled that she was free and keen to come. With less enthusiasm he rang Alex who readily agreed when he knew Kate was going too. Sam arranged to collect them on Friday evening. Maria said she would drive up late that night from London. She was due at a meeting and rather curt on the 'phone. For once she didn't manage to hurt his feelings.

The weekend was a resounding success. Elizabeth made her guests so welcome and they warmed to her hospitality despite being rather overwhelmed at first by the grandeur of it all.

'Why didn't you tell us you are so posh?' Kate asked as they drove up to Oriel Manor.

'We aren't really, you'll see' Sam assured her.

The time passed quickly. Elizabeth observed with interest the various emotional conflicts that emerged. Alex and Kate were old friends with a romantic link and, likewise Sam and Maria. With every passing hour it was increasingly obvious that Sam and Kate had eyes only for one another. Maria and Alex were not pleased and not attracted to each other in any way.

Elizabeth was relieved that Sam's interest in Maria seemed to be over. She was a single minded, brilliant girl with everything going for her. She was also utterly selfish and ruthless. It was good to see her a little deflated for a change and the experience would be salutary. Elizabeth didn't like hard women and was becoming very sick of feminists. They seem to think they had a right to steam roller their way over people willy nilly.

Alex was rather a different matter. He seemed sensitive and vulnerable. Elizabeth felt deeply for him after the loss of his mother whom he clearly loved. She spoke to Sam about Alex, asking whether Kate wasn't really Alex's girlfriend.

'No Ma, but they are old childhood sweethearts and still very good friends. He's very protective towards Kate and has a very soft spot for her. His current girlfriend is a student at Keele University.'

'Well I do think he's a little jealous dear.'

'Wouldn't you be with a fabulous girl like that' he laughed happily.

The four of them walked the dogs in Blenheim Park after Sunday lunch. They came back full of chatter with the labradors bounding ahead.

Maria had to leave immediately to drive to her office in Muswell Hill prior to flying to Paris for an important working lunch next day. If she had any qualms about Sam they didn't show any more. Maria was in gear for work and the adrenaline was beginning to flow.

After she'd gone Elizabeth said 'If you don't mind I'd like to come with you when you drive to Ludlow. I must start getting out more again.' Sam was surprised but Alex and Kate both seemed pleased.

Alex went up to Woodstock church on his own. It was a mission he dreaded but felt he couldn't leave without seeing where his mother died. He found it strangely soothing sitting quietly in the church. He wondered where she'd sat and exactly what happened.

Walking back he stopped to look at the stocks opposite to the church entrance. A group of youths were fooling about pushing used coke cans through the holes.

Elizabeth was in the drawing room pouring tea when he returned. 'I hope I've not kept you waiting but I've been sitting in the church.'

She smiled understandingly and said 'Not at all. Sam's just gone to look for Kate. I hope she'll be all right; she seems to be spending rather a lot of time in the bathroom.'

Alex laughed. 'I expect she's playing with the perfume sprays and enjoying the luxury of it. We've never seen bathrooms like yours except in magazines. I like the huge piles of towels and books. It's a real pleasure just being in there.'

Elizabeth laughed too. It never occurred to her that they had such interesting bathrooms. Kate and Sam came and sat on the sofa. 'What's so funny?' Sam asked.

'Nothing really' said Elizabeth quickly 'We were just discussing the merits of comfortable bathrooms.'

Kate said 'I've just been sitting in the thick fluffy towels on that lovely big rocking chair and watching the birds through the window. Do I smell nice?'

'It's a bit strong but very sexy' Sam quipped and they all laughed again.

Elizabeth liked Kate and Alex and was keen to meet Alex's father. She hoped he'd be in when they reached Ludlow. More importantly she wanted to see the house where Faith lived and her painting of the 'Oriole'.

They set off after tea. Elizabeth insisted on sitting at the back and Alex got in beside her. Kate hopped into the front seat. She had been very animated all weekend but was rather quiet during the journey. Elizabeth talked to Alex about his work at Keele and future aspirations. They both noticed Sam and Kate were holding hands.

Elizabeth viewed Ludlow with interest. She admired the beautiful sweep of Broad Street as Sam drew up and parked.

'What a splendid, elegant street' she commented, glad to see windows open at the house. She was bursting with curiosity and also a little nervous.

'Yes, isn't it. My mum was thrilled when we found this house. I like it too. Please come and meet Dad.'

They all walked up the old stone steps to the pavement level. Kate said 'I won't come in now, Alex, but I'll see you around. Sam will take me home and then I'll ring you or something.'

'OK. See you then' Alex replied as he fumbled with his door key.

'Thanks so much for a super time Mrs Jefferson. I can't ask you to come and meet my parents as they'll be at church. It's been a fantastic weekend.' Elizabeth shook the offered hand and gave Kate a little hug. 'I've enjoyed it too. Perhaps Sam will bring you again soon.'

Sam and Kate drove off. Alex was holding the door open for Elizabeth and, as she stepped inside, she met an older, even more handsome, replica of Alex.

'Dad, this is Mrs Jefferson, Mrs Jefferson please meet my father, David Green.'

They shook hands formally. If David was surprised he didn't show it. Alex just hoped David wouldn't let him down or say something embarrassing.

'Come and sit down. I'm afraid I'm not very organised these days. Faith always saw to everything in the house. Did you know Faith, Mrs Jefferson?'

'No, I'm sorry that I never met her. Please call me Elizabeth. I don't know how Charles knew your wife but you will appreciate he had such a wide range of friends and colleagues. I'm only sorry that we meet through such sad circumstances.' She found her curiosity mounting.

Alex hovered about uneasily collecting up unwashed beakers and waiting for an opportunity to offer Elizabeth a drink. She was sitting in Faith's chair with Tabitha on her lap. Tabitha was kneading and purring. Elizabeth was torn between her love of animals and trying to stop Tabitha drawing threads and ruining her dress.

She accepted a sherry and David began to warm to her company. Alex left them talking and went to his room.

'How are you managing to cope without your husband? You are so much younger than I expected, if you don't mind me saying so.'

'The family are good to me and I've had Charles' mother staying. But it is lonely even when surrounded by other people. I'm afraid we take so much for granted when life is going well. And what about you David?'

'It came at a very inconvenient time for me. Alex does his best but young people are so selfish and thoughtless aren't they?'

'I find the young refreshingly honest. On the whole they are easier to deal with as long as you share your grief with them. Their self absorbed side is pleasantly distracting and takes me out of myself. My daughter is more difficult.' Elizabeth sighed as she spoke of Rachel.

'Alex doesn't talk to me much, but I suppose I'm not very good at it really. It was Faith who kept the peace. She was always here, a very reliable wife, which made it such a shock.'

'Did you know Charles too?' Elizabeth asked.

'No, I'd never heard of him until that dreadful day when it all happened.'

Elizabeth took a deep breath and said 'Sam tells me you have a picture of Charles' boat that your wife painted. May I see it?'

David looked startled. 'First I've heard of it' he said tetchily and then recovered his manners. 'What sort of boat? As you can see we're littered up with her paintings everywhere. She seemed to be drawn to water. Always painting water. Can't see the attraction myself.'

'I believe it hangs on the stairs' Elizabeth said quietly. 'It's a barge on the river called 'Oriole'. Sam saw it when he came here the day of your dear wife's funeral.'

'Oh that one. Yes I know. I'll get it shall I?'

'Perhaps I could see the others too. I'm very interested in watercolours.'

David led the way and Elizabeth followed him up the badly lit staircase. He leant over her to switch on a light and accidentally brushed against her breast with his arm. It was like an electric shock. He apologised, covered in confusion and noticed how deeply and becomingly she blushed. To Elizabeth's astonishment it was a pleasurable sensation. She hoped he hadn't noticed her reaction.

At that moment the door bell sounded and Alex let Sam in.

'I think they're still upstairs, they'll be down in a minute.'

'Upstairs?' said Sam in surprise.

'Yes, they've gone to look at some of Mum's pictures.'

'Oh, I see' said Sam as Elizabeth emerged looking rather flushed and David, lumbering bear-like behind her carried the painting of the 'Oriole'.

Sam was on a high and also flushed. The conqueror returns, thought Elizabeth. He winked at his mother and she found herself blushing once more, to her great annoyance.

'Isn't it a good picture' Sam said realising he'd somehow come at an awkward moment. Alex was puzzled by the heightened atmoshere which seems to involve everyone except him.

David passed the painting to Elizabeth who sat looking at it for some time. A tear ran down her left cheek at the familiar sight of Charles' beloved boat. She swallowed hard and pulled herself together.

'Do you know when this was painted?' she asked at last.

'There should be a date on the back. Mum always dated her work.'

Elizabeth turned it over to find 9/10/89 in neat figures. 'That was when I was looking after Charlotte in Chelsea after her fall. I was there most of October.' She tried to think back to that particular day.

'I'd like you to have the picture of your boat Elizabeth' David said with a rare spark of generosity. He could see she was very moved and upset.

Elizabeth looked at Alex, who nodded his approval, and then thanked them both profusely. She didn't really want it but felt it would be churlish to refuse when they seemed so eager to give it to her. Also it was the only proof of their association. Proof, proof of what? Her mind was in turmoil.

Sam talked non-stop all the way home. Elizabeth closed her eyes so that she couldn't see the speedometer. Sam drove well but too fast – just like his father. She tried to picture Faith and imagine how she and Charles met. There must be a thread running through the events somewhere but so far it was a complete mystery.

CHAPTER 4

Elizabeth propped herself comfortably against the pillows and poured out another cup of Ceylon tea. It was just beginning to get light and the radio was on.

'The population of a bee-hive have to fly 50,000 miles and visit four million flowers to make just one pound of honey' she was informed by the presenter. She switched to Classic FM and thought about those enormous figures. She tried to visualise four million flowers and marvelled at how they reach these conclusions.

Until Charles' death she had loved the bees and was intelligent enough to realise there was nothing malevolent in their action. Her initial response had been to get rid of them, like a dog that has bitten a child, but she appreciated that it was a tragic sequence of events that would not be solved by petty action. She had started to take an active interest in them again.

Elizabeth had moved into a smaller bedroom which contained the reproduction Queen Anne walnut bedroom suite that she had as a child. It gave her a more secure sense of well being rather than looking at the empty side of a king-sized bed. She missed Charles most at night. She was worried sick about Rachel and now had no one with whom she could discuss her wayward daughter. How upset and mixed up she must be feeling. Sam refused to listen to anything about his sister. He was seething about her disappearance after the funeral.

Today was going to be fairly trying. Elizabeth was still being visited by kindly, well-meaning acquaintances trying to ensure that she wasn't lonely. If only they understood her need to be alone. There were also those that were taking the opportunity of the excuse to nose round Oriel Manor. It seemed so unfair to have to suffer these people at a time like this. Three such women were coming in for morning coffee but at least the occasion would be diluted by Charles' mother's formidable presence. With a bit of luck she would eat these three up in one easy mouthful.

Charlotte Jefferson was a force to be reckoned with at best and a lethal snare for the unwitting and unwary. She was a fine, handsome lady with a real presence. At eighty-five she was as quick and informed as ever and dressed beautifully with impeccable taste.

Elizabeth admired her mother-in-law and they had a good working relationship. She had been shocked when Charlotte did not attend Charles' funeral and insisted on staying alone in her apartment in Oxford. She still couldn't understand it. Elizabeth tried to persuade her to stay with them but Charlotte was adamant. 'Ladies of my generation do not attend funerals. I shall come to stay with you later if you care to ask me.'

So now she had come to be with Elizabeth in Woodstock. On the whole Elizabeth was pleased to have her and was astonished by her stamina despite losing her son. Charles was her only child. Elizabeth missed her daughter terribly and wished she could see her. It was a shock to discover she'd left without saying good-bye after the funeral.

By the time the coffee group assembled in the morning room Charlotte was installed on a comfortable, upright chair by the fire-place. At her side was a copy of 'The Times', her tapestry and a library book.

The three women arrived together and were introduced to Mrs Jefferson senior and looked suitably intimidated. They sat perched on the edge of their chairs and admired the artistic arrangement of delphiniums, larkspur, stocks and roses which filled the fire-place.

Charlotte peered over her glasses guessing that their first question would be 'Are the flowers out of the garden?' She didn't have to wait long before the little plump, rosy woman said 'Aren't the flowers beautiful? Are they from the garden?' Charlotte agreed that they were and smiled to herself. The herbaceous border to the right of the front door was ablaze with colour and unmissable. Blooms of every shade from blues, mauves, purples and pinks into the richest burgundy reds stopped all comers to the front door.

Elizabeth carried in the coffee tray with its perfectly starched drawn thread work tray cloth and gleaming silver and china. Charlotte was glad that Elizabeth's standards were as high as her own.

As Elizabeth took over as hostess Charlotte was happy merely to listen and observe. Even these particularly dull people were better than television. Church will be next, I expect, she thought. They don't look lively enough for politics. Her prescience didn't let her down.

'There's still a bother going on about women priests. Margery Bodger thinks we should get the church exorcised.'

'I thought only ghosts were exorcised.'

'Well they are usually, but you can use it for all sorts of reasons apparently.' (Just like tissues or elastic bands thought Charlotte. She couldn't think why on earth women wanted to be priests anyway. She'd known a deaconess once, clearly a lesbian and odd besides. Nasty, nicotined fingers she recalled.)

During her musings they had moved on to recycling. The long lady was asking Elizabeth what she thought about the Prices. Weren't they wonderful the way they turned their lawn mowing clippings into paper. It seemed there was little the world could offer that they couldn't recycle into something else.

'You must know Mr and Mrs Price, they come into the museum for coffee most Fridays.'

Elizabeth said she was afraid she couldn't recall the Prices. Charlotte took off her spectacles and said to Elizabeth 'Have the Prices got any children?'

Elizabeth asked the trio whether or not the Prices had children. It seemed not, they all agreed. 'No, they haven't got the recipe for that have they?' Charlotte said tartly and picked up her tapestry.

That put an end to recycling and hastened the visitors to ask whether they might look at the garden. Elizabeth's eyes were laughing at Charlotte's wicked put down, but it had certainly worked.

'Good-bye' said Charlotte ensuring they didn't come back indoors, 'it was kind of you to call.' With much fussation they gathered up their handbags and said good-bye to her in awed unison and followed Elizabeth out into the garden.

Both black labradors rushed up with an over enthusiastic welcome. Elizabeth did not check them so Charlotte watched to see who would be jumped up on first. She maliciously hoped it would be the pale beige woman – beige hair, beige complexion, beige dress and matching beige accessories. She looked like a plain biscuit. Jasper left two muddy paw marks on her skirt as he was called off.

Charlotte was pleased that Elizabeth was learning not to be quite so warm and welcoming to everyone. She would need to grow tougher to cope with life without dear Charles' protection, especially where men were concerned. Elizabeth seemed utterly oblivious to the effect she had on men. She had always been a most attractive and appealing woman. Even more desirable, she supposed thoughtfully, as a wealthy widow. Charlotte wondered just how much money Charles had amassed. Neither he nor Elizabeth were extravagant in anything beyond running a beautiful home. They had both been left legacies a few years ago.

She felt rather guilty that she was not more upset by her son's death. Was it the shock that had numbed her completely she wondered, knowing it was unnatural for a mother not to be devasted by the loss of her only child.

Actually she found it rather agreeable staying with Elizabeth whom she secretly admired enormously. As a daughter-in-law she was exemplary and had, clearly, made Charles very happy. Charlotte envied her easy manner with people from every sort of background. Even in mourning Elizabeth had apparent serenity.

She came in from the garden with the two dogs carrying sticks.

'Are those lovely creatures going to make a dreadful mess on the carpet dear?'

'Yes, Charlotte they probably will, but none of those thing really matter, do they? What's a bit of mess on the carpet when we're feeling so....' Elizabeth broke off realising that Charlotte was thoroughly composed and seemingly unaffected by Charles' death. It was unnatural somehow and she couldn't understand it.

'You are much closer to your son than I was to Charles. I feel I know you better than I ever knew him. He was a good son to me but I never let him get too close. You'll have to watch Sam now and make sure Charles' death doesn't keep him at home with you too much.'

'You needn't worry on that score. He seems more than usually occupied on the romantic front,' Elizabeth answered, with a smile, 'and is back in his flat in Oxford.'

'Oh, and what's that supposed to mean? Is he planning to become engaged to Maria? An opinionated little baggage if ever I saw one.'

'They still see one another but Maria always puts her career first I'm afraid. But there's another girl on his mind too. Ever since he went to that funeral in Ludlow he has talked about Kate.'

Charlotte looked pleased. She liked a romance in the offing. It would be better still if it despatched Maria.

'Have you heard anything from Rachel?'

'She came to the funeral of course but rushed back to London the same night.'

'She should be here with you. Is she any more stable? How did she look?'

'She looked remarkably well, much better than the last time we saw her. If I'd known she was going to dash off like that I would have tried to talk to her more.'

'She always pleased herself and much good it's done her' Charlotte said.

'She's certainly been a worry from the first day she went to school. A real rebel I'm afraid.'

'High time she grew out of it and faced up to life. Is she still on drugs?'

'I don't know. She looked quite normal but we were all so upset…'

'I could do with a stroll round the garden dear, my knees are very stiff and painful. I won't be long.'

She could see she had upset Elizabeth and left her to cry if she could. It would help her to let go a little.

Charlotte bent down to dead-head some flowers. Old age really had very little to recommend it. She felt like wringing Rachel's neck. Yet in some ways she saw some of herself in her granddaughter. She supposed she should have come to Charles' funeral and then she would have had a chance to talk to Rachel. So different from Sam she thought picking a few raspberries and eating them.

David woke up and leapt out of bed still affected by a vivid nightmare which refused to fade. The bedclothes were strewn over the floor. He stood, sweating profusely. His reflection in the mirror was grim and wild – eyes bloodshot and blazing, beads of sweat on his brow.

So it was an affair Faith had been having with Charles Jefferson. In his dream he had seen it all. The cover of Charles' fishing trips and Faith's outings to paint. Their secret safe until now, their lovers nest the 'Oriole'. Just one careless move, he thought, and that was hanging the painting of that wretched boat in their house. The only key to a network of deceit. Who would have thought Faith capable of such duplicity?

'The bitch,' he yelled, 'the bloody, scheming bitch and that smooth bastard.' Tabitha fled down the stairs, yowling with fear, as he ranted. David bulldozed his way round the house like a mad man, knocking over small tables and ornaments, crazed with revenge and hatred.

He snatched Faith's picture's off the walls with such venomous vigour that many of the hooks flew out too, sprinkling plaster dust about. He hurled them into a heap on the kitchen floor, smashing the glass on some of the old quarry tiles. He kept on until the walls were stripped apart from a calendar and some photographs. Tabitha sought refuge on the hall windowsill, half hidden by the curtain.

The front door bell rang. David stormed to the door and flung it open. Mrs Morgan, from next door, said nervously, 'Are you alright? I heard some crashing like broken glass and....' She stopped as she took in his wild appearance. 'Oh David, you seem to be bleeding. Where's all that blood coming from?'

'My bleeding heart I should think. Where else?' Mrs Morgan backed away nervously as she saw the mess everywhere. 'Well if there's nothing I can do...'

'No, there's nothing you or anyone can do, thank you' and he banged the door to behind her. 'Interfering, bloody busybody.'

The interruption broke the tempo of his frenzied outburst and he noticed the havoc he had wreaked. He licked his bleeding wrist and tied the dish cloth round it. His pyjama trousers were streaked in blood and he realised he'd torn the front opening and was fully exposed.

'That'll give the buggers something to talk about.' Bet she's not seen a dick as big as mine, he thought with some satisfaction.

He went into the garden shed at the back to fetch the wheel barrow, yard broom and shovel. Seeing the next door curtains move his fury started to mount and he crashed the metal barrow into the backdoor, grazing the paint work, and it stuck fast. David clambered over it, swearing as he caught his shin. He started shovelling the glass and pictures and broken frames into the barrow.

He managed to dislodge it from between the door jambs, he staggered awkwardly with the overladen barrow into the middle of the lawn. He sprinkled petrol from the lawn mower can liberally over the barrow and set fire to it. It burned quickly making a crackling blaze. Mrs Morgan watched in horror from her landing window, twisting her hands and wondering what to do. She was both frightened and concerned. He must have gone mad.

David felt calmer as the blaze subsided as if his anger had burnt out too. The bottom of the barrow was full of charred, smoked shards of glass. The effect was cathartic. He wrapped the smoky glass carefully in newspapers and put them into an old tea-chest in the shed. After brushing out the barrow he went indoors streaked with smoke and blood and flushed with his exertion. He was surprised to discover that he was still in his tattered pyjamas.

David luxuriated in a deep hot bath with plenty of disinfectant and examined his cuts and bruises. He usually made the most absurd fuss about the slightest injury and felt rather cheated that he wasn't able to make any mileage out of these. The bath soothed his damaged pride and gave him the incentive to clear up the chaos in the house before settling to read the paper with a mug of coffee laced with whisky.

He knew now that there was one more destructive move he wanted to make and that was to burn the tryst boat. It would have to wait though and be carefully planned.

* * * * *

Alex waited for his father to collect him from Newcastle. He had piles of books and files as well as the usual luggage to take home. He would sooner remain in his digs than return to Shropshire but felt his father needed some company. He'd had a very strained conversation with him on the 'phone and decided to have a couple of weeks working at home before leaving for France.

David arrived on the dot at eleven o'clock. He looked a mess. His clothes were creased, and not too clean, and he had sticking plaster on his hands and a large one on his wrist.

'Someone been giving you some grief?' Alex asked looking at the hands. David winced at this mode of speech but, simultaneously, thought it entirely apposite if taken literally.

'Yes, but I've dealt with it. Oh, these cuts, you mean; just some clearing up I've been doing.'

'You look tired Dad. I thought we could go to an exhibition at the City Museum in Hanley, if you like. It's supposed to be great.'

'Not pictures is it? I've had enough of pictures to last me a lifetime' he said meaningfully.

'Oh well let's go up the Vic Theatre for lunch. It'd make a change for you and save us bothering.'

David nodded. The hours that followed were some of the most companionable they'd had together in years. They went for a long walk on the Longmynd on the way back to Ludlow. The rolling hills were quiet apart from the sheep and occasional walkers. They eventually arrived home pleasantly tired and relaxed as dusk fell.

As Alex unloaded his gear he couldn't think why the house looked so odd. When he switched more lights on he noticed the lack of pictures on the walls. He went from room to room mystified. There wasn't a single painting to be seen, just marks on the paint where they'd hung and holes where some of the hooks had been.

David was putting the car away as Alex looked round the house. He noticed the damaged back door and general state of neglect, but there didn't seem to be anything else missing. He checked his own room carefully and it was just as he'd left it.

He met David coming in through the back yard. 'Has someone broken in Dad?'

'No. Why?'

'The door must have been forced back and the frame's a mess. Look at it.'

David didn't look at it. 'Just a little accident I had with the wheel-barrow. It's nothing to bother about.'

Alex thought it a very strange answer. What on earth would he be doing with the wheel-barrow in the house?

He said 'I take it you're redecorating. I'll give you a hand while I'm here.'

'I'm not decorating. Your mother was the painter. Do you think it looks that bad then?'

'I thought that was why you'd taken the pictures down. No, it'll look OK. When you put them back. It just looks weird with all those frame marks everywhere.'

'I'm not putting them back. I've got rid of them. Couldn't stand seeing them all the time reminding me of Faith and....'

Alex misunderstood the emotional hesitation but was shocked by what he heard.

'I'll take some to my digs if you don't want them here, Dad.'

'You'll mind your own damned business. I told you, I've got rid of them' David said snappily.

'What d'you mean, got rid of them. Where are they?' Alex's voice rose as he tried to control himself.

'Burnt the lot.' David's face was incrutable.

'Whatever did you do that for? Mum's whole life's work destroyed. That 's terrible; how could you? What about me?'

'What about you? The days of being Mummy's boy are over. She's gone; they've gone and that's it.' He turned and lumbered out of the room.

Alex fought his rising anger, grabbed an anorak and went out. He was glad of the darkness as he took his usual path to the river. He certainly didn't want to meet anyone.

He wondered if his father was ill but was more inclined to think it was sheer nastiness. But why, why, why? he'd always thought Faith's talents were wasted because of David's macho, selfish demands on her time. And now there was no evidence of that talent left. It was too incredulous to take in.

Alex slipped on the marshy ground and over balanced into the river. The edge was shallow and he was on his knees in the cold water. The current was strong enough to make him counter-balance against it even there. He didn't move for some minutes finding the cold, wet, bruising discomfort a helpful physical diversion from his fevered thoughts. He found himself understanding how murders were committed in the heat of the moment. If he hadn't left the house when he did....but no, that was ridiculous. He deplored violence.

It also went through his mind why people killed themselves for no apparent reason. If he'd been swept away by the current no one would have known why he was there. Crazy thoughts raced through his mind one after another.

Alex reluctantly pulled himself together. He was soaked from the waist down. He had lost the impetus to go further in such a cold, bedraggled state. He walked home briskly, in an effort to get his circulation going, and forced himself to go in.

David was in the kitchen making a bedtime drink. 'Where on earth have you been? Good grief, you're all wet through.'

'I've been to cool off, if you must know.' Alex stripped off his jeans and socks and went up to the bathroom and locked the door. A long comforting soak in the bath was therapeutic and helped soothe his tormented feelings. He stayed there, topping up with more hot water, until he heard David's bedroom door close.

Although this was a very ordinary bathroom, it had the advantage of a huge, old fashioned cast iron bath. Alex thought how different it was from the bathrooms at Oriel Manor. He preferred the old, stained, white iron bath, with it's turned out feet, to the smart oval coloured ones. It was deeper too and the water stayed hot longer.

He looked at his skin, wrinkly and crinkly from so long in the water. His thoughts turned to the prospect of spending time with David with increasing gloom. At least there was the biking holiday in France to look forward to. He closed his eyes and imagined blue skies, hot sun, rugged mountains, lots of wine, himself tanned with scantily dressed birds.

'Are you going to be all night in there?' David's voice interrupted his musings. The door knob rattled.

'I haven't decided yet. Why? Do you want a pee?'

'No, I just want some peace and order in my house. You've been there for over an hour, running off all the hot water, no doubt.'

'Suppose you've got a stop watch ready. Don't know why I bothered coming home. Doesn't feel like home any more.'

'Plenty of people would be grateful for your advantages. When I was your age…'

Alex threw the soap at the door. 'Bugger off and leave me alone, can't you.'

There was a long silence and finally he heard David's door close. Alex sighed and sat and dried himself slowly, thinking of his good intentions only twelve hours before.

CHAPTER 5

Elizabeth's mind kept returning to Faith's painting of the 'Oriole'. She wished the date wasn't during the time she was away in Chelsea. If only she'd been here when Charles returned, he might have told her about meeting Faith. She also understood he might never have met her at all and those dates might be an odd coincidence.

Elizabeth tried not to even consider the possibility of there being anything between them. She and Charles had a good marriage and gave one another space to develop their separate interests. After all, she thought, if Faith hadn't died at the funeral she would never have heard of her other than being a name on a list. There were many unfamiliar names among those she'd written to, thanking them for their donations and letters.

She had formed a picture of Faith, mostly from Alex's conversation. She needed to talk to someone about it and yet didn't want to admit any doubt about Charles' fidelity. Not least she didn't really feel any doubt, but there just seemed too many strange coincidences. 'I was the last to know' kept coming back to her from wives' letters to magazines and stories in the papers.

Elizabeth decided she would try to discuss it with Charlotte. She certainly wouldn't gossip and could be relied upon for an honest opinion.

It was a fine, sunny morning but with a hint of autumn. Charlotte was sitting in the conservatory writing letters. 'There you are Elizabeth. Do you think Jasper has got fleas? He keeps scratching and biting bits of himself, and I keep itching watching him.'

'No I don't think so, it's propably the seeds from the long grass' and she called Jasper over and examined his fur and skin. Oscar came too inviting inspection. 'It's a good day to give the dogs a bath,' she continued, 'and that should get rid of your itches too, Charlotte. If they have picked up anything the shampoo I use from the vet will get rid of it.'

'What about the cat, he could be the culprit. He'd do it just to spite me.'

'Poor Tobermory. You've never liked him and he senses it.'

'I suspect he was a criminal in some former life.'

Elizabeth laughed; she loved all their animals equally.

'You seem rather twitchy yourself this morning Elizabeth. Why don't you bring us some fresh coffee and come and enjoy this lovely sunshine.'

Elizabeth brought in a tray and placed it on the table between them. Charlotte had put away her correspondence, taken off her spectacles and was ready to talk. Perhaps now would be a good moment. Elizabeth hesitated, after all Charles was her only child. Charlotte scratched her shoulder thoughtfully.

'I don't think Charles was having an affair with that woman, do you?' she said leaning forward to get better eye contact.

Elizabeth was so taken aback by this calm, prescient question that she choked over her coffee on a wrong swallow.

'Ever since you brought that painting back from Ludlow you have been pre-occupied. I wondered about it too.'

'Did you?'

'Yes. But I've come to the considered conclusion that there was nothing in it. You and Charles were well matched and happy together. I don't think he was enterprising enough to live a double life. After all, one has to put a lot of effort into a successful affair. He was basically lazy despite all his success.'

Elizabeth considered these extraordinary observations in silence. She valued Charlotte's astuteness but was astonished by being confronted in this way.

'I've been trying not to think about it, but there does seem to be so many coincidences.'

'Did you have these feelings before the picture came to light?'

'No, it never occurred to me.'

'There you are then Elizabeth. Listen to your instinct more; you're a sensitive and intelligent woman. Have you ever had an affair?'

'Certainly not. I deeply resent that Charlotte. I thought you knew me better. Not only was I devoted to Charles, I also believe in my marriage vows.'

'I do – but you need jolting out of all this brooding. I had a glorious affair and believe me it takes a lot of time and effort. Well worth it though' and her eyes glinted with the piquancy of the memory. She sighed with a sort of resigned contentment.

'You must trust your intuition. What does it tell you?'

'That Charles was faithful to me.' Elizabeth felt better as she said it, as if a great burden had been physically lifted from her. Even the rhythm of her breathing went back to normal.

'What are you going to do with the painting?'

'I shall keep it, I think.'

'If you're going to hang it somewhere I hope you'll get rid of that nasty, vulgar Constable-style frame. There's nothing wrong with the painting itself, quite good really. I took the liberty of examining it the other day. What about the boat?'

'Sam wants to keep it.'

'Whatever for? That boy's never shown any aptitude for fishing or boating.'

'He thought he'd use it as his country retreat,' Elizabeth said smiling.

'Oh, I see! Perhaps Kate likes boats. When am I going to meet her?'

'You're very perceptive this morning Charlotte.'

'I'm perceptive every morning. You are not always so receptive my dear.' Charlotte stroked Oscar absentmindedly and then rolled up her sleeve, examined her arm and scratched it.

Elizabeth cleared the coffee away and called the dogs into an outhouse. Charlotte dozed in the warmth of the sun. She was awakened by the labradors tearing round the garden, shaking themselves and chasing each other. Tobermory shot up a tree out of the rumpus and eyed Charlotte hoping she would open the door. He looked rather dusty and kept shaking powder off himself.

'So you've been seen to as well? Perhaps it will take that superior look off your face, grinning all the time like the Cheshire cat.' Charlotte didn't open the door.

Elizabeth came back to report the complete absence of fleas.

'Jasper has a slight skin irritation which I've treated.' She had also washed all the animal's bedding and felt much better for the whole experience releasing her nervous tension.

'Thank you for sorting me out Charlotte. I feel fine now and yet nothing has really changed.'

'You have changed and that makes all the difference.'

'Would you like to tell me about your lover?'

'Some day perhaps.'

'Did Charles know?'

'Of course not. At one time he was one of Charles' patients.'

Elizabeth looked at the old lady, whom she'd thought she knew very well, with new eyes.

'What's for lunch today?'

'I thought we'd have an omelette and green salad. Are you hungry?"

'No, but I'm sure you are dear. You've been picking at your food lately.'

She was right. Elizabeth enjoyed her lunch and settled down to read the paper surrounded by two clean, sleeping dogs and an offended, rather huffy cat.

Elizabeth took a bowl of sweet peas, freshly cut from the garden, into Charlotte's room and checked that Mrs Tickle had changed the bed linen. It was a comfortable room with a view across Blenheim Park. Through the half open door she could see Charlotte in the bathroom. She was sitting on an upright chair by the window.

'May I come in Charlotte? I'm just checking round to make sure there are enough towels, soap and toilet rolls.'

'Yes, come in dear.' Charlotte was sitting with her sponge bag on her lap and put a plastic box inside.

Elizabeth stifled a scream as she said, 'I don't want to frighten you but there's a huge black spider on the window sill. I'll go and get something to catch it in.'

Charlotte calmly picked it up and put it into the box in her sponge bag. Elizabeth froze at the thought of touching it.

'Sorry about Basil. I forgot to put him away. Did he give you a fright?'

'What on earth are you doing Charlotte. Yes, it really made me shudder. I don't mind small spiders but can't bear those big wobbly ones. They run so fast.'

'Basil doesn't move at all, he's made of plastic.'

'Oh Charlotte, how could you?'

Charlotte struggled with the box and shook out the plastic spider. It was remarkably life like.

'There now, meet Basil.'

Elizabeth burst out laughing and put Basil into the bath where he looked even more real.

'But why do you keep it in a box?'

'It's my bug viewer. I've just been examining one of those beetly spidery creatures that I call 'speedles'. I was putting it back where I found it, crawling about on the edge of the fig tree plant, when you came in.'

She rooted about amongst the lowest leaves, produced the plastic box and captured the insect again.

'Eureka! Have a look yourself.'

She peered into the clear viewing box with its magnifying lid in fascination. It had six shapely legs, each joint clearly defined, and sort of shoe-like suckers. The body part was finely patterned with little black dots on an amber colour. Its feelers were exploring the sides of the box. To the naked eye it looked a rather dull dark grey insect.

'Where did you get it?'

'From the catalogue of the Natural History Museum. I sent away for it. Interesting isn't it?'

'Yes, it really is. It never occurred to me you were so keen on creepy crawlies. You really are an enigma Charlotte.'

'There's a design fault with the lid. I suppose it's more my arthritic fingers that are the problem. I find it difficult to unscrew.' Charlotte struggled, as she spoke, but managed it and went to return the 'speedle' to the plant pot.

'If you don't mind I think we'll shake it out of the window' said Elizabeth firmly.

Then she picked Basil up. 'Why do you have a plastic spider Charlotte?'

He came with the bug viewer and I've become rather attached to him.' Charlotte put him inside and closed the lid.

'What else do you get up to when I think you're resting quietly in your room?'

'You'd be surprised.' Charlotte smiled to herself.

'There's always a strong smell of nail polish remover in here. The bottle isn't leaking is it?'

'That's peardrops not acetone.'

'Peardrops? You never said you liked peardrops. You never accept sweets or chocolates when they're offered to you.'

'I'm in my peardrop period at present. It'll pass and there are worse smells.'

'But why peardrops?'

'They remind me of my childhood and cheer me up when I'm bored to distraction by old age. Taste and smell are the most evocative senses you know. When I was a child we were only allowed barley sugar, wrapped boiled sweets and butterscotch. Peardrops were considered nasty, cheap and vulgar. The maid used to buy them for me and I sucked them out of doors. I had to chew parsley and mint from the garden afterwards to disguise the smell.'

'Did you give your pocket money to the maid?'

'No. I was given a brass threepenny bit each week for church collection and four farthings for charity and myself. One farthing into the 'League of Light' lantern box for orphaned children and the other into the 'Missions for Seasmen's' box. That left me with a farthing for savings and a farthing for myself.'

'How things have changed. When you think what childlren spend now.'

Charlotte continued reminiscently and her eyes gleamed with nefarious pleasure. 'I found a way to take money out of the 'League of Light' lantern. I kept a knife from the dining room in my toy box. I used to dip it into the black treacle and then lower the blade of the sticky knife through the money slot into the lantern. If you were very lucky you might draw out a sixpenny bit but usually it was a farthing. They stuck to the knife as long as you withdrew it very carefully, not catching the slot on the way out.' Her eyes narrowed as she recalled the skill required. 'I became quite expert and made no mess. It was this money I gave to the maid.'

Elizabeth hugged Charlotte. 'You are a dear. I was feeling quite low this morning and you've really brightened my day. Fancy you being a thief.'

'Most children go through it one way or another. I'd have been regarded as a deprived child nowadays. I expect I'd have needed a support group and a social worker for my special needs.'

'I shall have to come to your room more often. Better still, why don't you bring your bug viewer downstairs?'

'And have your friends think I am as mad as Mrs Rochester? Certainly not. I may be eccentric but I have my dignity to consider.'

'You do indeed Charlotte. They are filled with respect and admiration for you.'

'You mean terrified of me.'

'Sometimes, perhaps.'

'There are few acceptable devices left to one in old age. One gets talked over, shouted at or addressed in slow monosyllables, all of which are insulting if one has managed to retain most faculties.'

'You seem to cope with people adeptly.'

'Thank you my dear, but it can be most tiresome.'

'The sweetpeas are coming to an end early this year.'

'Many of the best things in life are short lived but more precious because of it, Elizabeth.'

The telephone rang as Elizabeth was half way down the stairs. After some minutes Charlotte slowly descended and heard her say 'We shall look forward to seeing you on Friday then. Come about noon and we'll have lunch at one-ish.'

Charlotte's face lit up 'Visitors dear?' she asked.

'Just David sounding in need of cheering up.'

'Who is David? Do I know him?'

'Alex's father. No, I don't think you've met.'

'Ah, the missing link. I shall look forward to meeting him. Alex is an agreeable young man, is he like his father?'

'Only in looks. David has been made redundant, poor man.'

'Oh dear, that's unfortunate on top of his wife's death. Is he likely to find another position?'

'Not at his age and after this long recession.'

'How old is he?'

'Mid-fifties I believe.'

'Oh really past it with one foot in the grave' Charlotte said sarcastically.

'I didn't mean to be offensive, you know perfectly well what I mean. In business it's a cut-throat world.'

'Where experience counts for nothing. No wonder we're in such a mess. Like our nice Mr Major. Couldn't pass his examinations but became Chancellor of the Exchequer before Prime Minister. A curious advertisement for our education system. He's got a clever wife though.'

'I don't know much about Norma apart from her being an opera buff.'

'That's clever in itself not providing much fodder for the gutter press. I don't suppose she needs a support group either.'

'You've got support groups on the brain, a real bee in your bonnet about them.'

'Ah bees! I'm glad you reminded me Elizabeth. You seem to be looking after them rather well. Will you bring me one to look at in my viewer?'

'Can things breathe properly in there?'

'There are air holes, remember I bought it from the Natural History Museum' Charlotte said testily, 'not a tinker at the door.'

'Yes, of course, but bees don't like being tampered with. Leave the box open on the terrace with some honey on a leaf. I'll set it up for you shall I?'

Charlotte nodded, rather wishing she hadn't pushed Elizabeth into the subject of bees. She had been looking forward to a good argument about Mrs Thatcher and realised how adroitly Elizabeth had manipulated her away from politics.

She settled down with the newspaper to discover it was the Queen Mother's birthday. There's a woman who knows how to enjoy old age. Apart from swallowing fish bones she seemed to thrive on gin and horse racing. Charlotte had read somewhere that she smoked in bed and wondered if it was true.

*****

'How good to see you Sam. Your mother's gone to have her hair done and have lunch with an old school friend. How are things in publishing?'

'I was up most of the night following a print run through. It's always frantic when we are passing for press. I didn't realise you were still here, but you're looking very well.'

'Elizabeth waits on me most kindly and I can manage fine when I'm here, but I think I shall have to part with my flat.'

'Oh what a pity; why?'

'Don't tell your mother, Sam, but I'm considering going into a sheltered scheme for retired people. I went to look at it before I came here and have been trying to make a decision since.'

'Whereabouts is it Charlotte?'

'This side of Oxford, quite near to my friend May.'

'Do you want to go there?'

'No one in their right mind wants to be herded into an unnatural grouping. I don't like old people much either.'

Sam tried to keep his face straight. 'Why not?'

'They do nothing but complain. Growing old has little to recommend it, but one must make the best of things and adapt. These moaning folk are often the ones with the least wrong with them and they're always wishing they were dead. A whiff of illness and they're swallowing antibiotics by the bottle and clinging onto life like mad.'

'Would you like me to take you to have another look at it?'

'Yes dear, I would. I rang the warden and she tells me that there are two other people interested in the apartment I looked at.'

'Why don't we make an appointment for this afternoon and then Ma won't be any the wiser. It's a quarter to twelve now, shall I ring them for you?'

'I should be most grateful Sam.' Charlotte rummaged through her capacious handbag and pulled out her diary. 'The number is on a piece of paper clipped to the first page.'

Sam rang and made arrangements to view at 2.30pm.

Charlotte's face lit up. 'Thank you dear. Now I must think about your lunch. Elizabeth left me some smoked salmon sandwiches but there won't be enough for both of us.'

'No problem. We can either go out or I can nip down to Thorns and bring back something interesting to go with the sandwiches.'

'What a good idea. The young couple who own that excellent shop are charming and they work so hard. Bring a bottle of wine too.' Charlotte passed Sam £10.00.

When Sam returned, Charlotte had set the table in the breakfast room and was sitting by the window deep in thought. Jasper and Oscar raced across the lawn to greet Sam again. He poured Charlotte some wine and arranged his various purchases on the table. Taramasalata, pitta bread, savoury rice with pine nuts and olives and goat's cheese.

'That looks good dear, what a treat. I like trying all these sorts of things better than a proper meal.'

'How do you like the wine Charlotte?'

'An excellent choice, but I don't know what it is.'

'Picoul de Pinet. It goes well with our fish buffet doesn't it?'

'Yes but I mustn't have any more. I shall need to muster my remaining wits to deal with that dragon.'

'Which dragon?'

'The warden. I've forgotten her name.'

It was precisely half past two when Sam rang the warden's door bell.

'Ah Mrs Jefferson. How nice to see you again and right on the dot too. I like my ladies to be on time.'

'I am always on time Mrs Er, remind me of your name please. I can't read your label without my reading glasses.'

'Mrs Weaver. Having trouble with our memory are we? It comes to us all sooner or later' she grinned flashing her too white, too even dentures.

'WE are not having any trouble with OUR memory at all,' said Charlotte crisply. 'This is my grandson Sam Jefferson.'

'Pleased to meet you I'm sure she replied rather huffily. 'Nice for grandma to have some support.'

Sam didn't dare to look at Charlotte. A few more remarks like that and Mrs Weaver might be in need of some support herself.

The warden picked up her keys and accompanied them across the car park. They were aware of many pairs of eyes watching every movement.

'There's a lot of interest in this flat and there are two for sale on the other side. The other side of The Close is more interesting as you can see everything that goes on.'

'God forbid and the saints preserve me' Charlotte muttered.

'I didn't know you were religious. There's communion in the common room on the first Thursday in the month. Such a nice young man comes and gives it to them. We are taking names for the harvest supper. Those that can't get about are given nice big boxes of goodies. He does the funerals really lovely too.'

Sam intervened quickly. 'Don't let us take any more of your valuable time, Mrs Weaver, you must have such a lot to do. I'll return the key to you when we leave.'

'Very well then, just as you like. I've left a chair inside incase she needs to sit down. I'll see you before you go dear' and she patted Charlotte's arm. 'Don't overdo yourself.'

Charlotte looked close to apoplexy as Sam closed the door firmly.

'One would be willing to swing for a woman like that' she said.

'Let's look round. So this is the sitting room. It's a bit small but it's good to have a door opening into the garden.'

'This is the entire living area for daytime Sam, but the garden is very pretty. The gardening, outside maintenance and decorating and window cleaning are included in the service charge.'

'Not much room in the kitchen but I'm sure it would be adequate. It's quite a nice bathroom. What a low bath! You couldn't have a good swim in that. Sensible having so many bell cords though.'

'I'm sure the residents find a reserve of energy to get themselves out of the bath. The thought of that dreadful woman on the end of the bell is no mean incentive.'

'It's better than I expected Charlotte. With your beautiful old furniture and good taste, it would be transformed. I shouldn't rush into anything though. You and Ma get on so well that you could stay at Oriel Manor if you wanted to.'

'That's what I'm afraid of Sam. Elizabeth may not want to stay there when she's had time to find herself again. I don't want her saddled with me and, indeed, I need my own front door. That reminds me, where is the back door?'

'Well, you have two outside doors, the front door and the one to the garden from the sitting room.'

'So when you want to empty the tea leaves out of the teapot you have to go through the sitting room or out of the front door. How extraordinary.'

'They probably used tea-bags.'

'Don't you start talking about 'they' as well. When I was a child I hated 'they'. 'They' don't do this and 'they' don't do that. Now it's gone into reverse and one is supposed to be one of 'they'. What a ghastly idea. Let's try to leave without attracting any more attention.'

Sam took an envelope out of his pocket and slipped in the key. He wrote a note to Mrs Weaver on the outside and pushed it through her letter-box.

'They're all watching. I can feel them can't you?'

Sam had to agree.

'It looks like a floral barracks with all those hanging baskets.'

'I know what you mean. Modern architecture does seem to lack style and character, but it's well laid out.'

They were back in Woodstock and having tea when Elizabeth returned. She found them deep in discussion about mountain bikes and poring over maps of the South of France. She thought how good it was to see them together. She had enjoyed her lunch and break from home.

'Have the dogs been fed Sam?'

'No. We've been so busy I forgot to do it. Tobermory has though. He demanded his when we had lunch. I think he smelt our smoked salmon.'

'I hope you found something for your lunch Sam.'

'No problem Ma. We had a good lunch.' Elizabeth was aware of something going on between them.

'What have you been doing Charlotte?'

'I've been learning about Muddy Foxes dear, most interesting too.'

Sam grinned. 'They're mountain bikes. I've got to get my act together for the holiday in France next week.'

'It looks like a beautiful village. I quite envy you going off with your friends. Does Kate have a mountain bike?'

'Yes, and Alex is a really keen biker. I shall be the only novice.'

'I might consider a holiday before . . . before . . .'

'Before what Charlotte?'

'Before I get too old to enjoy it.' Sam and Charlotte couldn't stop laughing. Elizabeth knew there was no point in trying to get them to share their secret. Whatever they'd been up to they had obviously had fun. She went to give Oscar and Jasper their dinner.

David wished that he hadn't accepted the invitation to Woodstock when it came to Friday. He was uneasy all round. He found Elizabeth overpoweringly attractive and spent too much time fantasising about her. He was full of revenge where Faith and Charles were concerned, to the point of obsession.

With Alex in France he was tired of his own company and was confronted daily by his new situation. His home was a mess without Faith to see to things. He'd had various attempts to keep up appearances and failed each time. Cooking was a total disaster.

He had bought two grapefruits thinking they would be simple and make a change. The first one seemed to have a pithy fault running through the middle when he cut it in half. The second one turned out to be the same. It was only when he put the halves together again and cut them the other way that he discovered there's a right and wrong way to cut a grapefruit. Finally he squeezed them into juice and ended up with only a small glassful of it. There was a sticky mess of pulp everywhere and his shirt was sprayed with juice which left pale coloured stains. The washer had gone wrong full of clothes, and he hadn't found a way to drain the water out. It was a front loader so he decided to leave it until Alex came home.

Tabitha had taken to disappearing for days at a time, not even bothering to come back for meals. Someone must be feeding her as she looked plump and sleek. She had never been given to hunting apart from the occasional mouse.

Faith's friends didn't call anymore and Alex's friends knew he was away. David began to wonder whether he had any friends of his own and came to the conclusion that he hadn't. He had never thought friends important before now, but now he longed for someone to call or ring to break the awful monotony.

It wasn't so bad when he was still working. Being made redundant really was the last straw. It had come as such a shock too. He supposed he was secure enough financially, having always been thrifty and having sound insurance policies and investments. But he noticed how much more he was spending than he did when Faith was alive. He couldn't manage the weekly budget on Faith's amount of housekeeping money. Not only this but his quality of life had plummeted in every way.

He had always scoffed at people who ate junk food but now found himself doing it more and more. He chose not to look at the amount he was spending on drink. However, he was amazed by the number of empty whisky bottles accumulated in a few days. He went to the bottle bank more often and usually at night.

He dressed carefully to go to Woodstock. It was a shock to discover how many shirts required buttons or had stains that didn't wash out. He thought he'd better wear a suit despite the hot day. Alex had told him it was a big, impressive house and he didn't want to look impoverished. In fact he wanted to cut a dash with Elizabeth the first time he met her alone. This thought made him go back and change his boxer pants for a new pair. It was an unlikely precaution but if the chance presented itself he wouldn't like to be found wanting. Be prepared he thought – the old scout (was was it guide?) motto – and laughed to himself wryly, amazed at his own thinking.

David stopped at a stall at the side of the A44 and bought a large bunch of flowers. He couldn't think when he'd last bought flowers apart from red roses on their wedding anniversary each year.

He arrived at Oriel Manor at 12 o'clock and, as he drove up the drive, felt rather intimidated by it all. Two large black labradors bounded, barking, up to the car. David didn't like dogs. He got out warily as they sniffed his ankles. 'Get off' he said anxiously, but they stood their ground growling purposefully.

Elizabeth came out of the door looking even more alluring than he remembered. She called 'Jasper, Oscar stop at once. Come here' and they obeyed immediately.

She was wearing a simple dress in briar rose pink. Her legs were bare and she wore sandals. He felt thoroughly overdressed.

'How good to see you David,' and she held out her hand. 'Don't you like dogs? They're usually quite good at sorting out who's who.'

'No, I'm not very used to them really. You look very . . .' he hesitated and checked himself '. . . very well, Elizabeth.'

They went indoors and the dogs disappeared round the side of the house.

David followed her into a chintzy room with windows onto the back garden. There was an old lady sitting by the French window.

'May I introduce David Green, Charlotte. David please meet my mother-in-law, Charlotte Jefferson.'

They shook hands formally and sized one another up. David thought 'and now we've got a bloody chaperone.' Charlotte was impressed by his good looks. In spite of the awful suit he was an extremely handsome man. He was clearly rather ill at ease and both Charlotte and Elizabeth's good manners made an effort to minimise his discomfort.

Elizabeth said 'I had a card from Sam this morning. They seem to be having a wonderful time in Olargues. It will do Alex and Sam good to be away from home pressures after the events of recent weeks. Have you heard from Alex?'

'Yes I had a card. He didn't say much but seemed to be enjoying himself.'

'These are the times when one wishes one was younger. I love wild mountain scenery. Are you a mountain man David?' Charlotte asked.

'Apart from the Welsh mountains I haven't much experience. There are fine hills in South Shropshire where I like to walk.'

'What do you do?' Charlotte enquired.

'I used to be with a firm of estate agents in Hereford but have recently retired.' David caught Elizabeth's look of surprise and added 'Well actually I've been made redundant.'

'Oh dear! I am sorry, that's awful for you. You've had more than your share of misfortune lately without that.'

Elizabeth intervened 'What would you like to drink? While you're thinking I'll get you a dry sherry Charlotte.'

David didn't see any sign of whisky and couldn't decide what was in the crystal decanters. He took a deep breath and said 'Whisky please.'

'What do you like with it? Water, soda, ice, dry ginger?'

'Just straight for me.'

Charlotte sipped her sherry, drinking and driving she thought. A handsome man but the victim of a charisma by-pass operation.

Elizabeth put a small silver tray on a wine table beside David's chair. On it were a splendid squat, square decanter and a glass.

'Do help yourself.'

Charlotte made a comment about the garden looking well. It prompted David to remember the flowers he'd left in the car. Those blasted dogs he thought. I hope they've gone in.

'Excuse me a minute. I've just remembered something I left in the car.' The dogs weren't there.

Elizabeth and Charlotte looked at one another thoughtfully without speaking.

David came back with the flowers and gave them to Elizabeth. 'I thought you might like these, although I can see it's very much coals to Newcastle.' He poured himself another whisky.

'How kind of you. I love flowers. I shall put them in water right away. Thank you so much.'

Charlotte's eyes narrowed as she weighed up the situation all too accurately. She decided to take the bull by the horns before Elizabeth came back.

'It's strange the way we have come to know one another's families through the sudden deaths of Charles and Faith. Do you know why your wife was at my son's funeral?'

'No. They must have met somewhere I presume.'

Charlotte left it at that as she heard Elizabeth's footsteps returning. The flowers were prettily arranged in a brown jasper jug. She set them on a table against the wall.

'There. Aren't they beautiful? Lunch is ready when you are. No rush.'

They finished their drinks and Elizabeth waited for Charlotte to go first and then invited David to follow.

Lunch was an elegant but not formal occasion with delicious food. The only surprise was the wine.

Charlotte said 'Don't open that for me Elizabeth. David may not want wine, as he is driving, so only open it if you want it yourself. I should like some Malvern water please.'

Elizabeth was irritated by this manipulation but privately agreed with the sentiment.

'What do you think? The choice is yours David.'

'Don't open it for me either. I'd rather have a glass of beer if you have it.'

Charlotte said 'My husband drank beer but didn't care for it in bottles. Too gassy I believe. Do you prefer draught beer?'

'Yes I do, but some of the canned ones are quite good too.'

'I like the occasional draught Guinness myself, especially at midday with a good ploughman's lunch.

Elizabeth was astonished. 'You never fail to amaze me Charlotte.'

Charlotte beamed. 'Elizabeth doesn't care for beer, do you dear?'

'I can't get past the smell of it I'm afraid,' and she went to get the beer.

'I believe you have an elderly mother David. Does she live with you?'

'No, she's in a home in Church Stretton.'

'That's a pity. Is she very frail?'

'She's eighty and they're better looked after in homes.'

'Being eighty isn't an illness. I am eighty five. There are difficulties as one grows older. Now that you no longer go to the office you will be able to spend more time with her perhaps?'

David shot Charlotte a look of revulsion. 'I hate going there. They all sit round the room staring. It's most embarrassing. Alex doesn't mind going to see her. They seem to understand each other. She misses Faith though. They always got on well together.'

'Elizabeth is kindness herself when I stay here.'

'Oh, you don't live here then?' David brightened up.

'No. I have an apartment in Oxford.'

Elizabeth returned with a lead crystal tankard of beer. She poured herself some water. David appreciated the excellent lunch and had a second helping of chocolate fudge cake for pudding.

As they rose from the table, Charlotte said 'I think I'll take my coffee up to my room and have a little rest if you will excuse me.'

'I'll bring it up to you in a minute' Elizabeth replied 'Shall we have ours in the garden? The dogs are in the paddock' she added tactfully.

David strolled round the manicured lawns looking at the weed free flower beds and the extensive variety of mature flowering shrubs and trees. He was followed by Tobermory at a discreet distance. David tried to persuade the cat to come to him but it wouldn't.

Elizabeth put the tray down on a table on the terrace. Tobermory ran to her purring loudly, his tail held high.

'What a handsome cat. Isn't he huge?'

'Yes. This is Tobermory. Named after the cat in the Saki stories.'

As they talked David gave up any hope of getting close to Elizabeth that day, but the more he saw of her the more interested he became. She had no idea how provocative she looked although she was aware of his scrutiny and felt rather flattered by it.

As he was leaving they passed through the house. He saw a photograph of a man in his forties in a silver frame. 'Is this your husband?'

'Yes. It was taken at a book launch only last year.' Her eyes filled with tears as she spoke.

He looked a very distinguished, refined man with many of Charlotte's features.

'Thank you again and please say goodbye to Mrs Jefferson for me. I won't disturb her rest.'

'I do hope things start looking up for you. Do you think it will be difficult to get work?' What a stupid question, she thought. Like the hunt asking the fox if he's had a good day.

'I haven't tried yet. My motivation isn't very good at present.'

'It's understandable. There are some excellent adult education courses if you want to have a complete change.'

'Can I see you again? I find it very hard to communicate with people at present. You make it so easy.'

'Of course. When Alex comes home you must both come over for a weekend.'

That wasn't quite what David had in mind. He leant forward and kissed Elizabeth on the cheek. 'Thank you for lunch.'

As he drove away he tried to think how he could entertain Elizabeth in Ludlow. He was determined to get her on her own and on his own neutral ground.

CHAPTER 6

Lying on his back, basking in the blazing sun, Sam stretched happily knowing that Kate was asleep within reach of his fingertips. What a stunning place this is, he thought. In all his travels he'd never been anywhere so remote and beautiful – perfect for a romantic holiday.

He was the lucky one being included in the party through another not being able to make it. He was the least proficient mountain biker of the ten, with Kate coming a close second. This had great advantages as they took the less strenuous routes and spent more time à deux. After swimming in the pool beneath a waterfall in the dramatic gorge they lay on the warm rocks drying off. The rugged, rocky skyline of the Caroux glinted magnificently against the Botticelli blue backcloth of the sky. It was truly fabulous, the stuff of dreams.

Small camouflaged lizards ran over their legs and quickly disappeared into crevices. Butterflies of every size and myriad of colours were a constant source of fascination. The delicate tracery of their wings and the stencilled brilliance of jewel coloured patterns were breathtakingly beautiful.

The dragonflies were huge too. There were large numbers of topaz and turquoise coloured ones flitting over the water, their reflections were perfect silhouettes. The whole gorge was alive with activity. Always the sound of water rushing from the waterfall and keeping the crystal clear pools topped up before spilling away to form the next one. Sam had never imagined the South of France could be so wild. He'd been to much of France before but never deep into the mountains of the Languedoc.

Time seemed to have stood still for centuries in Olargues where they were staying. The medieval village, dominated by the eleventh century bell tower of the old chapel, had an almost fairytale look about its narrow cobbled streets. A timeless place, slumbering in the sun, now an espace protégé after its bloody, historical past.

The twelfth century Pont Diable must be one of the most beautiful old bridges in the world. It was the only way over the River Jaur, a tributary of the Orb, to the cité in days gone by. Even the trout seemed protected as they lazed undisturbed in its shadows. The weir was dry in summertime but Sam could imagine the torrents that flowed from the surrounding mountains in winter. There was a clear high water line shown by the trees and walls.

Kate woke up during Sam's daydreams but feigned sleep whilst squinting through slits of eyes. She was in love with Sam. She had thought she was in love with Alex but now realised the difference between a pash and a real passion. Her emotions were at once wonderful and frighteningly powerful. She thought her virginity would probably come as a surprise to Sam. She was ready to give herself to him and knew it would be today.

Sam looked at the wakening Kate and longed to make love to her. He wasn't always so sensitive and considerate. Somehow he knew he must contain himself until Kate was ready but he also knew that his emotions were building up almost unbearably.

Kate inched herself into the shade and dabbled her feet in the water. As he drew near she splashed him laughing. He sat behind her with his legs astride hers. Kate's heart was pounding as she felt Sam's pressure hard against her body. He kissed the back of her neck and she turned and knelt facing him. Their eyes met tellingly and they kissed and caressed.

Sam spread their towels under a fig tree and came back to the rocks. 'It's a bit lumpy. Is it . . . will it be . . . OK?' Kate took his outstretched hand and nodded.

She was a little tense at first but melted and relaxed as he caressed her body gently and encouraged her to explore his. He was as gentle as he knew how and her passion was at its peak as he entered her. 'I love you Kate and I don't want to hurt you.'

She could hardly breathe with his weight on her and they rolled onto their sides. 'Are you alright my love?'

'Oh yes. I do love you Sam' and she settled herself into the crook of his arm. They lay together for some time. Suddenly she jumped up in alarm.

'What was that?' Kate squealed.

'What was what?' Sam grinned, thinking how sexy she looked. What a figure and those long brown legs.

'That' she yelled. 'Look the ground's moving. Whatever is it?'

He couldn't help laughing although by now he had her in his arms to calm her down.

'Is it a snake?'

'No darling. It was just the earth moving like you said.'

'I'm not joking' she was trembling with fright 'something went through here,' and she pointed, 'something big.' She scrambled back onto the rocks and put on her shorts and top.

Sam gathered together the remains of their picnic. They had planned to go on but it was much too late now and they'd lost interest in adventure for today. It could have been a snake and he didn't want Kate frightened by anything to spoil their romantic day.

High on a rocky outcrop above them was a mouflon. 'There you are my love. There's your snake. It was a mouflon.' She believed him, to his surprise. She was so happy she could believe anything.

'Isn't he magnificent? I love those curved horns. But it could have been a snake. I'm terrified of snakes.'

'I don't like them either. I know there are snakes here but none of us have seen one. I've never seen so many different kinds of lizards and they're harmless.'

Kate was too happy to really worry about snakes. As they cycled down to Mons la Trivalle she also realised she was a little saddle sore. They stopped at the café for a break and coffee, in no hurry to rejoin their friends.

When they arrived back at the chambres d'hôtes, the others were all sitting on the terrace drinking beer. Alex noticed how radiant Kate looked and felt a pang of jealousy. Sam was a decent guy and he had to admit they looked good together.

Their host was setting up a barbecue on a higher terrace. The views were fantastic and the setting sun painted the sky with slabs of warm, vibrant, brilliant colours before sinking behind the mountain backcloth. As the trout cooked, a group of cats gathered in the shadows optimistically.

*****

Alex walked up to the tower before breakfast and sat watching the villagers going about their daily tasks. A steady stream of women winded their way up the cobbled street to the boulangerie. It was their first social meeting of the day. The baker's wife would lean her elbows on the counter ready to exchange any local gossip. The choice of bread often depended on her husband's intake of pastis the night before. He spent the day delivering to the mountain hamlets in his Renault van. They were a hardworking couple and mines of information. If madame was in a good mood then the queue had to wait for as long as it took to impart the titbits of news.

Most of the men left early for the vineyards. In these mountains the vines are still cut by hand and the grapes collected in comportes. What a different style of life these peasant people lead. They worked hard, ate and drank well and seemed pretty contented. No teenagers loitered about and those they met in the bar at night were friendly enough. No vandalism or litter anywhere. Apart from the campsite outside the old cité wall there were few foreigners. Even the campers were predominantly French with a sprinkling of Dutch, Belgians and Germans. Everyone was friendly although the older locals had a courteous reserve.

He became aware of another presence close by, it was a girl picking berries from a shrubby tree. He recognised her from the bar the previous evening and knew she came from the village. Either she hadn't seen him or was giving that impression.

'Bonjour Mademoiselle' he called.

She turned, smiled and came towards him.

'Ça va.'

'Ça va,' he replied and went on 'comment vous appellez vous?'

'Je m'appelle Martine,' and she held out her hand.

'Parlez-vous Anglais Martine?'

'Mais oui,' she said laughing. 'I am a student of English at the Université of Montpellier. It will 'elp me to talk with you and you can correct my mistakes.'

'I'm sorry my French isn't better. I find the Midi pronunciation difficult to follow.'

'If you come from Paris or the north you find it difficult also. Are you 'ere on 'oliday?'

'Yes. We're a group of mountain bikers staying at the chambres d'hôtes and completely gob-smacked by it all.'

'What means gob-smacked? Is it good?'

'Yes, in this instance. It means you're amazed beyond belief. Do you live in Olargues?'

'I live near to the bar. My parents 'ave the shop there. I expect you know it.'

Alex nodded. 'Do you like to cycle? We go mountain biking every day.'

'Not much. I used to like it when I was young. Now I enjoy escalade, and to walk in the mountains and swim in the pools.'

'Rock climbing. Are you good at it?'

'Yes. I started when I was at school. It is a natural activity in this region with so many gorges and rocky mountain outcrops.'

'I've never had a bash at that. Would you like to teach me?'

She laughed. 'I might. How long do you stay?'

'Another week and the time is flying by.'

'Where is your 'ome?'

'In the Midlands, near the border with Wales.'

'Ah! le Pays de Galles. It is very beautiful, yes?'

'Yes, but we get too much rain.'

''ere it rains also. We 'ave the same rainfall as London.'

'Are you sure? It doesn't seem possible.'

'Yes, but we 'ave the sun for three 'undred days of the year. When it rains 'ere it comes 'eavily. We need it for the cherries, vines and marron.'

'Have you ever been to England?'

'Yes. I was for one month in Brighton to look after some children who were on 'oliday. I 'ope to go back to practice my English.'

Alex became thoughtful. It would be good if Martine could stay with one of their party if she wanted to. He would mention it to Kate and see what she thought.

'What are you doing today?' he asked.

''elping at the Museum on guided tours of the cité. In the evening I work in the bar. I 'ave to earn money. What do you do for work in England?'

'I am a student too. My mother died very suddenly in June and I have hardly studied at all since.'

'That is very sad for you. 'ave you a big family?'

'No, just my father at home and we don't hit it off too well.'

'That is very 'ard for you. I 'ave two brothers and a sister all younger. What are you going to do?'

'I was planning a career in educational psychology but I'm convinced I made a wrong choice.'

'I want to work as an interpreter if I can be good enough with languages. I speak German better than English but there is a long way to go.'

'It's a brilliant time to study European languages. Where we are staying the English owner's children speak French fluently and they are only six and two years old.'

'I know the children well, beautiful blonde hair. They come with their parents to the café bar. They are such 'appy children. Is the 'ouse very big?'

'It has five double bedrooms for guests. We all share rooms and there are ten of us. It costs less to come in a party. It is very French in style, they haven't Anglicised it at all.'

'They 'ave a party at New Year and my parents go to it. For many years the 'ouse was empty. Everyone is interested to see what 'appened to it and the old shop.'

'Why don't you come for dinner one evening when you're not working?'

'What about your friends?'

'They'd make you welcome Martine. I'd better get back for breakfast. We are tackling Fontfroide today.'

'It will be very 'ot again. I shall think of you all après midi as I rest in the cool 'ouse.' She continued to pick more ripe sloes.

*****

Kate was walking on air. She felt fantastic and knew that she looked her best too. What a good thing she had seen the doctor before the holiday and started to take the pill. She was also pleased that she hadn't given herself fully to anyone before. This was partly because she was very old fashioned and also she wanted love and sex to go together. Most of her friends were much more casual about sex but this had never appealed to Kate. Now she was so thankful that she had followed her own instinct rather than her friends.

Sam had told her later about taking precautions. She told him quite candidly what she had done. He was both relieved and flattered. He teased her saying 'So you planned to seduce me did you?'

They spent more and more time together. The others watched their romance burgeon. Even Alex didn't seem to mind. Kate noticed he seemed very interested in Martine who worked in the bar. Martine, if she responded, did not show her feelings overtly.

There was another whole week before returning home. They decided to hire a car for two days to get farther afield and away from the others. There were books in the house about the Cathare Castles which had really caught their imagination. Kate had never been abroad before and found every day an adventure.

It was too complicated to hire a car properly at short notice because of the distance to the nearest town, so they decided to hire one belonging to the family. They had the choice of an ancient, battered old Renault van or a relatively new eight-seater Citröen CX. Thinking of the twisting steep roads they chose the old van. It didn't look wonderful but went like a bomb. Also it wouldn't show a scratch that easily if they caught it on a rock or anything.

The insurance was OK and they set off the next morning for Carcassonne. It was a scenic south westerly drive, at first through the mountains and later in the plain where the vendange was in full swing. The little tractors with their trailers piled high with black grapes making for the nearest co-operative cave.

The ancient cité of Carcassonne was impressive. The exterior was used for the film setting of 'Camelot' and still seemed like a film set in some ways. It looked too perfect to be real. It was full of tourists of every nationality, especially Americans. After a week of not seeing a single coach the sight of full coach and car parks was quite a shock.

The restoration had been cleverly done and a whole town lived within the cité walls from the cathedral to the school. Lots of restaurants, a hotel mingled with souvenir shops and more expensive boutiques. There was much to see here but they were both glad to leave all the commercialism and bustle behind and hit the open road towards the Pyrénées.

They picnicked choosing a corner of a vineyard beside a peach tree and under the shade of a fig tree. The fruit was plentiful and it was great to pick fresh, sun-warmed peaches and delicious black figs. They found some ripe walnuts too, the stains from which wouldn't wash off in the stream. A shady siesta before driving on was both romantic and therapeutic.

They made for Peyrepertuse – the name means pierced stone – which dominated the skyline. They had to walk the last part along an access path that wound and zigzagged up steeply to the battlements. Once through the threshold there was not just a fortress but a small, medieval town at 800 metres. Every bit of the top of the rocky massif was used. No sign of tourists here and it was a magical place to be. The stunning views sparked the imagination and wonder at how it came to be built. In the ninth centure it had belonged to a Catalonian Count of the House of Barcelona. It was not given to the French until two centuries later.

The terrible loss of life during the building and the sieges let alone the crusades that followed were awesome to contemplate. The Cathares fought against the Roman Catholic Order as well as the Royal Order for a whole century. The large military operation known as The Crusade of the Albigenses was triggered off by Pope Innocent III in 1209. It was interesting reading history from the French point of view.

What a vantage point enabling the naked eye to see as far as the Mediterranean, Pyrénées, Montagne Noire and the plain. They resolved to come back here one day as they dragged themselves away reluctantly. The attraction was like a strong ineluctable magnetic force.

They drove onto Rennes-le-Château where treasure of untold value is believed to be buried. Much controversy surrounds this little mountain-top town. The book shop at the museum has writings of countless authors, in many languages, on the subject.

The message engraved over the entrance to the church reads 'This place is Terrible.' A dire warning to all who enter. Kate shivered as she consulted her guide book. The disturbing message was said to have been engraved by two priests. The twelve treasures of Rennes-le-Château are legendary and fascinating. The Curé Henri Boudet's account books show that he spent as much as 130 million francs over a period of twenty years.

Did the Curé Beranger Saunier call his dog Pomponnet and his monkey Mela in order to remind us that the Spanish writer Pomponnius Mela located Pyrere and its fabulous riches buried south of Carcassonne?

Sam and Kate read about the Celts, the Romans, the Visigoths, the birth of Rhedae, the Arabs, the Francs, Rhedae as a royal city, the House of Barcelona, the Trencavel, the King of Aragon, Catharism, Simon de Montfort, the Lords of Voison, the Routiers, the Plague, the Count of Trastamarre, the end of Rhedae, the House of Voisins, the House of Hautpoul, the Lords of Blanchefort and the last of the Hautpoul family of Rennes.

On 17th January 1781 the Hautpoul family disappeared forever with the death of Marie de Negre Dables, Dame d'Hautpoul de Blanchefort, aged 67. But, as if the city of Rhedae refused to die, the date of that end marks the beginning of a quite unbelievable story.

By now they felt bewitched by Rennes-le-Château and could easily believe they were walking on top of fabulous, buried treasure. Dame d'Hautpoul died without an heir and so she passed on the guardianship of a great secret to her confessor, Antoine Bigou, the Curé of Rennes-le-Chateau along with important documents. What the priest learnt terrified him as France was in the throes of the political upheaval which, eventually, led to the 1789 revolution.

After much serious thought he hid the documents in the Visigoth pillar which held up the altar of St Magdalene Church. He feared for his life if he was to pass on the secret to a worthy successor and decided to entrust a stone slab with the information for future generations. It was engraved with Latin inscriptions and placed on the Marchioness's grave. This cryptogram was to provide the key to the secret in the right interpretation.

Sam and Kate spent a long time in the church where they re-lived some of the stories they had read. It was a relief to come out, blinking, into the sunshine. There was a swarm of wild bees settling onto a tree near the church door. Kate remembered the fate of Sam's father.

'Are you afraid of bees now Sam?'

'No, but I've always had a healthy respect for them.' Sam looked sad and serious. Kate took hold of his hand and pulled him away.

'Let's go and find somewhere to stay the night.'

'Couiza or Quillan seem the obvious choice. Which one do you fancy?'

'Quillan I think. I've never stayed anywhere beginning with Q.'

'That's as good a reason as any,' and Sam started up the Renault's engine.

They found a quiet house offering chambres d'hôtes and Sam booked a double room. Kate felt so happy. They made love as they changed for dinner and fell asleep in each other's arms.

It was quite late when they woke up, ravenously hungry. They strolled across to a little restaurant with traditional red checked tablecloths covered with white paper ones. Madame was enormous and spoke no English. They chose the cheapest menu at 60 francs and this included a pichet of wine. It was striking midnight as they finished with coffee with cognac. The creepy stories of buried treasure now seemed a million miles away.

Kate woke first in the morning. With the closed shutters she had no idea what time it was and it didn't matter. As she stretched Sam rolled over towards her. It was the start of another day of history and romance.

The next night was spent in a fèrme aubèrge close to Brassac run by a young couple with five children. After two days of being steeped in Cathare history it was good to drive back to Olargues in time for dinner. They were a lively party that night. Martine and a young Belgian couple joined them round the table. Witty repartee kept up until the early hours when they gradually trooped off up the spiral stone staircase. Sam went back to sharing with Alex and Kate with Sally. Alex came to bed hours later after he had taken Martine home. Kate feigned sleep to avoid Sally's questions. She thought through the magical hours alone with Sam and hugged her memories to herself.

CHAPTER 7

David found himself counting the days until Alex returned from holiday. He was not looking forward to explaining his redundancy but craved the company of someone to talk to. It would soon be time for Alex to go back to university and the financial situation had to be discussed.

David went to the job centre regularly but there was nothing suitable. The girl was not very helpful and made David feel really past it. He had to sign on every fortnight to keep his pension right credits in order. This he found a humiliating experience like many of the other people there.

The loss of his job had been a double blow as he had expected promotion. It seems that he had completely misjudged the mood of his employers for the past year. When he thought he was in line for a colleague's position it transpired that he was merely dispensable, his role was phased out.

David's preachings about using time well were to haunt him repeatedly. Left to his own devices he found it difficult to structure a day purposefully. He was conscious of the irony of it all and wondered how Alex would respond. He went round the house with a notepad jotting down what needed to be done room by room, He made a shopping list. He noted jobs to be done in the garden. The garden had never looked such a mess. He made a start by mowing the lawn. The machine just managed the length of the grass with the blades at the highest point. David felt so much better after working in the garden, that he made himself a daily timetable to get as much done as possible before Alex came home.

During the next days his moods swung from elation to depression alarmingly. He found it difficult to follow one good day with another. His sleep pattern tended to reflect the amount of anaesthetising whisky he consumed.

Faith's ghost hung about in the early mornings but his night-time dreams were more inclined to feature Elizabeth. The recurrent nightmare of Charles and Faith on the boat was powerful and disturbing. The shock of Faith's death still sent ripples of anger through him. He tried to work out how he might have felt if she had died in more ordinary circumstances without the possibility of involvement with anyone else. He would have been upset and able to grieve properly, as a normal husband should, instead he felt cheated and full of self pity and anger. He had always been faithful and loving and Faith had met all his needs most fully. He had never been tempted to stray and, until now, he would have sworn that Faith was the same.

He was amazed by the power of the surges of anger and jealousy that swept over him when he thought of Faith with Charles. He knew that a large percentage of murders took place within family circles and close friends, now he could really understand how matters could escalate out of control. Yet he had always prided himself on his self control and discipline. It was frightening and alarming to discover how circumstances could alter everything beyond belief.

Alex came home looking bronzed and fit and happy. David was immediately struck by his appearance and felt envious and rather peeved.

'Had a good holiday?'

'It was brilliant. None of us wanted to come back. How's things with you Dad?'

'Fair to middling I suppose. There's a lot we need to talk about when you've had time to unpack and settle down.'

'OK. Why don't we talk now? You've clearly got something on your mind. Go ahead; shoot, give.'

David fiddled with the top of one of his socks playing for time, before launching into his prepared speech.

'As you know I have been made redundant. There seems little chance of me obtaining suitable employment in the foreseeable future. All this means taking great care with money and economising to keep solvent.'

'Dad you've always been careful with dosh, there doesn't seem to be much scope for cutting down other than with me.'

David shuffled uncomfortably. He stood up, wound the clock and took his time before looking directly at Alex.

'That is the terrible truth. I am wondering how we are going to managed to keep you at university for another year.'

'Don't give yourself any grief on that. I've already decided not to go back to Keele.'

'You mean you're dropping out, just like that?'

'Yes and no. Yes, I'm quitting, no, not just like that. Even if you hadn't been given the push I would have come to this decision.'

David looked uncertain and puzzled. He should have felt relief not a rather irritable resentment. Alex seemed so casual about it.

'Look, I'll go and chuck my dirty gear in the washer and then we can talk over a coffee.'

'Oh dear! Yes, now there's a problem with the washing machine. It has broken down and I can't empty the water out. Will you have a look at it?'

Alex went into the kitchen. David winced at the expletives that accompanied the bangs and bumps and then the sound of water sloshing across the floor. He resisted the temptation to try to help thinking it more politic to keep out of the way.

Half an hour later there were promising washing machine noises and David ventured into the kitchen. There was water all over the floor but at least the washer seemed to be working. Kitchen towels and teacloths were strewn over the floor to blot up the worst of the puddles.

'Well done Alex. I couldn't make it work at all. What's this awful smell?'

'Stagnant water. However long has this lot been left? It really stinks.'

'It happened just after you left, I think it was the next day.'

'It's a bloody awful stench. I've put your clothes on a hot wash to try and get rid of it. They have gone rather slimy so I don't know how they'll be. There was a sock in the drainage pipe. The filter was out of position and blocked. Probably needs a new one.'

Alex rinsed his hands well with water containing bleach. He sniffed at them gingerly and said 'That's better. I'll do my stuff tomorrow when I'm sure it's working OK.'

David felt ever more inadequate. He put the kettle on. 'Tea or coffee or there's lager in the fridge.'

'Coffee please' and he swished the towels round with his feet, mopping up the water. 'I'll leave the door and windows open to try and get rid of his putrid stink.'

David nodded feeling horribly helpless. 'I'm afraid I'm not much use when it comes to household matters. They were always your mother's concern.'

Don't I know it, Alex thought, but his irritation with his father was tempered by pity and he held his tongue.

'Has Kate enjoyed her holiday?'

'Yes, she and Sam had a great time. They're not such keen bikers as the rest of us, but they found plenty to interest them. It's a fabulous place.'

'It must be. Your mother and I planned a holiday abroad this year, the first since our honeymoon.'

'I know. Mum was really hyped up about it. Shall you still go?'

'No. I cancelled it. Fortunately I had taken out a reliable insurance policy. Always a prudent measure, you'd do well to remember that.'

'You could do with a break and now you're not working you could get a good deal off-season.'

'Do you think I'd like Olargues?'

'No.' Alex replied too firmly.

'Why not? You seem full of it and you all enjoyed it.'

'You wouldn't fit in there. You don't like foreign food. You wouldn't like everyone sitting round the same large table to eat. There's no telly in the house. You don't speak French.'

'I thought the owners were English?'

'They are but they live a French lifestyle.'

'All right, all right. Aren't there hotels there?'

'There's one, but they don't speak English either. It's not a touristy place. The scenery is touristique but it's not at all commercialised. It really isn't your scene. It's ideal for painters, fishing, walking, biking, trekking, swimming, kayaking, climbing, natural history, archaeology,' and Alex ran out of breath, 'wouldn't suit you at all.'

Alex went to peg the washing out on the line leaving David feeling more depressed than ever. He recognised the truths he was hearing, he wasn't interested in any of those activities other than a bit of walking. He asked himself what he liked doing and scribbled his ideas on the back of an envelope. Football, television, growing dahlias, car maintenance, darts at the pub, those used to be his interests. Apart from watching television he no longer pursued any of his hobbies since Faith died.

Alex disturbed his thoughts. 'I'll leave the washing out overnight to freshen it up. I think most of it is OK but some marks haven't come out.'

'Quite the little housewife aren't you?', David sneered. Alex coloured and felt his hackles rising.

'Don't start anything Dad, we can do without more grief.'

David longed to tell him he used the word grief improperly but bit his tongue.

'You are quite right son. Now what about your degree course. What are you going to do?'

'I shall have to write formally and then go and see them at Keele about finishing. They won't be very pleased but I'm sure it'll be for the best.'

'What will you do?'

'Look for a job and re-think my plans. I made a wrong choice I guess.'

'I never could understand what you wanted with all that psychological clap-trap. Your mother seemed to understand it better. But it's bad to start things and not see them through.'

'But you virtually said we couldn't afford it. Anyway I feel right about it. My motivation isn't there any more.'

The telephone rang. Alex answered it. David heard 'Oh hi . . . yeah . . . pretty shitty . . . fab . . . brilliant . . . more hassle I guess. I've got to get some dosh together pronto . . . right, see you. Ciao.'

'Can't you people speak comprehensible English when you talk to each other? No one would ever think you'd had any education Alex.'

'I wasn't talking to you. I try to use parent-speak when I talk to you and I really make an effort. Why are you winding me up all the time? I've only been back a few hours.'

'I'm sorry but I cannot stand hearing our fine language corrupted by people who have had your opportunities in life. When I was your age . . .' David stopped as he realised he was talking to himself.

Alex was outside calling the cat. 'Dad, where's Tabitha? Is she OK?'

'She has taken to going off for long periods but looks fine when she deigns to appear. I haven't seen her today though.'

'Strange. She never used to wander. I hope she keeps away from the road.'

'What shall we have for supper? There's some corned beef and salad and . . .'

'I'm going out soon' Alex interrupted.

'Going out? But you've only just got back.'

'I'm meeting some friends at the pub at eight.'

'Want to eat something before you go?'

'No thanks. We've eaten fantastic food for a fortnight. I'll just grab a cheese sandwich later. They really know about cooking over there.'

David looked disappointed. Alex knew better than to feel guilty. Given another couple of hours they'd be at each other's throats.

David felt very cross with himself after Alex had gone. He had wanted to give him a good welcome home. He also felt rather hurt and sorry for himself. Alex seemed so confident and on top of things.

The nights were beginning to draw in and David viewed the prospect of autumn and winter with gloom. He couldn't understand people who raved about autumn tints. It was just a mess of leaves everywhere ruining his lawn and making more work.

He must find some way of occupying his time better. He thought about other retired men he knew. They seemed contented enough doing bits of shopping, going to the library and belonging to organisations. There again, they didn't have wives who had affairs and dropped dead at other people's funerals. Their wives were at home cooking their dinner, mending their clothes and doing the ironing. He supposed some of them must be widowers or divorced. Perhaps they answered those extraordinary adverts in the papers 'Attractive widow, early fifties, seeks tall man with a view to companionship. Photograph essential.'

The door bell jangled his thoughts. It was Kate looking for Alex.

'No I won't come in, thank you, but I need to see Alex.'

'He's gone to the pub, he didn't say which one.'

'Is he on his own?'

'No, I think he's meeting some friends. Is there anything wrong?'

'Parent trouble. I'll find Alex. He's very good at sorting things out when the going gets tough.'

'Anything I can do to help?'

'No thank you Mr Green. I'll find Alex, 'bye.'

David liked Kate and thought how pretty she looked. Parent trouble, he thought, she made it sound as common as 'flu'. Perhaps Alex regarded him as parent trouble, what a horrible idea. He was surprised that Alex was considered such an authority on the subject. Pity he didn't marry Kate, but how could he with no job and no prospects worth considering.

Kate's parents had treated her badly. Her father was always in debt and had been out of work for years. Her mother worked nights as an auxilliary nurse. Kate and her mother had been subjected to violence at times.

David poured himself a large whisky and turned on the television. A close-up of a couple having athletic intercourse attracted his attention. One consolation about being on his own was watching this sort of soft pornographic film lasciviously. If anyone else had been there he'd have snapped it off smartly and called it a disgusting wanton display.

When the film was over, and the whisky bottle much emptier, he began to think of Elizabeth. His disordered thoughts turned into fantasies and, when he went to bed, became dreams. Dreams in which Elizabeth was there but always just out of reach. The faces of Faith and Charles loomed between them menacingly. He kept pouring buckets of water over their faces. They spluttered but would not drown and it seemed to go on interminably. He awoke in a crazed, dazed state, his bed wet from water. Consciousness jumped into action. He could distinctly smell urine. Oh my God, he had wet the bed.

He rushed to the lavatory to no avail, it was too late he thought wryly. His head ached as he stripped off the bed and scrabbled through the airing cupboard searching for clean sheets. At least the washer was working. He flung the sodden linen inside and set the programme.

He went to the sideboard cupboard to look at the level of the whisky bottle. It wasn't there. The sticky glass was on the table with two fruit flies stuck to the side. He searched feverishly for the bottle which he knew he had bought the day before. Eventually he found it in the waste bin.

He couldn't have finished it, it wasn't possible. Alex? No, Alex didn't like whisky. He must have spilt it. He sniffed around hopefully but couldn't smell anything. The washer changed gear and pitch.

The back door opened and Alex walked in. He was astonished to find his father stark naked in the kitchen, with the bin lid in one hand and an empty bottle in the other. The washer was on and David looked flushed and disorientated.

'You're late,' David muttered.

'You're drunk' Alex said under his breath. He went on audibly. 'Yes. A load of hassle with Kate's people. What about you? You seem busy.'

'Just tidying up a bit. Couldn't sleep, that sort of thing' he said lamely.

'I'm going to bed. Goodnight.' France seemed a long way away, as Alex climbed the stairs wearily.

Alex posted his letters to the university. There were three of them. He felt a great sense of release as he dropped the last one into the box. It was a start but he must find work, anything would do, immediately. There was no way he could live with David and he was determined to find digs as soon as his earning power permitted.

He was surprised that he had no reservations about not taking his degree. It seemed an entirely positive step. He realised that much of his enthusiasm for university had been the pressure from school and his mother's delight and pride. Alex was grateful for the experience and felt it would stand him in good stead in the long term.

It was a bad time, with the recession, to find work but he was determined. He had to see his bank manager soon about an overdraft facility. He had hoped to borrow from David but couldn't face the endless lectures and having to be eternally grateful. So he spent two busy days in Ludlow sifting through the few possibilities. By day three he had a shortlist of four menial jobs. Washing up and general dogsbody at a hotel at £3.50 an hour. Sweeping up and cleaning houses on a new estate, after the builders had finished, at £3.75 an hour. An application form for a temporary, part-time support worker in the Youth Service for five hours per week, evening time. The rate for an unqualified applicant, grade 2, being £5.28 per hour. Also a form for a community care worker, twenty hours a week at £4.10 per hour.

He accepted the housing estate work and filled in the forms for the Social Services job and the temporary one with the Youth Service. The closing date for both jobs was in three days time.

Less rewarding was his effort to find a cheap bedsit or lodgings. The only ones available were ridiculously expensive. So he put his name down on various lists with housing associations and estate agents. He didn't tell his father anything more that he was searching for work.

He started at the building site the next day. It was simple, boring and took much less time than the foreman allocated. He had to slow himself down to fit the system otherwise he would be shortening his own hours. He was paid for eight hours a day, three days a week with occasional extra days. He worked alone but enjoyed the crack of the men during the many tea breaks.

Two weeks later he started with the Youth Service working two and a half hours on Monday and Wednesday evenings. He ran a five a side football, table tennis and basket-ball sessions. His clientele were a mixed bunch, but he rarely had trouble that he couldn't deal with and thoroughly enjoyed the experience. It made a welcome change from the intertia of the building site. His employers suggested he take a qualification assuring him that his background in educational psychology would advantage his prospects.

This gave him around a hundred and sixteen pounds a week. He gave David twenty, put fifty in the building society and kept the rest for himself. After living as a student he found himself relatively well off. He enrolled for French classes one night a week at the adult education centre.

David was amazed how quickly he sorted things out and, grudgingly, admired him for it. Admittedly it was work that anyone could do, but it showed initiative and grit. It also added to his own sense of inadequacy.

Alex was buoyant, a letter from Martine came back quickly in reply to his. It was a chatty account of life in Olargues and her preparations for the coming academic year. She asked him to correct any grammatical or other errors. He was glad he couldn't find any as he had no intention of parting with the letter. He had managed to get hold of a photograph of her from Kate. It was in his room in an old Victorian frame he'd picked up cheaply in the Sunday flea market. He would be able to write her quite an amusing letter about his new lifestyle.

Alex was concerned about his father's apathy and the amount of whisky he was consuming. It occurred to him that the twenty pounds a week he was chipping in to the household budget would scarcely keep David in whisky for three days. He wasn't eating properly either and this was a bad combination. If he said anything about it there was an immediate flare up between them and it didn't take much of a spark to light up the touch paper these days.

Kate came round most weeks and was a calming influence on David. Alex and Kate's friendship was now on a safe, platonic footing which suited them both. Sam was a frequent visitor and he and Alex were on very good terms since the holiday.

Sam told Alex that his publishing firm were advertising for a production assistant and suggested he applied for the job. The money wasn't brilliant but the training was good and would put him on a rung of the ladder towards production management. To Alex the money seemed relatively good but the hours were long and irregular. He decided to apply for it. He liked the idea of moving to Oxford but didn't really hold out much hope of getting the post despite Sam's optimism.

At the weekend David and Alex went to clear his room in Newcastle. With a borrowed roof-rack they managed to move all his gear in one go. Alex had no second thoughts at all. His friendship with flatmates would continue. They'd all had a fantastic time biking in France and would keep in touch.

He managed to see one of his lecturers but all of the others were still on vacation. Alex felt he had really moved on in life since the last time he was at Keele. His last assignment was in his locker and was not up to his usual standard. He would not have to heed the cryptic comments of his tutor again.

David showed more interest in Keele that he had ever done before. Alex was proud to show him round the campus. There was much activity everywhere in preparation for the start of the academic year. Every room smelt of fresh paint and there were signs of workmen all over the campus.

'Aren't you going to miss all these facilities Alex?'

'No, I don't think so. I've made good use of them over the past two years and I'm not going to have time to look back.'

'What about your friends?' David asked.

'We shall meet up again. We've had some riotous times I can tell you.' Alex went on to recount some hair-raising stories that shocked David. It was a wonder they ever did any work, wasting taxpayers' money. What a contrast to his early life.

David felt more relaxed than he had for a long time. Alex was in high spirits and suggested stopping in Shrewsbury for a meal on the way back. He insisted on treating his father and kept up an animated conversation. David hadn't been to an Italian restaurant before and found the food surprisingly good.

The relaxed atmosphere lasted until they arrived home and finished unpacking the car. Then a cloak of uncompanionable silence fell over them, as if they were different characters behind closed doors. The gloom weighed on them both heavily. Alex spent the evening sorting out his room. It was crammed full of boxes and plastic bags. He made a pathway through to the bed and stacked the boxes of books and belongings neatly. It looked a mess but he hoped he wouldn't be here much longer.

By the time he went downstairs David was asleep in the chair, television on and the inevitable whisky bottle on the table.

Alex went up to David's bedroom. He had hardly been in there since Faith died. He pulled open the dressing table drawer and there were her brush and comb, face cream, powder and lipstick, hankies and oddments. Her familiar smell wafted out as he handled her things. He opened the wardrobe and her clothes were all hanging there. David kept his where they'd always been. At the bottom of the wardrobe on Faith's side were her writing case and small jewel box.

He wondered whether his father was keeping her things like this for sentimental reasons or whether he just hadn't bothered with them. It didn't make any sense to keep everything exactly as it was and yet burn all Faith's paintings. Alex still felt very sore about the destruction of Faith's creative work. He closed the door full of mixed feelings. They would have to talk about it but it was important to catch the right moment. He wanted to keep the gold locket she always wore and slipped it into his pocket for safety.

CHAPTER 8

Charlotte was disappointed in Elizabeth's lack of reaction to her pronouncement that she was planning to move to Cherwell Close. What she didn't know was that it was Elizabeth's third shock in one day. Charlotte had timed it for maximum impact but it had become one of the after shocks following the earthquake in the sequence of events.

Elizabeth was still reeling from an obscene 'phone call at breakfast time. Not only was the content abhorrent but she recognised the caller. He made no effort to disguise his identity. He was a close friend and colleague of Charles from their earliest days in medical school and was best man at their wedding. They went on fishing trips together in recent years.

He started singing a song to the tune of 'Making Whoopee'. It was sickening:

'Now you are free
I'm offering me
From bended knee,
Oh can't you see
Us dear Lizzie
When we shall both be
Making whoopee.'

She was sure of the voice but had to be certain she wasn't making a terrible mistake. The error, in the event, was that she listened at all. For a second she thought it was a silly joke. She quickly realised it was not.

He didn't sound drunk, every word was clearly annunciated and nauseating. She was affronted by the explicit nature of sexual proposals and the bragging about his expertise. She put the 'phone down and switched on the answering machine.

She was still shaking when she walked into her Solicitor's office at 10.30 for an appointment to sign documents for the probate office. It was a relief to get out of the house though.

'Are you alright Elizabeth? You don't seem your usual self today. You'll have to start getting out more.'

'Yes, I'm perfectly all right. I didn't sleep too well last night, that's all.'

'You poor dear. You need someone to keep an eye on you', and Roderick put his arm round her reassuringly. When his other hand started to purposefully explore the front of her neckline she pulled quickly away.

'Roderick, how dare you.'

'Very easily my dear. You're looking better already. The colour's back in your cheeks; I know what you want.' As he spoke he advanced with a menacing leer. Elizabeth slapped him hard across the face, knocking his glasses to the floor.

'And I know what you want' and she gathered her papers and swept out of the room. He called after her 'I think you've broken my new spectacles.'

'Good,' she snapped to the surprise of the receptionist.

In the street she paused to collect herself and decided to go to the library café. Thankfully there was no one in there that she knew. She ordered coffee to calm herself. She couldn't recall ever feeling so angry and vulnerable.

She supposed she should feel flattered, in a way, but she definitely did not. Since Charles' death she found she had to be on her mettle where men were concerned. It was disconcerting after years of protection to be thrown into the chase again. The rules seemed to have changed since she was young to no holds barred. Charles' presence had kept her free from anything more than the pleasure of admiring glances and the odd innocent flirtation at parties. She had been able to enjoy male company from the safety of her marital status. She knew very well the level that conversation could sink to at dinner parties given by doctors and surgeons. If patients heard even a fraction of the crudity they would be horrified. She always thought this a sort of necessary evil, a safety valve, a letting go of the considerable strain and responsibility that they bore through their work.

Her solicitor was the last straw. Who could she turn to when professional friends behaved like alley cats. Elizabeth paid for her coffee, took several deep breaths and set off home. She had planned to look for a new blouse but had lost the inclination and just wanted to get home. The rhythm of walking was helpful. The leaves were starting to fall and the trees wearing their autumn colours.

As she entered the house she heard the answering machine clicking off. To her horror the tape was full. She tried to tell herself not to listen to any of it, to clean the entire lot off but she ended up playing it through. There were various ordinary calls, including one from the solicitor's secretary, but mostly it was the depraved caller from breakfast time. She wanted to get rid of it before Charlotte came from her home in Oxford.

The song went on
'You're on my knee
You're feeling me
Inside you free
My dear Lizzie,
'twas worth the waiting
Anticipating
Making whoopee.'
There were more verses that became more lewd and crude.

She thought of his wife who had written such a kind letter when Charles died. She had always found Lynn a tense, twitchy sort of woman – difficult to talk to. Perhaps she had more to contend with than anyone knew . . . did she know? . . . poor Lynn, how dreadful to be married to someone as warped as that.

Elizabeth went to look for the tablets that her doctor had given her when Charles died. She had never taken them. She poured a glass of water and took one now. She toyed with a sandwich but left most of it. She took the telephone receiver off the hook and sank into a comfortable armchair. Tobermory jumped onto her knee. Hugging him to her she fell asleep, soothed by his warmth and rhythmic purring.

Charlotte found her sleeping and was vexed at having to contain her news. Elizabeth looked tired but very beautiful and Tobermory's tail swished angrily at the sight of his adversary.

'Horrible creature', Charlotte muttered as she tried to creep quietly out of the room. Her arthritis caused her to stumble. Elizabeth was aware of Charlotte's presence and wearily pulled herself together. She felt a little light-headed and her mouth was dry.

Charlotte was in the kitchen struggling to fill the kettle. 'Let me do that for you, it's heavy.'

'I've done it thank you. You can carry the tray when I've made the tea. I've some news for you Elizabeth.'

'Why don't we have it here, kitchens are such comforting places.' In another mood Charlotte would have picked up on this but she was bursting to tell Elizabeth what she'd done.

'I've decided to move into Cherwell Close and sell the Oxford apartment.' Charlotte waited for Elizabeth to react, but she didn't. After a long pause she said 'If that's what you want Charlotte I'll help you all I can. You are always welcome to stay here, but you know that already.'

Charlotte felt deflated. At the very least she expected some opposition and surprise. She looked closely at Elizabeth and was about to suggest she saw her doctor for a tonic when the telephone rang.

'That'll be for me I think. I asked Mary to ring here.'

'I thought the receiver was off the hook.'

'It was dear. I put it back on when I came in.' and she went to answer it in the sittingroom. Elizabeth drank her tea, but could hear Charlotte's clear voice.

'I beg your pardon, who do you think you are talking to? . . . Yes, I am Mrs Jefferson, who are you?'

Elizabeth hurriedly picked up the hall extension. To her horror she heard the voice telling Charlotte about the size of his 'wedding tackle.'

'You sound sound thoroughly penalised to me. If it's as long as you say I suggest you wrap it tightly round your throat and throttle yourself. Good afternoon.'

Charlotte caught Elizabeth putting the receiver down, convulsed with laughter.

'I take it you have been having problems dear. I thought you looked peaky. An educated voice too, making such a fool of himself. Couldn't bonk a butterfly. No wonder you weren't impressed with my news when you have that sort of silly ass to deal with. I presume it's a medical consultant.' Elizabeth nodded. 'Someone you know no doubt?' and she nodded again.

'How history repeats itself. You are more sensitive than me, I expect it has upset you.'

'Yes it has, but you've put it in perspective for me. That wasn't all,' and she told Charlotte about the solicitor.

'I shall go to see Roderick tomorrow.' Charlotte said firmly.

'Oh no, Charlotte. I am quite capable of fighting my own battles.'

Charlotte privately disagreed with that but said 'So you're going to deprive an old lady of one of her last chances for a good skirmish. How selfish and what a pity. I need a solicitor to deal with Cherwell Close, Elizabeth. All I ask is for you to give me first go at him. I shall not mention your name other than you recommending him to me.'

Elizabeth laughed. 'You're wicked Charlotte, truly wicked.'

'Speaking of wicked, you know these things are supposed to happen in threes. I suggest you watch out for the vicar to complete the trick of the key professions.'

Minutes later Elizabeth heard Charlotte making an appointment to see Roderick. 'My name is Mrs Jefferson of Oriel Manor.'

Elizabeth resolved to take a considerable interest in Cherwell Close tomorrow. Good old Charlotte, she's rescued her again, saved her from herself.

After a good night's sleep, with the help of a second tablet. Elizabeth's composure was restored. She drove Charlotte to the solicitors and went to do her shopping. They met at the library café for a light lunch. Elizabeth was itching to know what had happened, but knew better than to ask. Charlotte's eyes were gleaming dangerously brightly. She took off her gloves slowly pulling one finger after another.

'Have you managed to set things in motion to negotiate for your apartment?'

'I sorted out a good many things. Roderick is sending a partner to Oriel Manor tomorrow morning with your probate papers, if that suits you. If it doesn't you ring up and ask a girl called Diana for a different appointment.'

'What did you think of Roderick?'

'A tiresome little man, not as old as I expected. I asked him whether he'd considered going on a client relationship course under the auspices of the Law Society.'

'Do they have one?'

'No, I shouldn't think so for one minute. He rattled very easily. Your name wasn't mentioned but he knew exactly what I was getting at. Once I'd pinned his ears back he focused his mind on my contract and explained the conditions quite well.'

Elizabeth leant on her elbows full of admiration. They ordered sandwiches and coffee. She wondered how Charlotte maintained her sparkle and realised she thrived on challenge.

'If you aren't too tired we could go on to Cherwell Close and you could show me your apartment.'

'I should like to. I don't know what you'll make of it. Very different from our life style. Sam thought it was all right though.'

'He never told me about it.'

'No I asked him not to. He took me a couple of weeks ago when you were out. I didn't want to involve you until I'd made up my mind about leaving my home. You have always been most kind to me Elizabeth but you have your own life to lead.'

'Do we need an appointment?'

'Yes, but we needn't bother. There is some fearful activity going on on Wednesday afternoons in the community room. Someone with a key is sure to be there.'

As they drove into the complex Elizabeth was favourably impressed. It was well laid out and maintained with pretty gardens and hanging baskets.

'Voila! The floral barracks' said Charlotte.

'I know what you mean but it's rather attractive. A lovely quiet position and so near to Mary.'

'That's a very big plus. The warden lives over there' and she pointed to a particularly floral corner. 'Mine is on the other side. That one with too many fuchsias outside.'

The warden wasn't there but her husband gave them the key. Charlotte was disappointed that Elizabeth didn't meet the dragon.

A pleasant little lady came out of the next door flat. She was walking with difficulty with the help of a stick. She was well dressed, rather plump with short, white, permed hair and wore powerful spectacles.

'They all look like that' Charlotte said waspishly. She came to their door.

'I believe you are to be my new neighbour. I am Florence White. I hope your mother will be very happy here.' She smiled warmly.

Charlotte bristled. 'I am Charlotte Jefferson and this is my daughter-in-law Elizabeth.' They shook hands.

'Do you play?' she said to Charlotte.

'Play. Play what?' Charlotte asked rather testily.

'Bridge of course dear. We play three afternoons a week. You don't look the bingo sort so I quite thought you'd be bridge. We could always teach you.'

'Thank you but no. My mother's advice when I married was 'never, but never, resort to bridge'. I never have.'

Florence looked puzzled and shuffled away. She turned back and called 'If I can be of any help you only have to say,' and she went indoors.

'That was kind, she seemed a nice little woman.'

Charlotte sniffed, 'I'm sure it's teeming with nice little women. There are a few men here too, several couples I believe. How they cope with the confined space I can't imagine. Can hardly swing a mouse, never mind a man. One could go off anyone in a place this size. Now, Elizabeth, have a look round and give me an honest opinion.'

Elizabeth went from room to room checking heaters and thermostats, turning on taps as she went. Charlotte was busy with a tape measure in the small kitchen when Elizabeth joined her.

'Well dear?'

'It's small but well thought out and gets plenty of sun everywhere but the bedroom. Everything seems to be in order apart from small things like tap washers. The bathroom suite has no damaged surfaces or stains and the lavatory is clean. With a change of décor and your own furniture it would look quite nice. I think it's fine if you're sure you want to move.'

'I must stay as independent as I can and it's getting difficult to manage at home. There's a splendid laundry room with all the latest machinery, a guest room suite and that community room.'

'Is it very expensive?'

'It isn't cheap. You buy your apartment and pay a hefty service charge but it does mean that you can forget about all outside maintenance. It covers the warden and the alarm system and all the communal facilities.'

'Yes, it seems very secure and the gardens seem to be well cared for. It's good to have a door into the garden. It would be quite pleasant to sit out on the little patio on warm days. Have you met the warden?'

'Oh yes, a frightful woman. She didn't like me either and I could tell she thought me a real snob.'

'Well you can give that impression when you choose Charlotte. It would be wise not to get off on the wrong foot with her.'

They took the key back to the door marked Warden. The warden answered.

'So you're here again Mrs Jefferson. Have you made your mind up yet? What does your daughter think of us?'

'This is my daughter-in-law, Elizabeth Jefferson, Mrs Er . . .'

'Weaver dear, Weaver. We must try to remember.'

'Mrs Weaver, that's it. I have decided to take the apartment now that Mrs Jefferson has given it her seal of approval.'

Mrs Weaver patted Charlotte's shoulder and looked Elizabeth up and down.

'I think it will be very suitable and convenient' Elizabeth said, 'and near to friends.'

'We're one big happy family here I can assure you. Have you shown Elspeth the community room?'

'Mrs Jefferson's name is Elizabeth not Elspeth. No I haven't.'

'Well come along. You're just in time to see the end of the keep fit class.'

Charlotte shuddered but Elizabeth steered her firmly after Mrs Weaver.

The room seemed to be full of fat, sweaty women and two puny men. There was an unpleasant smell of human bodies wearing man-made fibres; the room was hot and airless.

'Hello ladies and gentlemen. I've brought a new lady to look at you. Show her what you can do.'

A younger woman put on a tape and they started throwing bean bags to each other in time to the music. Some were standing but most were sitting down.

Elizabeth, seeing Charlotte's face, said to Mrs Weaver 'Thank you so much, most interesting, but I'm afraid we shall be late for an appointment if we don't leave now. I didn't notice the time until I saw your clock.'

Mrs Weaver nodded and closed the door. 'Is mother all right? She's gone a funny colour.'

'Yes, she's just overtired I think. We'll be in touch soon. Goodbye.'

Charlotte mumbled 'Goodbye' as Elizabeth helped her firmly into the car.

As they drove out Charlotte said 'Bean bags! I haven't seen bean bags since I was in kindergarten school. Isn't that hatchet faced woman horrendous? And all that lolloping flesh and the smell, oh Elizabeth, heaven preserve me.'

'I should think Mrs Weaver is kind and efficient but she just isn't your type. I expect keep fit is quite beneficial to people who can't move much. Keeps their circulation going. But it was pretty awful that smell, they should open some windows.'

'I shall keep myself to myself unless I find a kindred spirit away from bridge, bingo and bean bags.'

You will be busy finding homes for your favourite bits and pieces. Remember Mary is close by and you'll be able to visit each other easily.'

'Dear Mary. She won't believe what those old folks get up to.'

Elizabeth smiled. Most of those old folk were quite a lot younger than Charlotte.

Charlotte moved the second week in October. Her flat sold quickly and the transaction went through smoothly. Elizabeth was extremely helpful and did everything possible to minimise the effort of moving for Charlotte.

Once she had decided to live at Cherwell Close, Charlotte adopted a positive attitude towards it. She had plenty of ideas about what she wanted and Elizabeth executed them efficiently. She was amused by the smallness of it and felt as if she was on holiday, like a child playing house. She was also exhausted by all the decisions involved in moving despite having so much help.

She had noticed a general slowing down throughout the summer caused by a heart condition. Her doctor kept an eye on her medication and they both agreed she was good for her years. The move seemed a sensible, logical step.

Since Charles' death, Charlotte had spent a lot of time with Elizabeth. She felt it had helped them both. She had hoped her grand-daughter Rachel would have filled this role and tried to improve relations between Elizabeth and her daughter. Rachel left home after a bigger than usual row on her eighteenth birthday. She had been a rebel at fifteen and was still a rebel at twenty-five. She hated their bourgeois lifestyle and took great pleasure in being an embarrassment to the family. She was a terrible worry too as she got into bad company and the drug scene, first in Oxford and later in London. She had moved into a squat in Hackney when they last heard.

Charlotte knew she would feel guilty after her father's death. She was composed at the funeral helped by her old friend Jane. She had even agreed to wear some of Jane's clothes with coercion. She had left that night and Elizabeth hadn't heard a word from her since. It was the one subject that Charlotte couldn't talk to Elizabeth about.

So when Rachel's call came out of the blue she was surprised and delighted.

'Hi Grandma! I've been to your old place and they said you moved last week. They wouldn't give me your new address but I guessed you'd keep the old 'phone number.'

'Where are you Rachel?'

'In a call box at the station and running out of money.'

'Get in a taxi and come to No 1 Cherwell Close. It's off the Woodstock Road, on the left. I'll pay the driver when you get here.'

'What about . . .' and the 'phone went dead as the money ran out. Just as well, Charlotte thought, saved an argument.

Charlotte checked she had enough milk. She knew she was well stocked up on groceries, Elizabeth had seen to her shopping. She felt uncharacteristically nervous. It was important to get this meeting right and not have Rachel flounce off the minute something didn't suit her.

Charlotte had the money ready when the taxi drew up at the door. She handed Rachel a ten pound note and she paid the driver. There was much blind movement and curtain twitching in the Close. Rachel looked dishevelled. She was wearing a sort of Paddington Bear hat pulled down over unwashed hair, faded jeans with holes at the knee and a long black jumper. She had Elizabeth's good bone structure, complexion and colouring but she was taller and had Charles' brown eyes.

'Hi Grandma, here's your change.'

'Lovely to see you Rachel. Didn't you give the man a tip?'

'No, why should I? He really pissed me off. Had loads of hassle getting him to bring me. Wanted to see the dosh first. Told him he could ring you and then he agreed.'

'That's largely your own fault. If you will go about looking as if you haven't got two pennies to rub together, what else can they go by?'

'Oh Grandma, I'm surprised at you. Fancy judging people by what they look like."

'For goodness sake grow up. If you were a cab driver with a few unpaid fares you'd see it differently. But I don't want to quarrel, I'm so pleased to see you dear. I began to think I might never see you again.'

'You're not ill are you?' Rachel shot her a concerned glance.

'My heart isn't too clever, I'm eighty five and I can't take shocks like I used to. One has to face the facts.'

'Don't talk like that, it frightens me. Let's look at your new pad. Do you like it?'

'I'm getting used to it gradually but I miss the big rooms and my privacy.'

'It's a dinky little bathroom. What a shallow bath, isn't it low down? I like your carpets, a really gen colour.'

'Your mother found it and brought samples.' Charlotte noticed Rachel's face cloud over at the mention of Elizabeth. 'In fact she has looked after me as if I was her own daughter. I always regretted not having a daughter and so I am very blessed.'

Rachel thought this over for a few minutes then asked 'How's Ma?'

'Coping very well. She has a lot to do and a new life to build. She needs as much support as we can give her.'

Another silence. 'But she's got everything; money, looks, big house, car and loads of friends.'

'She has lost the most important person in her life and material things are not much compensation.'

'I suppose Sam is still the blue eyed boy.'

'Let's make some coffee and then you can tell me all your news.'

'OK, Shall I do it?'

'Yes please dear. The coffee is in the cupboard over the fridge.'

'Instant OK or d'you want proper coffee?'

'Instant will be fine for me.'

Charlotte was interested to notice Rachel rememembered her dislike of beakers. Charlotte's came in a cup and Rachel's in a beaker. They sat opposite to one another companionably.

'Now tell me about you. Where are you living now?'

Rachel told Charlotte she had moved to Islington and helped out in a café. She was living with a boy called Jethro who had just lost his job. She had received a letter from the family solicitors telling her she was a beneficiary in her father's will. The money would be held in trust during Elizabeth's lifetime but there was a discretionary clause.

'How much do you think I'll get Grandma?'

'I have no idea. You will have to discuss it with the solicitors or your mother.'

'Jethro says I can get a copy of the will from Somerset House.'

Charlotte bristled. 'Jethro may well be right, but it's not necessarily the best way to approach matters. And what do Jethro's people do?'

'His father was a miner and his mother sticks handles on cups at the Wedgwood factory.'

'Is his father dead?'

'No, but the mines have closed down. He used to work at Trentham which is near Wedgwood. I've been there and they're really nice.' She was looking out of the window. 'Who's that old bag messing about in your garden?'

Charlotte laughed. 'That is the warden. Don't let her see you or she'll be wanting to come in.'

'She's already seen me, that's why she's hanging about.'

Mrs Weaver came to the French window. Charlotte opened it reluctantly.

'Everything all right Mrs Jefferson? Got a visitor have you? That's nice.'

'This is my grand-daughter Rachel Jefferson, Rachel this is Mrs Weaver who is in charge here.'

'Pleased to meet you I'm sure,' and Mrs Weaver looked Rachel up and down. 'Features her mother doesn't she?'

'Do you think so. I've always thought myself more like my father' said Rachel in an uppity voice.

'Well I'd better be getting on and let you have your coffee while it's hot. Cheerio. I expect I'll see you again soon.'

'I don't think she thought much of me, do you?'

'I shouldn't let that worry you. She seemed rather interested in your clothes.'

'My grunge you mean, it's what I wear always.'

'Grunge. What is grunge?'

'Comfy clothes. These are my favourite jeans. Aren't they a fantastic colour?'

The telephone bell saved Charlotte answering the question. She picked up the receiver instead.

'Hello dear. You'll never guess who's here . . . How extraordinary, right first time . . .'

Rachel took the coffee things into the kitchen. Hearing her mother's voice brought tears coursing down her face. She closed the kitchen door and wept.

After a while she went into the bathroom and looked at herself in the mirror. Her mascara had run. She cleaned it off with a tissue and came out to face Charlotte. She was sitting looking out of the window.

'That was your mother. She's coming at twelve and hopes you will join us for lunch at the wine bar.'

'Oh I don't know,' Rachel began, 'I haven't seen her since the funeral' and her eyes welled up with tears again, 'I didn't even tell her I was leaving or anything.'

'You must miss your father, and your mother misses him and you very much indeed. Make it easy on yourself and meet her on neutral ground. You won't lose face, it was she who asked you.'

Rachel looked at her watch nervously. Charlotte said 'Why don't we have a drink while we're waiting. Make us both perk up a bit. There's wine and lager in the fridge. I'll have a small dry sherry. It's in the cupboard here.'

Rachel twizzled the stem of her wine glass. 'I suppose Sam will marry Maria and have a big vulgar wedding.'

'No. He doesn't see Maria much now. He has a girlfriend called Kate, she's a lovely girl from all accounts.'

'Is she horsy or debby?'

'Neither. She's a straightforward girl from a quite ordinary background I believe.'

'They won't like that at Oriel.'

'On the contrary, Elizabeth and Kate get on well.'

'What does she do?'

'I'm not sure. They've been on holiday together in France. Had a marvellous time from all accounts.'

'I don't believe it. My little brother taking his bird to gay Paree. Was she at Pa's funeral? I can only remember Maria there.'

'No. They couldn't have met until afterwards. It's a long story.'

'Why didn't you go to Pa's funeral Grandma?'

'Ladies of my generation do not attend funerals Rachel. I sat quietly at home and talked to God.'

'I can hear a car outside,' Rachel jumped up and looked out.

'Why don't you go and let Elizabeth in. It will make it easier for both of you.'

It was an emotional reunion but a joyful one. Charlotte felt drained with the effort. 'Do you mind girls, if I don't come out? I'm tired after the removal and would be better resting quietly.'

'Rachel turned to Elizabeth and said 'Can we go to 'Gees'? It would be a fabulous way to celebrate.'

'Why not, as long as they're open at lunch time. Are you sure Charlotte?'

'Let Grandma rest if she wants to. Thank you for everything' and she flung her arms round Charlotte's neck. Then she looked at her mother's neat suit and added 'Will I be all right like this?'

'It won't worry me darling. I'm just thrilled to see you.'

Charlotte let out a contented sigh as she waved them off with fingers crossed.

Rachel was astonished how easy it was being with her mother and how much she wanted her affection. She couldn't stop talking and Elizabeth listened avidly and responded.

As they approached 'Gees' Rachel suddenly longed for the security of home.

'Ma, I'm sorry to keep changing my mind but please can we go home instead?'

'Of course. What a good idea. We can talk privately without any interested ears. I don't think they open until the evening.'

'Will Mrs Tickle be there?'

'No. She finishes at twelve although I'm hoping Hawley will come to do some work in the garden. He's getting old and we are finding it's getting on top of us. So much to be done in the autumn.'

'I like Hawley, he knows so much. Does he still only put his teeth in on Sundays?'

'Oh yes, some things never change. I like him better without them, I'm so used to it. He looks quite fierce with a mouthful of gleaming white teeth.'

Elizabeth stopped at Thorns delicatessen and chose a selection of ham, salami, garlic sausage, saveloy and fresh baguettes. Rachel followed her inside and was very taken with the aromatic smells and the vast selection of the little shop. Elizabeth was chatting to the servers and they were enquiring about Charlotte's move. She introduced Rachel to them and they turned out to be the owners. Back in the car Elizabeth told her how they'd put everything they had into the business and worked round the clock to make it successful.

Jasper and Oscar gave Elizabeth a rapturous welcome. 'You silly dogs, I can't have been out above an hour. Why don't you welcome Rachel home instead.'

Rachel realised they hardly knew her and resolved to remedy that. 'Shall I take them out later?'

'Yes, they'd be pleased. Why don't you give them a run in the garden and see whether Hawley is there.'

Elizabeth watched from the window thrilled to see her daughter throwing sticks and chasing the dogs, and looking so happy. If only she could keep this rapport going.

She quickly set the table in the kitchen and spread a buffet lunch on top of the units. She heated some home-made soup. She rang the ship's bell outside the back door just like she did when they were children. Rachel came bounding back with the dogs at her heels.

'Do you want the dogs in? Hawley is here.'

'No, they can stay and keep him company in the garden.'

'He calls me Miss Rachel. I told him to drop the 'Miss' but he wouldn't. Sounded really weird. Umn! Something smells good.'

'Just some chicken, lentil and herb soup I made the other day.'

'Do you eat in the kitchen now, it's much better?'

'Sometimes; it's strange only having myself to please after all these years of doing what the family want.'

Rachel tucked in and enjoyed her lunch.

Elizabeth asked her about her life in London but was careful not to be intrusive. She didn't like the sound of it all but was interested to learn as much as possible.

'Aren't you scared of burglars here Ma? It's such a big house for you on your own.'

'Not really. I've got the dogs and I give them the run of the house when I'm out and also at night. There are the alarms of course. I'm pretty fatalistic about things like that.'

'It's hell in Islington. I've had my music centre nicked three times during the day time.'

'Have you ever thought of leaving London? It must be very expensive and horrid during the summer.'

'But it's where it's all happening Ma. At least I used to think it was', there was a hint of wistfulness in her voice. Elizabeth knew better than to push it.

'Let's have coffee in the conservatory. You go through and I'll bring it in.'

'What about the washing up?'

'To hell with the washing up. It'll keep and there's nothing much anyway.'

Elizabeth put the kettle on and warmed the cafetière.

When she carried the coffee tray in, Rachel was sprawled on the sofa cuddling Tobermory.

'Isn't he huge and very heavy. You big, fat cat Toby. Don't you have a dreamy life here. Ma, what's Sam's place like?'

'It's small and central and ideal really. He was lucky to get it in the centre of Oxford but the rent is extortionate.'

'Is he still going to be a publisher?'

'Yes, and doing very well. He must like it to work the long hours.'

'Grandma says he's got a new bird and they've been to France on holiday.'

'That's right. Ten of them went and had a splendid time. I think you'll like Kate, she's the exact opposite to Maria.'

'Can't be bad, a real bitch and such a snob. Let's go across the park to the lake and take the dogs or are you too knackered?'

Elizabeth was tired but was not going to miss this opportunity to know Rachel better.

'Lovely, I'll just get my anorak and walking shoes.'

'Walkies boys, come on' and Rachel put on their leads which they picked up and carried in their mouths, play growling at one another.

In Blenheim Park they let the dogs loose. They had permission to walk them on the far side of the lake as long as the dogs were controlled. The labradors were obedient to command and reliable.

'Isn't Grandma fantastic? I hope she lasts forever.'

'Yes, she is a marvellous woman but none of us last forever. She has been good to me and we are the best of friends.'

'Why didn't you get on with your mother?'

'She didn't want a daughter and I cramped her style. She regarded me as competition when I grew up. I saw very little of her as a child. I was nanny-reared and sent to boarding school when I was seven.'

'Did you like school?'

'I did when I was much older but I was very homesick for some years. Although my mother didn't love me, I adored her.'

'That must have been really tough.'

'It was. If I hadn't met your father I don't know what would have happened. It wasn't so easy for girls to earn good money and have their own flats then. She even tried to take the spotlight off me at our wedding.'

'Are you disappointed with me, Ma? Did you hope I'd be deb of the year?'

'Not disappointed exactly, but saddened. I so hoped we'd be friends and share confidences and swap clothes and gossip.' Elizabeth watched Rachel's reaction. She was silent and pensive. 'I just miss you darling, I can't help it.'

Rachel looked Elizabeth straight in the eyes and said 'I'm just beginning to see how selfish I've been. I was angry when I left, sick of the money and all that went with it. I was pretty out of it when I was doing drugs. I think I'd be dead by now if I hadn't been helped by good friends.'

'Why wouldn't you let us help you? We tried everything but you wouldn't let us near you. You do realise how much we cared, don't you?'

'I do now. I just felt a complete failure and thought you were ashamed of me. I was ashamed of you. I hated living in a big house surrounded by all that bloody success. I couldn't seem to be good at anything. You were so bloody reasonable, it really pissed me off.'

Elizabeth put her arms around her. 'We love you because you're you. There's no more to I than that. Don't blame your father for being successful though.'

'I don't now, and it's too late to explain. You were all so bloody perfect, I couldn't stand it. Why did he have to die before I could put it right?"

'Because we are not perfect Rachel, we are not God, we are not in control of our destiny.'

'I never thought of you as one of the God squad.'

'I don't go to church every Sunday if that's what you mean. I say my prayers and I try to lead a good life; it sounds pompous but I don't mean it like that.'

'Pa went to church every Sunday and look what happened to him. He saved so many people's lives and couldn't survive a bee sting. It's crazy, doesn't make sense.'

'It's hard to understand and often we can't and don't. That's where faith comes in.' Elizabeth stopped and pointed to the dogs. They were sitting waiting, heads on one side, wondering what was going on. Rachel ran towards the lake calling 'Come on dogs, I'll race you,' and she sped off. Elizabeth sat down on a fallen tree stump watching. There were so many thoughts racing round in her head. She did some deep breathing exercises to calm herself, she must not put a foot wrong now. She felt happier than she had since before Charles died.

After a while she stood up and called the dogs. They tore back up the field to her. Rachel came after them flushed and panting and smiling.

'I know what you want,' Rachel said, 'a nice cup of tea.'

'You must be clairvoyant or I am very boringly predictable.'

'I'm really into tea these days especially some of the herbal ones.'

'I've got peppermint, apple and cinnamon and wild raspberry I think.'

'And you'll want Early Grey!'

Shortly before seven Rachel said ' Is it all right if I stay the night?'

'Of course darling, what a treat for me. Your room is just as you left it. Help yourself to clean towels in the bathroom, there should be plenty. I'll just check everything's all right.

Elizabeth moved a flower arrangement from a table on the landing into Rachel's room and turned the bed down and drew the curtains. She made sure the clock radio was plugged in and put some magazines and a Jane Gardam novel on the bedside table.

'Do you want to ring Jethro or anyone?'

'No, I told him I was going to see Grandma. I might give Sam a bell later on.'

CHAPTER 9

Sam was surprised to find a message from Rachel on his answering machine saying she was staying overnight at Woodstock. He was also very pleased. By the time he returned the call she'd left for London, but Elizabeth sounded over the moon. It seemed Rachel was coming back at the weekend.

'Is she all hippie and greenie?'

'A bit, but she seemed to be so pleased to be home. I've felt a different person since, so relieved.'

Sam was really glad. He had been furious with his sister after the funeral. She had cleared off afterwards without a word to anyone. He'd made no effort to contact her since and swore he'd never speak to her again.

He went to see Charlotte to find out what she thought about Rachel. He also wanted to use her as a sounding board for his own plans.

She was in high dudgeon when he arrived.

'These people are driving me mad. I'm besieged by do-gooders from morning till night wanting me to join activity groups. Some of them are dreadful people, the sort Noel Coward described as having 'their brains too close to their bottoms.' What do you think the health visitor said to me?'

Sam didn't even hazard a guess, just shrugged his shoulders.

'She informed me I am very well preserved. I ask you, does she think I'm a stuffed tiger or a jar of jam? Preserved indeed!'

'What did you say?'

'I told her to stick a conservation order on me and leave me alone. That's enough about me, have you heard that Rachel came to see me?'

'Yes, tell me about it, Charlotte, it's quite a surprise after such ages.'

Charlotte brought him up to date with family gossip. Charlotte was clearly thrilled to find herself the focal point of family affairs. She had done an excellent diplomatic job and she relished the role. It was very satisfying.

'And how's your young lady?'

'I want to get engaged Charlotte. What do you think about a Christmas engagement?'

'Well, you'll have known her for about six months, no doubt very well after your stay in France, about right I'd say. Have you mentioned it to Elizabeth?'

'No, I thought I'd try it out on you first.'

Charlotte purred with pleasure. 'And what does Kate think?'

'I can't say for certain yet but I'm sure she'll agree. She's ever so old fashioned though and her father's a difficult chap.'

'Nothing wrong with being old fashioned. You'll have to speak to him of course. Can you afford to keep a wife? Have you thought about where you would live?'

'Yes, I can afford it and no, I don't know where we'd live. I'd have to buy somewhere. I don't think Kate would like city life.'

'Sensible girl. I hope she stays like that. You'll have to think about a ring. If she likes old family jewellery, she will have a good choice and save you a lot of money.'

'That will be down to Kate' Sam said firmly.

'Why do people all say 'down to' nowadays? It always used to be 'up to' people to do things not 'down to'. All part of the degeneration of modern living. We all need to look up not down if we're to progress.'

'The Government all say 'down to' don't they?'

'Don't talk to me about the Government. All the parties seem to talk about is level playing fields, kick starts and infrastructure and other inane expressions. They need kick starting on a level playing field and then see if they can build any infrastructure. It's all words, sheer gobbledygook if you ask me. Good English is as scarce as rocking-horse droppings.'

Sam grinned but felt it prudent to change the subject back to Ludlow.

'I'm going over to see Kate on Sunday. I was going to spend the weekend over there, but now Rachel is coming to Oriel I feel I should see her.'

'Is she bringing her young man?'

'Ma didn't seem too sure about that. I expect you're curious too, we all are.'

'What are Kate's people like?'

'Her father's horrible, a nasty piece of work. Mother is all right but very timid and unemancipated. His temper is dreadful and he gets violent at times.'

'Oh dear, poor Kate. Why does she live at home?'

'She can't really afford to leave as her money is a major part of their income. I think she's really frightened of her father.'

'Well the sooner you can take care of her the better. I had no idea. Why don't you have a Christmas wedding? Everyone will decide there's a baby on the way as a result of your French holiday. Then you can prove them wrong.'

Sam grinned again. 'How are you getting on here Charlotte?'

'I am perfectly all right when I'm left in peace. I suppose it's very good for people who like being organised. There are lots of outings and tea parties. It seems to be a staple diet of bridge, bingo and television. The warden tells me 'they all watch snooker on the telly'. She wanted to know if I watched it, called it the old people's friend. I told her straight that in my book pneumonia is the old folk's friend. She was absolutely horrified! I also told her that I'd never been reduced to the pursuit of balls.'

Sam laughed. 'You wait until she catches you watching Wimbledon.'

'Wimbledon doesn't count as balls, it's part of the social calendar like Ascot and Henley' Charlotte replied loftily.

'Game, set and match to you Charlotte.'

Charlotte grinned wickedly. 'All I need is a good broomstick and a horrible black cat! It's a pity I don't like cats isn't it?'

'I expect Tobermory misses you as a sparring partner.'

'I don't miss him at all with that supercilious grin on his fat, furry face. There are plenty of birds in this garden and I wish I'd brought my bird-bath and table with me. It never occurred to me at the time.'

'We could go to the garden centre and choose some new ones, couldn't we?'

'I suppose we could. You've enough to do. I'll ask Elizabeth when she's not too busy.'

'I shall have to go now, we're short staffed in the office. I've got to see a tricky print run through tonight. Don't get up, I can let myself out. See you again soon.'

'Goodbye dear, thank you for coming.'

Sam went to Oriel Manor on Saturday afternoon. Elizabeth and Rachel were finishing a late lunch in the kitchen and Sam joined them for coffee. He was surprised how matey and relaxed they seemed to be. He couldn't remember Rachel ever being as pleasant as this before. She even looked well groomed and attractive in her second-hand clothes. It was almost like meeting a stranger in that he found himself making conversation. There was no mention of her bloke. He relaxed more as time went by. He worked in the garden for a couple of hours raking the lawn and sweeping up leaves. While he worked he thought out how he'd approach Kate's father tomorrow. He was excited and apprehensive. He wondered whether they could be married by Christmas. Deep in thought he didn't hear Rachel behind him and jumped visibly as she spoke.

'Do you want a hand?' she asked.

'OK. I'll rake the grass if you'll sweep up the leaves and moss. Do you like gardening?'

'Dunno really, never do it, but it's good to be outside and smell the wet leaves. Do you see much of Ma?'

'Not that much. I come over each week to see if she's OK. I stuck around after Pa died for some weeks as there was so much to see to.'

'I suppose that's what I should have done. I'm sorry I ran away and dropped you in the shit but I just couldn't face it.'

'Well you should have damned well made yourself, anyway it's history now. Ma won't ask for support but she does need it.'

'OK. OK. Don't get all preachy. I've told you I'm sorry. Tell me about Kate. Where did you pick her up?'

'I met her at a funeral just after Pa's.'

'Sounds real jolly stuff. How macabre.'

'Do you remember that woman who died at Pa's funeral?'

'Yes, hardly the sort of thing you forget. Faith someone and no one knew who she was. Really creepy and weird.'

'I went to her funeral in Ludlow the following week and Kate was there. She's practically one of their family. She's great and a looker too.'

Sam went on to tell Rachel about David and Alex and the painting. She listened to the whole story in silence.

'Do you think they were having an affair?'

'No, of course not. What a ridiculous idea. Pa wasn't that sort of bloke. He and Ma were always good together, you'd have known that if you'd been around a bit more.'

'OK, you've had your dig at me. I was just wondering that's all. You must admit it's odd about the painting of the Oriole. Can I see it or has Ma got rid of it?'

'It's in the garden room over Pa's chair. It's quite a good little watercolour.'

'What's David like?'

'Dull and boring. He's started hitting the bottle rather.'

'You can't really blame him.'

'No, but it's grotty for Alex getting the backwash of his moods. He's been made redundant which doesn't help.'

Elizabeth came down the garden laughing. 'You two look exactly like council workmen leaning on your broom and rake. You've been standing like that for quite half an hour. I'm not complaining but it looks funny.'

'We've done a fair bit but started talking about how I met Kate at Faith's funeral.'

'Of course, you wouldn't know about all that dear,' she said to Rachel, 'such a lot has happened.'

'Really bizarre isn't it?'

'I suppose it is. Alex is an interesting young man. Has he applied for that job with your firm Sam?'

'Yes, and he's had one interview. His second interview is on Tuesday, I expect he'll get it.'

'Suppose one word from you will be enough to clinch it,' said Rachel sarcastically.

Sam lunged at her with the rake. She ran and he went after her brandishing it in the air. The dogs followed. Elizabeth laughed. 'Just like Mr MacGregor chasing Peter Rabbit.'

The light was fading and there was a good smell of woodsmoke.

Elizabeth had lit the sitting room fire and they sat round cosily eating muffins dripping with butter and sprinkled with cinnamon sugar.

'This is the life' said Rachel licking her fingers. 'I'd forgotten how delicious muffins are. They taste better by the fire; I love the smell of wood smoke.'

'I like them too. I usually just have a cup of tea but Charlotte enjoys proper afternoon tea when she stays here.'

'She's giving the old dears a good run around at Cherwell Close. I called to see her yesterday. Get her to tell you about the snooker on telly.'

'She is really brilliant. Made me ever so welcome and told me off for not tipping the cabby.'

Elizabeth drew the curtains and went to turn on more lights. 'It's a privilege to know Charlotte, we're lucky to have her.'

'Please leave the lights Ma. It's lovely with just the table lamp and firelight, so romantic like an old film' Rachel pleaded.

They stretched their legs and listened to the crackle of the fire. Tobermory didn't like the apple logs spitting and jumped on to the back of Elizabeth's chair.

'I suppose you sit on bean bags and cover the wall with posters like a teenager' Sam teased.

'It's pretty basic and I'm not letting you wind me up. It's great being home, even with you here, and I don't want to spoil it.'

'Point taken. It's good to have you back. I mean it' and he found he really did mean it.

Elizabeth slipped away, tears in her eyes, happy to hear their banter. She sat in the dark, in the drawing room, playing the piano.

'I haven't heard her play for ages' Sam said.

'I think she's happy to have us together after all the trauma.'

The 'phone rang. Elizabeth answered it and was talking for a long time. She came in all excited, 'That was my childhood sweetheart. The only romance I had before meeting Charles . He read of your father's death, waited a suitable time and now wants me to meet him for dinner.'

'What's his name? Is he handsome? Do we know him?' Rachel quizzed.

'He's Rex Barker, you don't know him and I haven't seen him since I was eighteen. Do you think I should go?'

'Of course you should' they chorused.

'I did agree and he's coming here at 6.30 a week on Tuesday. He lives in Sheepscombe, near Painswick.'

Sam and Rachel smiled at each other. They'd never seen their mother all flustered before. They were also rather impressed by her being dated by an old flame.

'It's really like an old movie now Ma, a romantic weepy. I love 1920's films' Rachel teased.

Sam switched on the television and flicked through the channels. Then he went through Elizabeth's videos and chose 'Brief Encounter'. Elizabeth's hankie was soaked by the time it finished. Even Tobermory, now on her knee, was also a little damp.

As he drove to Ludlow early next morning, Sam rehearsed aloud what he thought he'd say to Kate's parents. It was possible, he reminded himself, that she might not want to hurry into being engaged or married but he was sure that she would.

His first call was on Alex to brief him for Tuesday and warn him not to be surprised at being interviewed by Sam in his role as production editor. Sam had managed not to be available at the first interview but he was involved with the appointment of all production staff. He was convinced Alex had potential and tried to view him impartially. Sam knew of course, Alex needed to get away from the constraints of home and menial work.

David answered the door and was most welcoming. Alex had gone to fetch the Sunday paper. David asked Sam about his work and what prospects there were for Alex if he started at the bottom of the production ladder. They were drinking coffee when Alex came in.

Alex suggested they walked down to the river and Sam welcomed the opportunity. After they'd discussed the interview situation Alex told him about the endless happy hours he'd spent in, on and by this stretch of the River Teme. The burnished trees were dressed in their blazing autumn finery, especially the beeches. It was wet and slippery underfoot as they walked along the bank. The squirrels rained acorns down on them attracting attention to their treescape of old oaks. Alex knew a great deal about wildlife and Sam was interested.

They discussed where Alex would live if he was appointed.

'You'll find Oxford expensive and accommodation scarce. There's so much demand with all the Colleges. You can bunk down with me until you get somewhere if that's any help.'

'That would be great but I've got to land the job first. Have you any idea when they want the appointee to start?'

'As soon as possible. We are short staffed in production and there's a mass of work with deadlines. You could use your bike to get around.' He heard the church clock start striking twelve. 'I must go. I'm meeting Kate at 'The Olive Tree' for lunch.'

Alex was about to suggest joining them and then thought better of it saying 'She could do with a break. It's getting very heavy at her place. I don't know how she sticks it.'

Sam quickened his pace. He left Alex in Broad Street and walked up to the restaurant. There was no point in moving his car. Kate was already there drinking coffee and looking drawn and tired despite her healthy tan. They kissed and sat talking. Sam insisted upon being told about the state of things at home.

'If I'm going to ask you to marry me, Kate, I need to know how best to approach your parents' he said in desperation.

She looked at him to be sure he wasn't joking, but of course he wasn't and her heart leapt and pounded. He held both her hands and said 'What about it Kate, shall we get married? I love you so much.'

'Oh yes, Sam, yes. I love you, you know I do.'

'I shall have to speak with your parents however awkward it is.'

'They like you Sam but they rely on my money. I know it isn't much but they need it.'

'Well they'll have to learn not to. You can't sacrifice your life to subsidise theirs. It's just not on.'

Kate nodded. 'What about your mother Sam?'

'That won't be a problem She liked you from the first day you met and I'm sure she'll be pleased for us. It's our choice in any case but it will be better if we can keep it hassle free.'

'When do you plan to talk to Dad?' Kate asked nervously.

'This afternoon seems as good as any. What do they do on Sunday afternoons?'

'Mum isn't working this weekend so she'll be busy in the house I expect. Dad usually falls asleep watching telly.'

They ordered lunch. Kate was too excited and worried to enjoy hers. Sam ate with relish and tried to keep the atmosphere light with banter. He was relieved that Kate hadn't hesitated and was anxious to get the hurdle of her parents over.

It was heavy going. Kate sat twisting her fingers while Sam and her father argued. Her mother's contribution was small and not really significant at first.

Sam was polite and patient and appalled by the selfishness of Mr Evans. Kate's happiness hardly seemed to come into his thinking. The only thing he would grudgingly agree to was a long engagement. Sam said this was out of the question, that no one these days had long engagements in ordinary circumstances.

Kate agreed there was no need for a long engagement and Mrs Evans timidly backed her up. Finally Sam's patience snapped.

'Mr Evans, we have discussed this for nearly two hours and we're getting nowhere. I came to see you as a matter of courtesy hoping for your blessing. As you are not giving it, we are going ahead anyway.'

'You can't just walk in here and think you can get your own way. Kate's a good girl and will do what I say.'

Kate intervened. 'I have made up my mind Dad, I'm old enough, and I want to marry Sam.'

'There it is then Mr Evans, Kate and I are engaged to be married.'

'I hope you'll be very happy,' and Mrs Evans kissed Kate and, rather shyly, gave Sam a little hug.

'You keep out of it Mother.' Mr Evans said sharply.

'No, this is an important day in Kate's life and we should celebrate not argue about it. Shall I go and put the kettle on?'

'I think we are going for a walk if you don't mind' Sam said firmly and Kate nodded.

When they emerged Sam breathed a sigh of relief. 'I'm glad that's over, it was pretty heavy going, wasn't it?'

'Not as bad as I expected. Dad can be very mean and unreasonable. Mum's pleased though. She'll have an awful time with him now.'

They walked towards the castle. 'What sort of ring would you like?' Kate's face lit up. 'I'd like an old one, perhaps Victorian.'

'Let's go and use my car 'phone and ring Ma. OK with you?'

'Yes, good idea.' Kate slipped her hand in his and they walked jauntily down towards Broad Street.

Elizabeth was delighted and asked to speak to Kate. She was so warm and welcoming and invited them to stay at Woodstock the following weekend. It would be a chance for her to meet Rachel. Sam had another word with Elizabeth and confirmed the arrangement.

Alex walked through Oxford after his interview feeling elated. Only now did he realise just how badly he wanted to work for Hackforths. It was strange being interviewed by Sam and he was impressed by his professionalism. So the job was his and he was to start on Monday, less than a week to move and tie up all loose ends in Ludlow. It was going to be pressure all the way at Hackforths and he would be starting at the bottom.

Now he had four hours free before meeting Sam at his flat. He decided to take the official bus tour of the City to see the colleges and general layout. It was a dull day but not raining and there were still plenty of tourists about. He felt uncomfortable wearing his only suit.

The commentary was live and quite witty. It was given by a Peter Ustinov look-alike. There was so much to see and it really whetted his appetite for living there. So many nationalities everywhere with especially large numbers of Japanese people. Some of the girls were most attractive with their deep limpid eyes and slim figures.

He got off at the Ashmolean Museum. The guide had suggested taking a look at the famous Randolph hotel opposite too. Alex went up the steps into the Ashmolean and discovered it was too expensive for the short amount of time he had left. He looked round the museum shop and bought two postcards, one for Martine and one to keep. The Randolph looked too grand to go into, so he sat on the steps outside the museum and wrote to Martine. Then he read through his letter of resignation to the Youth Service which he'd written before he left Sam's office. He dropped them both into the nearby letter box. What an extraordinary few months, he thought to himself, as he found his way to Sam's flat. If Faith had not gone to Charles' funeral so many events would never have taken place. It was no fair exchange. He'd give anything to have Faith back, but she was continuing to influence the way his life was going, through the connection she had caused to be made. He felt guided and sure of himself. It was good that some positive spinoff came from such a tragic event, though he doubted whether David would ever see it that way.

He rang Sam's bell and was told to come upstairs. It was a big Georgian house converted into apartments most successfully. There was a good feeling of space, given the well proportioned rooms and high sash windows. Sam showed him round. There was a large living room, small kitchen and interior bathroom and a double bedroom and box room. Sam was prepared to turn the box room back into a small single bedroom if Alex decided to move in. The rent was £125 a week of which Alex would pay £35 plus the usual outgoings. He jumped at it and agreed readily. It was a known quantity, he liked Sam, it was immediately available and had the use of a large back garden. It was agreed that Sam would collect Alex, and his possessions, on Sunday morning and move him in ready for work the next day. Alex couldn't make it any sooner because of working for the Youth Service.

Sam made coffee and cheese sandwiches which they shared before the drive back to Ludlow. He had arranged to bring Kate to stay with his mother. He told Alex about their engagement and how impossible Kate's father was being. Alex congratulated him and was genuinely pleased for them both. How strange, he thought, to have his ex-girlfriend marrying his new boss. He wasn't the least surprised about Kate's father.

Sam had insisted on Kate taking sick leave from the library, with the agreement of her doctor, to get away until after the weekend. 'I can take Kate back when I collect you on Sunday. Come to think of it we'd better make it early afternoon as we shall probably have a late night celebrating.'

'It's lucky for me that you and Kate are so involved isn't it?'

'Not your view when we first met I suspect.' They both laughed and agreed.

The house in Broad Street was in darkness when they pulled up outside. Sam wouldn't come in as he was already running late and Kate was waiting for him. Alex let himself in and found David asleep in the chair in front of the television. There was the usual bottle of whisky on the table. He woke up straight away and wanted to know how he'd gone on with the interview.

'Fine thanks. I start on Monday. Isn't that great?'

'Monday? You don't mean next Monday?'

'Yes. They want me straight away. My availability was helpful in the event.'

'Where will you live?' It takes time to find digs especially in a strange city. It will be a lot more expensive there than Shropshire.'

'Sam is putting me up for a while until I get some money together and can find somewhere. You're right about Oxford being expensive and short of digs. By the way I've got some good news about Kate. She and Sam are getting engaged this weekend.'

David looked astonished and rather disappointed. The already bleak outlook promised to get lonelier still. He ought to be pleased about Alex's success but could only think of the awful quiet of the house with only his own company.

'You seem to have taken it remarkably well. I always hoped you would marry Kate.'

'We were just good friends as they say. I like Kate very much and I think she will have a good life with Alex. You know how impossible her father is.'

'A real lout what bit I know of him. Yes.'

'Sam's taking her back to Woodstock until the dust settles.'

'You are very fortunate to be employed so quickly. I will say one thing for you Alex, you don't let the grass grow under your feet. I hope it turns out well, we could do with some good things coming our way for a change.'

'Have you ever thought of working dosh free, doing something for the community?'

'No, that's women's work. Your mother was good at that sort of thing.'

'What have you done with Mum's clothes and things?'

'Nothing. They are exactly as she left them, in good order.'

'She would have liked them to be of some use. Don't you think they should go to the Hospice Shop or somewhere?'

'Are you trying to tell me what I should be doing with my wife's effects?'

'No Dad, I'm not. I'm just trying to think what Mum's reaction would be and I don't think she would just leave things.'

'Just because you've landed a job doesn't mean you are in a position to interfere in my affairs. I shall do things in my own good time.'

Sam's request for Kate to stay with Elizabeth coincided with Rachel's decision to return home. Elizabeth was determined to make them both welcome and forgot her own worries in the flurry of arrangements. It was late evening when Kate arrived and she was in an emotional state. Sam had to get back to Oxford and left Kate and Elizabeth talking into the early hours. She poured her heart out, years of suppression were released in a torrent of anguish and resentment. Elizabeth acted as emotional blotting paper and finally they were both drained and spent.

Next day Kate felt a different person, lightened by off-loading so much pent up emotion. They met Rachel at Oxford station. The two girls eyed each other warily at first but soon relaxed and chatted freely. Rachel took up her role as daughter of the house quite unconsciously. Elizabeth was delighted, and they both set out to make Kate's engagement stay memorable.

They discussed whether they should throw an impromptu party. Sam and Kate both wanted a quiet celebration, so it was decided to ask Charlotte and Jethro to join them on Saturday and stay for the weekend. Sam and Kate spent their evenings together and the house was large enough for complete privacy. They talked about the engagement ring. Kate was adamant about wanting an old one. Sam asked Elizabeth to show her the family rings but stressed that he was equally happy for them to look round the shops in Oxford. Kate loved the idea of rings that had been worn by generations of the same family. Eventually she and Sam chose a diamond cluster set in platinum. All the Jeffersons chorused 'Won't Charlotte be pleased that you've chosen her engagement ring.'

Kate was horrified and said she couldn't possibly take it, but was assured that Charlotte had added it to the collection in the hopes that Kate would choose it. She couldn't wear it any longer because of the arthritis in her knuckles. It was not Victorian but late 1920's.

Kate couldn't stop admiring the ring. It fitted her finger perfectly.

Rachel talked confidentially to Elizabeth. She wanted to know about the sleeping arrangements for the weekend. Elizabeth had a ready answer.

'You and Sam and I will keep to our own rooms, Charlotte can have Pa's and my old room, Kate will stay where she is and Jethro can have the little room by Sam's. The beds are made up and aired so there's no problem.

'Aren't you going to put us together and Sam and Kate together?'

'Certainly not. It's an engagement not a wedding.'

'Jethro and I are used to sleeping together and I bet Sam and Kate did in France.'

'No they didn't. Kate shared with Sally and Sam and Alex were together.'

'Well Jethro's going to think it's pretty wacky.'

'You will just have to tell him it's house rules, won't you.'

'There's no such thing in the 1990's. Really archaic Ma.'

'Perhaps you'd like Charlotte to explain to him.'

'No way. She'd eat him for breakfast, you know she would,' and they both laughed.

'We would be asking Kate's parents to join us but I know she doesn't want them to come.'

'They sound really shitty. She's ace and can't deserve them.'

'I think her mother's quite nice but nervous. It's very sad.'

Kate was beginning to realise how different her life style was going to be. The luxurious quality of everything both fascinated and shocked her. Yet the Jeffersons were much more careful not to waste things than her own family. She was learning fast what to do and hoped she wouldn't commit any social gaffes.

Alone with Sam she was unaware of their differences. Although Rachel had been living a dropout life for a decade, she could soon slot back in without effort. Kate wondered about Jethro and looked forward to meeting him. She felt very much at ease with Elizabeth who had real insight where other people's feelings were concerned.

She wondered what Saturday's dinner party would be like and what she would wear. She asked Rachel what she would be wearing. She suggested they went round the charity shops in Oxford to see if there was anything they'd like. Kate sought Rachel's advice on what she thought Sam would like as an engagement present.

The two girls had great fun in Oxford. They tried on some really freaky clothes as well as well known labels. Kate found an Italian long skirt in a dramatic deep, rich violet velvet. It's lining was perfect and the skirt had hardly been worn. The hem had come down a little at the back, probably caught by a high heel. She whirled round in front of Rachel saying 'What do you think?'

'Fab colour, matches your eyes. You've go to have that. How much is it?'

'Five pounds and it's good quality materials.'

'What will you wear with it?'

'I've got a cream silk Laura Ashley blouse.'

'Just the business. You can't wear trainers with it.'

'I was just thinking about shoes.'

She looked through the shelves and boxes of shoes while Rachel was trying on a Liberty dress. She found a pair of plain black patent leather pumps, which fitted quite well, for £1.50.

Rachel was strutting round in the flowered Liberty dress and a curious fringed stole. She said 'How do I look?'

'I like the dress but not sure about the shawl.'

'I'm having the dress although it's got a ciggie burn here, look. Doesn't show much because of the pattern.'

'I could easily mend it. Just wants a bit of material from the back of the hem putting behind the hole. Do you sew?'

'Not if I can help it. Never was any good.'

'I'll do it for you. I'll have to catch the hem up on my skirt. Will your mother have cotton do you think?'

'A drawer full of every colour you can think of.'

They paid for their purchases and wandered round the shops. Kate was on the lookout for Sam's present and rummaged round the less expensive antique and bric-a-brac shops. She found a beautiful old glass paper weight and wondered whether Sam would like it. It was a Florentine design in subtle jewel colours. The price was £30 and she didn't consider it expensive.

Rachel watched her counting her money.

'Are you buying that for Sam?'

'Yes. Do you think he'll like it?'

'Yeah. How much shall you offer for it?'

'It's £30. It's priced underneath.'

'Offer her £25.'

'Oh I couldn't do that. It's not like the market.'

Rachel picked it up and took it to the desk. 'I've only got £25 and I want this for my fiancé when we ge engaged tomorrow.'

The woman looked first at Rachel and then at Kate.

'It's low priced as it is. We're not a charity shop.'

Kate felt most uncomfortable. Rachel went on undaunted. 'Oh well I'll have to put it back then.'

As she went to move it the woman sniffed and said 'All right then £25 being as you're getting engaged,' and she rummaged under the desk for some paper.

Kate quickly passed £25 to Rachel who paid for it.

'I hope your fiancé likes it and that you'll be very happy.'

'Thanks. I'm sure he will,' and they walked out into the street.

'I feel quite guilty about that,' Kate said.

'Well don't. She didn't have to go along with it, did she?'

Kate was pleased with the paper weight but would have preferred to have paid the full price. She felt very unsophisticated with Rachel being so street-wise and sharp.

Kate was fascinated by Oxford and the colleges. When Rachel discovered how interested she was, she suggested getting on one of the city tour buses. She admitted she had never looked round Oxford properly and they both enjoyed being tourists.

'I can't believe I'm going to live here one day. It's like being on holiday.'

'There's more to it than I thought, not that I'm into culture much. It'll make Jethro want to throw up. I wish he wasn't coming tomorrow,' she said confidentially.

'You'll probably feel different when he's here. Your mother makes everyone feel so welcome.'

Rachel still looked doubtful. They caught the bus back to Woodstock and Sam's car was outside.

'You two had a good shopping session?' he asked.

'Yes we've had a great time. We've been round the city on a sightseeing tour and shopping.'

'Alex did the bus tour after his interview on Tuesday. Kate, I thought we might go and move the boat tomorrow morning. Do you like boating?'

'I've only been on the ferry and trip boats and canoes. Is it the boat in Faith's painting?'

Sam nodded. 'Yes, I want to bring it nearer home so we can use it more.'

'What fun. Yes, I'd like that.'

'Can I come too?' Rachel asked.

'No you can't,' Elizabeth called from the kitchen. 'I need you to help me here.' Rachel pulled a face. 'Anyway you must be here when Jethro comes.'

'Oh yeah, I'd forgotten about his coming.'

Sam read the paper while Kate borrowed sewing needles and thread and carefully repaired Rachel's frock and her own skirt in her room. She wanted her skirt to be a surprise. She had never worn a long one before. She tried it on with her blouse and put on the amethyst and seed pearl pendant and earrings her god-mother had given her for her eighteenth birthday. The total effect was magical and she felt thrilled. She primped and prowled round the room looking at herself in the long mirrors as she preened. She sprayed some perfume onto a tissue and tied it round the top of the coat hanger when she put her skirt into the wardrobe. She didn't want it to smell musty.

Kate took Rachel's frock to her room. She wasn't there, so she left it on her bed. She was glad she and Sam would have some time to themselves tomorrow and she was interested in seeing the 'Oriole' too.

CHAPTER 10

It rained all night and Kate, too excited to sleep soundly, thought it was a pity it was going to be so wet. By morning it was blustery but bright. Since their return from France a friend of Sam's had moved the 'Oriole' along the river network until it joined the Oxford canal. It was currently moored in Aynho and the idea was to bring the boat to Thrupp to a permanent mooring. They left early with two baskets of provisions and would make lunch on board. Kate borrowed waterproofs and wellingtons from the big cloakroom. There was every size from a small child to a large adult to choose from. The dogs chased round excitedly, as they packed the car, thinking they were coming too. Sam patted them but said 'Not today boys. We'll take you next time.' Their tails and ears drooped knowingly.

Kate kept looking at her ring and letting the diamonds sparkle in the sunlight as they drove cross-country to join the A423 towards Banbury. Sam watched her ring catching the light and felt a surge of pride and happiness. He wanted her to enjoy today and had contrived the urgency to move the boat as a useful ploy to get away from the family. He hoped she would like the 'Oriole' as much as he was beginning to.

They turned off the main road and drove through the villages of Lower Heyford and Steeple Aston. The autumn colours were vibrant after the rain; a painter's palette from splodges of ochre and brown to brilliant reds and gold. The wind blew strongly making the sky puffed with cotton wool, then the clouds built up and suddenly the threatening change to the slatey greys of rain. The overlapping of sun and rain turned into pale apologies for insipid rainbows, present only for a few blinks of the eye.

'How shall we get the car back if we're leaving by boat?'

'I'll pick it up in the morning. Ma said she would drive us up to fetch it.'

'And how do we get from the canal to home?'

'It depends what time we get to Thrupp. There shouldn't be too much traffic on the canal at this time of year but you can never tell on the waterways.'

It was ten past nine when they parked the car and unlocked the boat. It looked smaller than Kate had expected from the painting and she was rather disappointed at first. Sam held the hatch open for her and she went inside.

'You explore and I'll fetch the nosh.'

She liked the compact, clever use of space and was surprised how much equipment there was inside. The galley was well fitted out and she found the kettle and matches. She ran the tap and nothing happened. She heard Sam laughing behind her.

'I'll fill up the water tank in a minute.' He opened some windows to get rid of the condensation and lit the gas heater.'

Kate had found the loo and shower. 'Whose are these clothes?'

'They're some Pa left on board. Fishing gear and stuff.'

'Does it make you very sad to come on the boat?'

'No, not at all. He used to come here to relax with friends, fishing and bird watching and generally messing about in boats.'

'Shall I put the food away? It's like playing house.'

'Yes. We won't bother with the fridge today, not worth it.'

As Kate put things away she discovered where crockery and cutlery lived and began to enjoy herself.

'Right are you ready for the off? I've watered up' Sam called from the aft deck.

The engine started up disturbing the Sunday morning peace. There was little sign of life on the other boats. The engine sounded loud and there was a strong smell of diesel until it settled down to a steady putter.

Kate went out and joined Sam as they left the mooring. He threw her a rope which she managed to catch. The water looked rather dark and dirty but made super reflections of the trees and hedgerows. The wind caught her hair as they left the shelter of Aynho and she anchored it down with a scarf. Sam handed her a Nicolson map book open at this stretch of the Oxford Canal. It was an ordnance survey equivalent for the waterways. The bridges were all numbered and so it was easy to follow and there was plenty of information about the surrounding countryside.

Passing boats and walkers on the towing path all called out in friendly greeting. Apart from the fishermen, who tended to scowl at them, there was a good sense of camaraderie. The pastoral countryside was typically English as the Brindley designed canal wound its way from village to hamlet. Grey herons stood still as statues, until the boat was almost alongside, before taking off with their wide wing span fully extended, long legs tucking up like a plane's undercarriage, silhouetted against the sky.

Kate went below and made two large mugs of hot coffee. It was warm inside and she turned the fire down to its lowest heat. She found some gingerbread and took it out with the coffee. She sat on the roof facing Sam with her legs dangling over the doorway relishing every minute.

'We could have our honeymoon on here' she said.

'Not a good idea love.'

'Why not? It's so peaceful and interesting.'

'We can come on the 'Oriole' anytime. Our honeymoon is a unique event. Although we seem miles from anywhere, friends could even walk and catch us up wouldn't that be naff? I don't want to share you with anyone. We shall go somewhere very exotic and choose it carefully.'

'Point taken. Do you kow why it's called a honeymoon?'

'No. It's a curious word.'

'The monks and nuns used to make mead and give it to newlyweds on their wedding night. Mead is made from honey and is meant to be an aphrodisiac. But you'll know all about honey, keeping bees.'

'I don't. It was Pa's hobby and now Ma looks after them.'

'Do you feel angry with the bees . . . after what happened?'

'No, it wasn't their fault. It was such a shock though, I can still hardly believe it at times. It's helpful being on the boat and dealing with the things that were his.'

'I've always liked bees until I heard about your father. I love honey especially from a comb.'

'You go on liking them and their honey. Anyway I don't need an aphrodisiac!'

'Where are your bees, I haven't seen any hives?'

'They've gone away to the heather at present.'

'You're joking, gone on holiday?'

'No I'm not, they go to the heather every year. We've usually fetched them back by now.'

'How on earth do they get there?'

'By Land-Rover in their hives, air head!'

'But how do you get them all in the hives ready to go?'

'Well you don't whistle them like dogs. You wait till it gets dark and then close the hive entrance. They're already inside. Bees don't go out in the dark or the rain.'

'Isn't that amazing. Don't they get lost in a strange place or is it that sort of radar that takes them back to wherever they started?'

'That's right. Brilliant isn't it.'

They stopped for lunch near Lower Heyford. Kate heated the soup. The rest of the meal was cold but they were both hungry and ate well. It tasted so much better than it would have done at home. It was necessary to press on because of the time and Sam started up the engine while Kate cleared up the lunch dishes. Even washing up was fun in the tiny, shallow sink and she soon learnt to be economical with their water supply.

Kate took her turn at the tiller but was nervous going through bridges and sometimes with oncoming boats.

'You'll be find as long as you remember to pass port to port,' Sam assured her. She would squeal with panic and he took over to the amusement of the experienced boaters.

She spent much of the afternoon on the roof where the view of the surrounding countryside was splendid. She had to lie flat through some of the bridges. Kate's expertise with a windlass was better by the time they were down in Thrupp. As Sam taught her to work the three locks his own confidence in boatmanship improved. It was the first time he had ever felt competent with it.

He tied the boat securely fore and aft on the mooring rings at Thrupp. Kate watched him proudly. She was getting better at throwing and catching the ropes. It was after five and the light had gone and the rain started again. Sam left Kate on board while he went to ring for a taxi.

Charlotte was looking forward to meeting Kate. She had heard so much about her that she felt she knew her already and she hoped Kate lived up to her expectations. She could hardly be worse than Maria. Charlotte despised Maria and her feminist views.

The effort involved in going to stay anywhere was irritating to Charlotte, just packing a few clothes shouldn't cause her so much tiredness. It was the energy needed to see they were washed, ironed and clean and the trying to remember all the little things. In fact everything was suddenly becoming a terrible effort. She found Mrs Weaver remarkably understanding about it. For the first time ever she began to feel her years. She seemed to have jumped from feeling sixty to being eighty-five in a matter of weeks. Perhaps the move had taken more out of her than she thought. So much had happened since Charles' death that it wasn't surprising she felt enervated. A taxi was taking her to Oriel Manor at 3.30 so she planned to have an early lunch and then rest on the bed until three o'clock.

She arrived in Woodstock in time for tea. It was just like old times. Elizabeth was busy in the kitchen being helped by Rachel. She was surprised by the change in Rachel. Her hair looked well cut and clean, and her shirt and jeans tidy. She spoke more normally too, which was a relief.

There was a lovely fire in the drawing room and Rachel settled Charlotte into a comfortable chair.

'When is your young man arriving?'

'He came earlier on. He's taken the dogs for a long walk so that we could get on with the cooking, Grandma.'

'How do you like being back home?'

'It's great. I would never have believed how much I've missed it.'

'You will be a great joy to your Mama especially now with Sam's mind being on Kate. What do you think of Kate?'

'Really great. Very unsophisticated and not street wise, but I like her.'

'Where is she?'

'She and Sam are on the 'Oriole' moving it nearer to Oxford. Ma didn't want her to be involved in the preparations and they wanted time together. Have you seen the dining room? We've really made it look good.'

'No but I think I'll let it come as a surprise,' said Charlotte who had just managed to get the painful part of her back comfortable.

Elizabeth wheeled in the tea-trolley. She looked flushed and pre-occupied.

'You must be busy my dear.'

'I have been but it's more or less in order now. Rachel's been a big help. Is Jethro back yet? I haven't heard the dogs.'

As she spoke there was a commotion, some shouting and the dogs raced into the hall all wet and excited. Rachel dashed out to stop them coming into the drawing room, banging the door in her hurry.

'You air head Jethro. What the hell did you bring them in for? You can see they're wet. Get them out quickly before they start shaking themselves. Come on Jasper, Oscar out you go. Out!'

Jethro was full of apologies when he came in with Rachel minutes later.

'Grandma, this is Jethro, Jethro meet my grandmother, Charlotte Jefferson.'

They shook hands. Charlotte wasn't sure what she had expected. It certainly wasn't this thin, bespectacled, earnest looking young chap. She was almost disappointed. Jethro was very impressed by the look of Charlotte. He was also aware of her interest in him.

'I believe you come from Staffordshire Jethro?'

'Yes, from the Potteries. Do you know Stoke-on-Trent?'

'Not really but I had a friend who lived in Barlaston once, in the Old Road.'

'I know Barlaston Old Road well, great big houses built by potters mostly, before the last war.'

'She's dead now. Most of my friends are, one of the perils of living too long you know.'

'I expect so, it must be awful.'

Charlotte bristled. 'It isn't awful at all. You have to rise above it.'

'I don't want to grow old. Do you believe in euthanasia?'

Rachel took several deep breaths as Charlotte replied.

'I used to. One tends to go off it rather the nearer one comes. Too many legal problems, families wanting to get rid of people, that sort of thing. You aren't at all like I expected.'

Jethro laughed. 'Did you think I'd be really off the wall?'

'Quite possibly,' Charlotte said faintly.

'I don't suppose Rachel told you much about me.'

'Not a lot really, I suppose.'

'She didn't go down a bundle with my people.'

Charlotte was needled again. 'Really, why was that?'

'Too wacky by half.'

Rachel fled into the kitchen where Elizabeth was filling the hot water jug. 'Ma it really is too bad. I knew I shouldn't have asked Jethro here.'

'It can be difficult for people from different backgrounds to cope with the country house set up at first. Just the same for Kate.'

'It's not that,' she wailed, 'he's really ashamed of me.'

'Don't be silly dear. I expect he's pleased to see you against your home background, gives him some perspective.'

'Can't you see, he doesn't approve of me. You all being so nice makes it worse.'

Elizabeth began to see what she was getting at and wondered what she had told him about them. 'Why is he so superior then?'

'Because he got me off the drugs. He gave me a really hard time.'

'It seems to me we owe him a debt then' Elizabeth said grimly.

'Don't you start, please Ma.'

'No darling. I'm just pleased to have you back with us.'

They returned to the drawing room where Charlotte and Jethro were deep in conversation.

'What are you two talking about so seriously?' Elizabeth asked.

'Minimalism.' Jethro replied.

'As a philosophy or an art form?'

'You can't separate the two it seems,' said Charlotte tartly.

'Much as I don't want to disturb the flow of your conversation, the time's getting on and I suggest we are all changed for dinner by 7.30 ready to celebrate Sam and Kate's engagement with champagne.'

'Are they back?' asked Charlotte.

'No, but they've arrived in Thrupp so they won't be long. You can use the bathroom before Sam gets in Jethro. I will look after Charlotte and Rachel can use my bathroom.' Elizabeth steered them into action leaving just Charlotte sitting there.

'Well what a turn up for the books he's turned out to be. I feel quite exhausted but I've enjoyed having to sharpen my claws. He certainly knows how many beans make five.'

'Why don't you rest quietly until dinner. You are the only one dressed already. I suggest you have a little p. and q. while you can.'

Charlotte meekly agreed. She must be in good form to meet Kate. Jethro had proved to be quite an experience. If a young fellow had spoken to her mother like that all hell would have been let loose. He was sincere though and didn't mean to be impertinent. She wondered why he and Rachel got on so well together, they made such an unlikely pair. It was much more stimulating than the petty squabbles of Cherwell Close.

It was six o'clock before they reached Woodstock. They had a cup of tea in the kitchen before going to greet Charlotte and Jethro. Dinner was to be at eight and Elizabeth suggested they met for drinks at seven thirty.

'What's Jethro like?' Sam asked.

'Shush! He'll hear you. We'll talk about it later. You'll see' she replied.

They went into the drawing room but Charlotte had fallen asleep. Jethro and Rachel were nowhere to be seen. Sam and Kate went to have a shower before changing. Kate couldn't wait to put on her new clothes and hoped Sam would like them.

Elizabeth cast a last look round the dining room and went up to have a bath. It all seemed to be going well. She'd never seen Sam look happier and Kate had obviously enjoyed her little cruise.

'Oh Charles, if only you were here I could really feel happy tonight.' Then it struck her, if Charles was still here Sam and Kate would never have met. Her grandmother used to say God moves in mysterious ways. Perhaps he really did, perhaps it was all part of his plan for them. She couldn't entirely accept that but thanked God for bringing Rachel home safely.

Her mind returned to dinner and the next jobs she must see to. She looked at herself in the mirror as she towelled off. Apart from shadows under her eyes she was looking more her old self again. If only Charles was there, but she knew the futility of 'if only'.

Kate lay on the bed after her shower thinking about the day and reviewing the evening ahead. Thoughts raced through her mind. She was looking forward to meeting Charlotte and hoped she would come up to scratch. She looked at her ring and remembered it was once Charlotte's engagement ring. She fell asleep and was wakened by Rachel.

'Come on, chop, chop. You're going to miss your own party if you don't hurry up.'

Kate looked at her watch and couldn't believe it was twenty past seven.

'Oh help! Is everyone waiting?'

'No, but they soon will be. I'll see you downstairs. OK' and Rachel disappeared.

Kate was cross with herself. She'd planned a leisurely, indulgent time in which to get dressed up. As it was she hurried into her finery, brushed her hair furiously and fastened her jewellery. There was a tap at the door and Elizabeth came in.

She gasped, 'You look beautiful Kate. What an inspired choice, Sam will be thrilled.' Kate blushed with pleasure.

'I like your dress very much too.'

Elizabeth was wearing a plain black Jean Muir dress relieved only by magnificent pearls.

'Thank you my dear. Will you do something for me?'

'Of course I will. What is it?'

'Will you come downstairs in exactly five minutes?'

'Yes of course. It will take me that long to finish getting ready anyway.'

Elizabeth went downstairs and Kate read the card she'd written on Sam's present for the umpteenth time. She took a last look at herself in the mirror. She'd never realised what the right clothes could do for one's confidence. She looked at her watch and descended the stairs. Sam was standing at the bottom holding two glasses of champagne. Behind him were Elizabeth and Charlotte, Rachel and Jethro all holding their glasses high.

Although Kate felt marvellous as she walked down she had no idea what a stunning entrance she had made. Charlotte said, in a quiet undertone, 'Absolutely to the manner born. What poise.'

Sam handed Kate her glass and stooped and kissed her.

'You look fantastic Kate, and very sexy,' he whispered in her ear. 'Come and meet my grandmother. Charlotte this is my fiancée Kate . . .' Before he could finish the introduction Charlotte stepped forward and kissed Kate warmly.

'I've waited a long time to meet you dear. It was well worth the wait. Welcome to the Jeffersons Kate. Sam is a lucky man and I congratulate him.'

'Thank you for letting me have your beautiful engagement ring Mrs Jefferson. I really treasure it and feel very honoured.'

'It is you who does me the honour Kate. I wish you both every joy in the world'

Kate went towards Rachel who looked almost demure in the Liberty frock. She spoiled the effect by saying 'Thank you for darning my fag holes. Come and meet Jethro. Jethro this is Kate.'

'How do you do Kate. I was expecting a country mouse not a glamorous film star. Sam looks completely gob-smacked.'

She turned to look and he did. She laughed with delight. Then she remembered she still had Sam's present and she gave it to him.

'It's nothing much but I hope you will like it.'

Sam opened it and smiled with pleasure. 'It's fabulous darling, thank you. I wasn't expecting a present.'

They followed the others into the drawing room where Kate had a chance to talk to Jethro. She wondered why Rachel had worried about him coming. She wasn't the least bit fazed and seemed thoroughly at ease talking with Charlotte. Kate was feeling quite light headed. She couldn't decide whether it was the champagne or sheer elation. If only her parents could see her now, her mother would be thrilled.

Elizabeth said 'Dinner is served, do come through. Sam will you bring Charlotte first.'

'Certainly not,' said Charlotte. 'I shall ask Jethro to escort me. Sam has his fiancée.'

He bowed and took her arm. They both laughed as he whispered 'I don't even know where we're going.'

Sam followed with Kate and Rachel said audibly 'Well bugger me!'

Elizabeth tucked her arm through Rachel's and went into the dining room. It was decorated with Michaelmas daisies and asters from the garden which, perchance, were the perfect setting for Kate's new skirt. The silver gleamed and the crystal shone, the napery was crisp and immaculate. The table was lit by deep purple candles.

On a side table was a large iced cake decorated with lavender coloured icing made into open books and violets. The books represented Sam and Kate's work. The colour was a compliment to Kate's eyes and, in the event, her velvet skirt and amethyst jewels. She was thrilled and amazed they had gone to so much trouble.

Conversation was animated and the food delicious. Salmon mousse wrapped in smoked salmon parcels, water-cress soup, roast pheasant with all the trimmings and crème brulée. Champagne flowed freely. No one could even look at the cheeseboard as there was still the engagement cake to come.

Charlotte proposed the toast with an impromptu speech straight from the heart. Sam replied briefly for them both. Kate, Rachel and Elizabeth all had tears in their eyes. Kate was thankful she didn't have to respond as she was too full of emotion to articulate. Elizabeth ached for Charles to share her joy.

Kate and Sam cut the cake and made a secret wish. They all adjourned to the drawing room for coffee. Rachel cut slices of cake into small pieces and handed it round. Kate sat on the sofa with Charlotte and answered many questions including some about her family. She told Charlotte she wished she could have asked her parents but her father wouldn't have come. Charlotte was kind and understanding.

Kate told Charlotte she realised she didn't have all the social graces. Charlotte silenced her with 'You have natural grace and good manners which are far more important Kate. Put those thoughts out of your mind and just be yourself.'

The rugs in the hall were rolled up and they danced and listened to music. Shortly before midnight Charlotte asked Kate if she would help her to bed. Kate was helpful and sensitive to the old lady's dignity without any trace of embarrassment.

In bed Charlotte looked older and more vulnerable. Kate hugged her and thanked her again for the diamond ring. 'Goodnight Mrs Jefferson.'

'Goodnight Kate. You must call me Charlotte, Sam does.'

I'll try to. Goodnight Charlotte, sleep well.'

When she came downstairs she said the music sounded quite loud from Charlotte's bedroom and suggested turning it down. Elizabeth soon wished everyone goodnight and went upstairs. It had gone well but she was tired. Rachel and Jethro said goodnight and disappeared into the kitchen. Sam and Kate were left together in the firelight in each other's arms.

CHAPTER 11

David's hangover was aggravated by the church bells. He registered it must be Sunday. There was something happening on Sunday and he struggled to think what it was. It came to him eventually. It was the day Alex was leaving for Oxford and he viewed the prospect gloomily. Although they had their differences it did break the monotony having him come and go. He would miss the practical help round the house and Alex's contribution towards the cooking as well as his company.

He stretched his long legs and turned over. He was pleased that Alex had found employment so quickly and was to work under Sam. Strange how this Jefferson family had altered all their lives. This brought him back to Elizabeth and he closed his eyes and fantasised.

The bells stopped and the silence was bliss. Alex was right, he would have to dispose of Faith's clothes and effects. He resolved to get on with it tomorrow. There would be Alex's things about the place today and plenty happening. He hated Mondays.

He could hear Alex downstairs and the appetising smell of coffee and toast wafted up. He could hear Alex talking to someone, not bloody visitors before nine on Sunday morning surely? David lumbered onto the landing and listened. He could only hear Alex's voice. Perhaps he was on the 'phone. He couldn't be talking to himself, only I do that David thought wryly. He splashed some water on to his face and put on the same clothes he wore yesterday. He sniffed at his socks, better find some clean ones.

Alex was in a good mood. He looked forward to starting a new life and he was pleased to find that Tabitha had come home. When he drew back the kitchen curtains she was sitting outside on the window sill looking back at him. She looked well fed and clean so presumably she had two homes. After a saucer of milk she sat purring on his knee, gently kneading with her front claws, as he ate his toast dripping with honey. Alex was very fond of Tabitha and told her how glad he was to see her back home.

David shuffled in relieved to find no one else there. He looked at Tabitha and said 'Finally deigned to come back, have you? Not very hygienic having the cat on your lap while you're eating. You don't know where she's been.'

'I know, but I'm pleased to see her and want her to know that. She's always been a very clean cat.'

'Thought I heard voices. Must have been you talking to the cat.' David poured himself some black coffee and three spoonfuls of sugar. 'It will be quiet here without you Alex.'

'I expect it will. If Tabitha stays she'll be some company for you.'

'Can't converse with a damned cat all the time. What time is Sam coming for you?'

'Early afternoon I think, depends how late they went to bed. He and Kate were having a family party to celebrate their engagement last night.'

'He's got a good girl in Kate. You missed your chance son. She's done well for herself though. Plenty of money and position and prospects.'

Alex resisted commenting and just nodded in reply. He didn't want any hassle between them and he was determined not to be drawn into any arguments. He wanted to leave their relationship on a good note. His gear was packed ready and he suggested they had a walk. David wasn't enthusiastic but he, too, was keen on keeping their relationship on a better footing and so he agreed. Alex's keen observation of wildlife made him an interesting walking companion.

'You will miss our lovely countryside when you live in the city.'

'Yes but I don't expect I'll have much free time for a while. There's some good country round Oxford but it's not so wild as ours, more populated.'

'I don't know Oxford, never been there. It must be very interesting, steeped in history and academia. Gown and town and all that.'

'When I get my own place you can come and stay but I'll have to get some dosh together first.'

They walked on in silence thinking their own thoughts. As they cut across the fields rabbits scampered up the sandy banks. Pheasants gleaning the stubble were untroubled by them. It was a good year for berries; clusters of hawthorn, fine polished rosehip and an abundance of holly berries brightened the hedgerows. The luscious claret coloured fruit that follows the honeysuckle flowers glistened richly, tangled with forgotten blackberries. The spiders were mending their webs on which the night air had hung its dew. It was good to be alive on such a morning.

'How are we going to cross the river or shall we have to turn back?'

If we keep working our way round to the right we shall join the bridle path and end up close to the bridge at Dinham.'

Alex spotted some field mushrooms and they picked as many as they could carry.

'I must make myself take regular exercise, it's very therapeutic. These are splendid mushrooms. What a pity we haven't got a bag with us.'

'I'm always happier outside. My bike will be useful to get out of Oxford to explore at weekends. Have you thought any more about getting away for a break?'

'Not really. I can't seem to think of anywhere I want to go. Your mother was always the one with the ideas.'

'There must be some place you want to see. Have you looked through the weekend travel supplements?'

'Yes. Nothing much of interest to me.'

They stood aside to let three riders pass. They were girls in their early teens who smiled and thanked them politely. One of the horses dropped a steaming pile by Alex and the rider burst out laughing. Alex laughed too. They were soon in sight of the bridge and the castle stood high and proud beyond.

'How far do you think we've walked?' David asked.

Alex looked at his watch and worked out the mileage. 'About five miles I think. We left at quarter past ten and it's half past eleven now. We've kept up a fairly brisk pace.'

'It has been most enjoyable but I'm ready to sit down now.'

'We shall have to eat lunch about one in case Sam is early. I don't want to keep him hanging about.'

'I should think not. Punctuality is courtesy in my book. What shall we have for lunch?'

'I set the oven timer for the jacket potatoes to come on at 11.30. The bacon chops won't take long in the oven with our fresh mushrooms and some tomatoes.'

David started feeling hungry at the thought of it. He had not fathomed out the mysteries of the oven yet. Tabitha was curled up on Faith's chair just as she always used to be. David stroked her and went to open a tin of cat food. She rubbed against his legs approvingly. Alex washed the mushrooms and left them in the colander to drain. He was pleased to see David looking more relaxed and cheerful.

It was not long after they had cleared up the lunch dishes that Sam arrived. He had taken Kate back home very reluctantly. He asked David if he would keep an eye on Kate for him. It would be a help if she had someone she could talk to nearby. David was glad to be of use and made a note of the Evans 'phone number. There would be pages of Evans in the telephone directory being on the Welsh border.

Alex and Sam soon had the car packed and the mountain bike tied securely on the roof rack. David could see Alex was excited and he noticed the easy rapport between the two young men. He suddenly felt old and passé and lonely.

'Won't you stay for some tea Sam? David asked.

'That's kind of you, Mr Green, but I'd like us to get off as soon as possible so we can off load in the daylight.'

'Very sensible. You will have done a long drive with the round trip. Congratulations on your engagement by the way. We are very fond of Kate aren't we Alex?'

'Sure thing Dad.' Alex grinned at Sam.

'Right, if you're ready we'll get off. Goodbye Mr Green. See you again some time.'

'Cheerio Dad. Thanks for everything. I'll give you a bell during the week.'

'Goodbye Sam, goodbye son.'

They waved as they drove away. David closed the front door and faced the empty house again. He was beginning to be afraid of his own company.

Elizabeth could not settle to anything after the weekend. It had all gone so well she felt positively high until Monday morning. Sunday had been another hectic day and already she missed having Kate around. It would be good for the spotlight to be on Rachel though, now that Jethro was returning to Islington. They had gone into Oxford by bus that morning to have a look round before Jethro's train.

Elizabeth quite expected Rachel might want to return with him but there was no sign of it. She couldn't make Jethro out, he was a real enigma. However she was extremely grateful to him for rescuing Rachel from the drug scene and she hoped they would remain good friends. It brought tears to her eyes thinking of Rachel addicted to drugs. On the rare occasion they'd seen her she looked thin, ill and dishevelled. She owed her life to Jethro after all was said and done.

Rachel had behaved well with Kate and not tried to steal her thunder. She was glad the girls seemed to like one another so much. Charlotte had gone back to Cherwell Close having thoroughly enjoyed herself. Elizabeth had driven her home before going to have her hair done after lunch.

Suddenly it was time for Elizabeth to think of herself and tomorrow's dinner date with Rex. She had been so busy during the ten days since he rang that she had hardly had time to think about it. She wondered whether he had changed much and what he'd think of her after all these years. She felt a surge of excitement tinged with apprehension. It must be about twenty-seven years since they last met. She took the dogs out into the garden.

When Rachel returned she found her mother burning garden rubbish. The dogs were dragging a long branch round growling at each other. When they saw her coming they charged towards her hampered by the branch. Oscar let go to greet her but Jasper took the opportunity to improve his grip on the branch. Their game went on boisterously. Elizabeth's face was streaked with smoke. Rachel was surprised by this display of energy after the busy weekend.

'Hi Ma! I thought you'd be lying down with pads on your eyes, swathed in towels and your feet covered with toe enhancing cream getting ready for your date.'

'That's tomorrow dear and I've had my hair done towards it. I feel rather restless and needed some air.'

'Your hair will reek of bonfires.'

'Yes, that did occur to me although I've had this scarf over it all the time. Isn't it a splendid fire? What is toe enhancing cream anyway?'

'The sort of gunge women's bathroom cupboards are supposed to be full of. Yes, it's a lovely blaze. Have you got any chestnuts?'

'No, what a pity. It never crossed my mind.

'What about dampers?'

'I'd forgotten about dampers. I haven't heard of them since you were little. We made them with flour and water and cooked them on sticks, didn't we? I think they are best left as childhood memories. They probably taste disgusting to the adult palate.'

'I suppose we'll be eating dinner party leftovers for weeks, like after Christmas.'

'No, there's next to nothing left apart from the cake and that will keep. I gave Charlotte enough for two main meals so we can have what we like.'

'Shall I cook some pasta?'

'That would be a real treat, thank you dear. I'll be in as soon as my fire dies down a bit.'

Elizabeth was still outside an hour later as the fire burned longer than expected. She was gathering her tools together when she heard the ship's bell ring. It was the first time she had been summoned to eat by the bell. She hurried across the garden obediently.

Rachel was standing by the back door smiling. 'We're into role reversal today. I'm sorry I started too soon. Your cooker's much quicker than my old thing.'

Elizabeth washed her hands, and the sooty smudges off her face, and ran a comb through her hair, and she sat down apologising for her scruffy appearance. Rachel served the pasta directly on to the plates. It smelled deliciously of Provençal herbs and garlic.

'Be careful, it's very hot.' Elizabeth thought how pretty her daughter looked as she leant over the table flushed from cooking.

'Mmn! Scrumptious pasta. You must tell me how to make the sauce. I like the crispy bacon, pine nuts and basil combination.'

Rachel was pleased with the result herself and said, 'I wonder what you'll be eating tomorrow night.'

'I've no idea where we are going. Presumably somewhere close by as it's quite a drive from Sheepscombe.'

'What will you wear?'

'I don't know. What do you think?'

'Something chic but not O.T.T. What about the dress you wore on Saturday night?'

'I wondered about that. You don't think it's too severe?'

'No, it suits you and it wouldn't matter where you ended up.'

'That's true, the conventional little black dress. I would feel right in black too, a mark of respect for your father.'
'What shall we have for pudding?'
'I'd like yoghurt and an apple. What about you?'
'I'll have a yoghurt with honey in' She went to get them clearing off the plates at the same time.
'That reminds me seeing the honey, I must fetch the bees back from the chase. They are usually back by the beginning of October but it's been so warm and sunny. It's a pity you don't drive. Why don't you have lessons?'
'I'd like to.'
'Well fix up a course with the driving school. We must discuss your allowance, you can't live on thin air. I'll arrange for your bank account to be credited if you give me the details.'
'I haven't got a bank account. I've had several and now I'm blacklisted by all the banks and credit card people.' Rachel put the yoghurts and fruit basket on the table.
'What about a building society? You could open a cheque account tomorrow,' Elizabeth was sharply reminded of Rachel's London lifestyle and went on 'You will need an account when you find a job, won't you?'
Rachel nodded, her mouth full of yoghurt and honey.
'Until you are working, and while you're living here, I'll make you an allowance of £200 a month.'
'Thanks Ma, that'll be great. Why didn't Pa leave me anything directly?'
'Because of the way you were living at the time he changed his will. He was not leaving you the means to kill yourself with cocaine and quite right too.' Rachel wished she hadn't brought up the subject and sighed.
'What a mess I've made of my life.'
'You are young and want to make the most of it from now on.'
'I'm not qualified for anything, so getting decent work will be murder.'
'That's up to you now Rachel. You have a good brain, security behind you and the opportunity to train. You must start believing in yourself if you want to convince others.'
'It really hacks me off when you talk like that.'
'If I can't talk sense to you, who can?'

'True. I hate reality.'

'That could be a serious problem if you don't deal with it and talk about it though. Perhaps Alex could be a help to you. He's easy to talk to and has a background in psychology.'

'Thought he was in publishing, not a shrink.'

'He started at Hackforths today but his educational background is in psychology. I'd like you to meet anyway. He's very much part of Sam and Kate's set.'

They cleared the table and washed up. Rachel scooped up Tobermory and took him with her to watch television. Elizabeth realised how very insecure Rachel was and still vulnerable. Perhaps learning to drive would help to boost her self confidence.

Rex arrived at 6.30 in a black turbo-charged Saab. She did not think she would have recognised him if they had passed in the street. The young man she recalled was slightly built and very handsome. Rex was now overweight with blurred features and greying hair. She wondered what he would make of her.

They kissed in greeting, each feeling slightly awkward. Elizabeth introduced Rex to Rachel and was glad that she was there.

He said to Elizabeth, 'I'd have known you anywhere, you haven't changed much. I compliment you on keeping your trim figure, more than can be said for mine,' and he laughed.

She offered him a drink and he chose gin and tonic and she joined him with one. Rachel drank Coke with lots of crushed ice.

'Nice to see a youngster who doesn't drink for a change,' he said.

'I often drink wine but not spirits.'

'And what do you do Rachel?'

'I've been involved with the drug scene and homelessness in London but I'm looking for a change of direction.' Rachel tried not to embarrass her mother.

'Very difficult work I imagine and not always rewarding. You've a charming place here, Elizabeth, have you lived here long?'

'About eighteen years. I think you were seven when we came here Rachel.'

'Have you any other children?'

'Oh yes. Sam is twenty three and working for Hackforths in Oxford. He became engaged last weekend so we've been celebrating. What family have you?'

'Four daughters ranging from eighteen to twenty four. I should have liked a son but it wasn't to be. I've booked a table at 'The Feathers'. I hope it isn't too uninteresting for you to dine so close to home. I'm told the food is good and couldn't find anywhere that sounded better in the vicinity. If you prefer we can go somewhere else.'

'No Rex. 'The Feathers' will be a real treat. I rarely dine out in the evening apart from the odd dinner party.'

'I will take good care of your mother and possibly see you later Rachel.'

'Ma's got her own key so I won't wait up,' she said with a straight face but laughing eyes.

Elizabeth was delighted to discover that Rex was the same kind, honest man that she remembered. They talked about his marriage and how he was coping with life on his own. His youngest daughter had just started a law degree at Birmingham University. His wife died of cancer seven years ago. Her sister had kept house for him for three years to help him bring up the girls.

'I notice you still like fast cars. You were the envy of us all with your XK120.'

'A lethal car for a young chap but I loved it. I've slowed down a lot since then and observe all the speed limits. The Saab made short work of the drive here and goes well.'

'Which way did you come?'

'Through Birdlip, Northleach and Burford, cross-country but good roads and a pleasant run.'

'Well I am flattered that you came all this way to take me out. It's lovely to see you and catch up on many years. You would have liked Charles I feel sure.'

'I remember him. The best man won I suppose. Shall you stay at the Manor? It looks like a big house for you and Rachel. I expect she will be off again before long.'

'I don't know. I'm not keen to rush into any changes and should like to be here for Sam's wedding. His fiancée's parents have been hit by the recession and she has some home difficulties. I shall start looking at smaller properties after the winter, by which time I may have a clearer view of where I want to live.'

'I moved to a bungalow with every convenience and still have a pied-à-terre in Holland Park.'

'We . . . I belong to the Royal Over-Seas League in London which I've often used on my own. One of the few places where standards never vary and Over-Seas House is so central and quiet.'

'So I believe. I've never actually been to it.'

'Perhaps we could meet there for dinner if you would care to.'

They talked about friends they both knew and had a long session of 'do you remember when' nostalgia which was fun.

'The Feathers' was busy and they took coffee in the upstairs lounge. Rex could see that Elizabeth was well known and respected there.

'I should really be letting you get home. It's a long drive.'

Rex went to settle up while Elizabeth spoke to the hotel's parrot in the hall. He helped her on with her coat.

'It was a delicious dinner, thank you so much Rex.'

'The pleasure was mine. We must do this again, that is if you'd like to.'

They drove the short distance to Oriel Manor chatting freely.

'You are a very attractive woman Elizabeth. You have to be careful with men friends. There are some dreadful types about, women too for that matter. Believe me, I know from experience.'

'Don't I know it. I've already discovered that even with men that I know, never mind strangers.'

'Present company excepted I hope.'

'Of course Rex, that must have sounded awful. You are the gentleman you always were.'

'Well just be careful.'

The outside light was on and Elizabeth unlocked the door with the dogs barking excitedly on the other side.

'Good guard dogs. I'll just see you safely inside and then I'll be off.'

Rex made sure all was well. There was no sign of Rachel, but she'd left plenty of lights on. Rex kissed Elizabeth goodbye and she stood in the doorway flanked by Oscar and Jasper until his car lights disappeared. She had enjoyed her evening and at last felt secure and comfortable in another man's company. She ached for Charles though. The company of Rex made her more aware of her solitary state. She sat in the kitchen for some time before she could face going to bed. She knew she was fortunate to have a secure home and no financial problems. She was blessed with two loving children, one of whom still needed her. She was grateful for all these things but longed for her husband.

'Oh God, will it ever get any easier?'

David turned more and more towards the bottle. The anaesthetic effect of the whisky added to his depression. Although he felt it was a helpful prop his nightmares increased and his tolerance grew along with his dependence. Always the same scenario in his tormented dreams. Charles making love to Faith on the 'Oriole'. Perhaps if he could destroy that confounded boat he could destroy them too. They would have nowhere to go.

His resolve the day Alex left was short lived. He sorted Faith's clothes and personal nick-nacks into plastic bags for the Hospice Shop. He found letters and photographs and all manner of oddments. There was nothing from Charles. He read the letters from Faith's old school friends and a cousin. The most interesting were from her oldest friend, Jennifer, living in Melbourne. He was astonished at the intimacy of the content. No man would write to another in that gossipy way. He began to wonder about Faith's letters to Jennifer. Surely she didn't write about him the way Jennifer wrote about her husband.

Jennifer's husband was a gambler and seriously in debt and she was having trouble with her teenage children. David remembered seeing photos of Jennifer's husband and family over the years. She and Faith had maintained their close friendship, despite the distance, since school days.

He found Alex's old school reports, drawings and paintings he did as a child and letters from school camp holidays. He was amazed that Faith kept them all.

David was concerned about the amount of whisky he was consuming. It was the tell-tale empty bottles that alarmed him. He told himself he didn't have a problem as he didn't hide bottles under the bed or start drinking when he got up in the morning. He did not understand the equally significant symptoms like his protection of the supply and the speed at which he drank. He was only secretive about the disposal of empty bottles and about not buying his daily bottles from the same shop. He knew he could not buy a case of bottles as he drank what was there until it was finished.

His functioning was increasingly affected. His memory was unreliable but he put this down to his age. He was very shaky in the mornings and had a tremor by the time he had his first drink of the day, usually mid morning. A couple of stiff tots steadied his hands. He no longer seemed to get drunk in an obvious way as by now he was continuously topping up. If he went out he needed a drink to get him there. When he returned he took another to get over it. The process was slow and insidious.

The bright spot of his day was Kate's visit. He kept his word to stay in touch with her and she was torn between the relief of being away from her father and the problem of David's drinking. Kate tried to talk to David about it. He laughed it off by saying he enjoyed a drink and there was nothing wrong with that. She knew it was more serious but didn't know how to deal with it. She mentioned Alcoholics Anonymous and he was furious.

'That's for addicts not social drinkers. People who drink meths and sleep rough and that sort of thing. Skid row stuff.'

'Plenty of professional people go to AA. Doctors, clergy, lawyers, as well as ordinary folk.'

'They've got real problems though.'

'Anyone who depends on a chemical substance to get them through the day is at risk of addiction.'

'That's all claptrap. Are you saying that all the heavy drinkers in the pubs are alcoholics?'

'No, but there can be a fine line and drinking alone is more dangerous.'

'Well you tell me how you can tell the difference between someone who drinks a lot, but can control it, and someone who is alcoholic.'

Kate thought for a while and David thought that he'd floored her.

'I think if it costs you more than money then you may have an addiction.'

'What do you mean, more than money?'

'If it costs you family upsets, work problems and affects friendships, that sort of thing.'

'Well I needn't worry then. I've got no family apart from Mother and Alex and they're not here. I've no job and no friends.'

'But you do put bottles out of sight when you hear me coming don't you?'

'Just tidying up I expect, I've never thought of it. You can't smell drink on my breath can you?'

'No, it's usually peppermints.'

David gave her a sharp look. He did use toothpaste and peppermints to mask the smell.

'Let's talk about you and your problems.'

They were both uneasy. David needed a drink badly and Kate wanted to go but didn't like to. She saw to David's mending and noticed there were shirts and socks on top of the sewing basket. She started sewing buttons on the shirts.

David offered to make coffee and she accepted. She distinctly heard the sound of a bottle being opened and put down and crept to the kitchen door. David had his back to her and was swigging whisky from the bottle. He jumped when she spoke and shoved the bottle behind the bread bin. It fell over.

'I shall have to get some more darning wool unless you've got more put away.'

'You're snooping on me, trying to catch me out.'

'If I was I must have succeeded then.'

Kate was upset and angry. She grabbed her coat and left without saying goodbye.

After she had gone David felt guilty. He had promised to keep an eye on Kate and help her. He was annoyed by her insinuations and felt she had spoken out of turn. He was also cross that he had been caught out. After all, if a chap on his own can't have a drink it's a poor show. He tried to justify his actions to himself. He had become adept at doing this and it bothered him sometimes and became the reason for his next drink.

He rang Kate and apologised for his bad humour and she was friendly and magnanimous. She sounded tense and troubled though.

'Is everything all right Kate?'

'No it isn't. My dad is in one of his moods. Will you ring Elizabeth for me and ask her if I can stay with her for a while until he comes out of it? I daren't ring from here in case he catches me.'

'Of course I will. Leave it with me.' David jumped at the chance to ring Elizabeth with such a good excuse. He poured himself a large whisky and rang right away. There was no reply and then the answering machine came on. He wasn't ready for that and so put the 'phone down. He prepared a suitable message and rang back. He read it out carefully and felt satisfied with the result.

He waited for the 'phone to ring, not daring to move far away. By late afternoon he needed to get to the off-licence to replenish his supply. He took his receiver off so it would sound engaged and hurried to the nearest place to buy his whisky. Kate was there when he returned.

'I rang you but it was engaged so I knew you were in. At least I thought you were,' and she looked meaningfully at the plastic carrier bag.

'I just needed some oddments of shopping. I rang Elizabeth but there's no one in. I've left a message on the machine.'

Kate followed him into the house.

'Perhaps she will ring while I'm here and I can talk to her.'

David privately hoped not. He wanted a chance to talk to Elizabeth and set himself up in a good light.

Kate made a pot of tea and they sat waiting for the 'phone to ring. They both jumped when it finally rang. David explained to Elizabeth why he'd rung and had no option but to hand the receiver to Kate. After a few minutes she gave it back to him saying 'She wants to speak with you.'

'David will you drive Kate over here as soon as possible? The poor girl is obviously frantic and needs help. I'm sorry to ask you but I'm tied up here for the next two hours and will have to be in.'

David agreed that he would. He looked at his watch and it was 7.40. 'We should be with you shortly after half past nine.'

'Will you stay the night? It will be too much to drive straight back. In fact you are welcome to spend the weekend here. Sam and Alex are coming tomorrow.'

'That is most kind of you,' he wanted to go but was thoroughly fazed by the spontaneity of the invitation. 'Yes that will be nice. It seems much more than a fortnight since Alex went.'

'See you later then. Don't rush but please keep an eye on Kate.'

Kate was following the conversation anxiously. 'I am sorry to be such a trouble. Will it be all right?'

'Yes of course. What what about your things if you are going to stay there. You'll need clothes won't you.'

'They are packed in my room at home. Please will you come with me when I collect them?'

'Yes, don't worry about that. I shall need some overnight things myself.'

Kate looked him straight in the eyes and said 'Are you . . . all right to drive?'

He held her gaze firmly and said 'Perfectly all right, at least I think so. If you think I'm over the limit what are you going to do about it? If you want to get to Woodstock then you'll have to put up with it' he added nastily.

'Don't think I don't appreciate it but I don't want you to get us . . . you . . . into any hassle.'

'We'll take our time and stop for a bite to eat on the way.'

Kate just wanted to get away from Ludlow as quickly as possible. David came downstairs with a small suitcase and a suit on a coat hanger.

They went to the Evans house. David kept Mr Evans engaged in conversation while Kate brought two large cases down. She told her father politely but firmly that she had asked David to take her to Woodstock. He was blazing with anger but contained himself because of David's presence. They left immediately.

The drive was uneventful as David drove at a steady forty-five mph and Kate was untypically silent. David put the radio on to make it easier for them both. They stopped for a coffee and sandwich but neither of them had any appetite.

Elizabeth and Rachel were very hospitable. David hadn't met Rachel before and found her very different from her reputation. She was frankly curious about him and asked him about his previous visit to Oriel Manor. Elizabeth whisked Kate off the minute they arrived.

David found the house much bigger than he'd imagined. He expressed his surprise and Rachel offered to show him round. He was amazed to discover they used all the rooms except the attics on a regular basis. The tour gave David an opportunity to note the room in which Elizabeth slept. His room was next to Sam's at the end of the same landing.

He confessed to Rachel his fear of dogs. She was most understanding and suggested he tried to overcome it by making friends with known quantity dogs like theirs. 'If you sit down in the kitchen I'll let them in one at time and let them come to you in the house. Then they'll be used to you when you meet them outside.'

He reluctantly agreed. Rachel let Jasper in first. He didn't bark but came up and sniffed him, tail wagging. It all seemed very straightforward. Then Oscar came in and, apart from them jostling one another a little, it was a repeat performance. He stroked their backs gingerly.

'Now you get up and walk to the Aga.'

David complied and the dogs took no notice of him.

'Now walk to the window.'

Just as he started to Elizabeth and Kate came in. 'What are you doing, Rachel, ordering David about?'

'I'm getting him used to the dogs Ma. What shall I call you?'

'I think David would be best.'

Elizabeth was quietly amused. Kate leant against the Aga. Rachel said 'Why don't we listen to some sounds. You look as if you could use something mind blowing,' and they went upstairs.

Elizabeth apologised for bothering David but felt it was imperative to respond to Kate's cry for help. They both agreed she wasn't a girl to ask readily.

'I hope you can stay for the weekend?' Elizabeth said.

'I should like to very much if it isn't too much trouble.'

'I've not arranged anything as I was expecting to spend it in the garden. We'll see what the weather's like tomorrow and go from there.'

'How much help do you have in a house this size?'

'I've a splendid woman who comes in three mornings from nine until twelve.'

'That's not very much but I suppose Rachel is a big help to you.'

'She's not keen on housework but she gives me a hand in the kitchen or garden. Our gardener comes three days a week but he's in his late seventies and can't do too much now. He's a real character and part of the local colour. We sort of inherited him when we bought the house. He regards it as his garden rather than ours.' She went on 'Shall we have a night cap before we go to bed? What would you like?'

'Scotch please.'

'I remember now, you're a whisky man. You like it straight too if my memory's reliable.'

'That's right Elizabeth. Thank you.'

She poured herself a very small tot and filled it up with water. She was aware of him watching her every movement.

'You are very beautiful but I expect you are used to compliments.'

'Thank you. I am having to get used to the attention of men again after a quarter of a century of never giving it a thought. It's not easy.'

They finished their drinks and she switched off the lights apart from the hall.

'I don't think the girls are coming down, it's gone very quiet up there. If you like to go ahead you know where your room is don't you. I'm going to let the dogs in now.'

'Yes I do. Where do the dogs sleep?'

'In the hall usually. I like them to have the run of the house at night. Good night David, sleep well.'

'Good night,' and he went upstairs. He looked through his hastily packed case to see if he had everything he needed. Most things seemed to be there but he couldn't find the bottle of whisky. He panicked, he must have left it in the car. He couldn't go and get it because of the dogs and the burglar alarm. Perhaps he could get into the drawing room for a good slug from the decanter. He crept along the landing and peered over the banisters. The dogs were lying at the bottom of the stairs. He was imprisoned until morning. He felt very threatened and nervy. He tried to read in bed, there were interesting books and magazines, but he couldn't concentrate. Eventually he fell into a fitful sleep but had panic attacks each time he woke up. The night seemed endless. His best sleep came when he knew he should get up and he dreaded facing the day. He was sweating profusely.

Rachel and Kate were having breakfast when he appeared. Elizabeth was clearly waiting for him. She observed how disorientated he seemed. He tried to pour orange juice from a jug and was shaking so much that they all noticed. Only Kate knew the reason way. He had difficulty in holding the glass to drink too. He made an excuse about tablets to go out to his car. He was soon back smiling broadly and smelling strongly of peppermints.

Elizabeth said 'You really should keep your medication with you. You looked quite distressed when you first came into breakfast.'

They made outline plans for the day. Elizabeth and Kate were going to do the weekend shopping. Rachel suggested she showed David round Woodstock and Blenheim. The only time they arranged to meet up was drinks before dinner when Sam and Alex arrived.

David made his bed and moved his whisky into the wardrobe ready for tonight. He would buy half a bottle in Woodstock which would fit into his anorak pocket. It was a welcome change to have company and Rachel seemed pleasant enough. Perhaps Alex would like her. It wasn't going to be so easy to get Elizabeth on her own but he was determined to find an opportunity.

CHAPTER 12

Rachel proved to be interesting company. They wandered round Woodstock and for the first time he went into the church where Faith had died. It was a strange, detached feeling wondering where she sat on that fateful day.

For Rachel it was full of ghosts and she was relieved when they emerged into the sunlight. She suggested coffee at a café. David said he would meet her in there in a minute, he needed to get something from the chemist. He found a grocer with a wine counter and bought two half bottles of whisky. It was far more expensive than his usual off-licences but he wasn't fussed about that. With his security in his pockets he could go and drink coffee.

David steered the subject round to boats. He told Rachel he was interested in them and believed they had one. She didn't like power boats but rather fancied sailing. She told him Sam was the one to tell him about the 'Oriole'. She explained that she hadn't lived at home for years and her father bought the boat while she was in London.

'Where is it kept?' David asked casually.

'Sam moved it recently to Thrupp. He and Kate spent their engagement party day moving it to a secure mooring nearer home.'

'Do you know the way there, I'd like to see it?'

'No, but it's on the Oxford canal and so it can't be any hassle to find it. Wouldn't you rather see Blenheim?'

'Perhaps we could do that tomorrow.'

Rachel shrugged her shoulders. 'OK then. Will you let me drive your car? I've got a provisional licence and I'm having lessons.'

'No, my insurance isn't suitable,' he said firmly. It was fully comprehensive but he didn't want to be driven by a learner. 'We could have a pub lunch somewhere. How would that suit you?'

'It's OK with me. I like eating out.'

They walked back to The Manor and everyone was out.

'Have you got maps so we can find Thrupp?' Rachel asked.

'Yes, there's a good road atlas in the car.'

They sat in the car looking at it and David chose the most direct route. On the way Rachel asked David's advice about work and tried to discover what it was like working for an estate agent. He advised her against it and reminded her of the tragic demise of two female agents in recent years. They soon arrived in Thrupp and parked near to the boats. It was a pleasant place and they looked at the moored boats as they walked along the towing path. They saw a pair of working boats chugging along carrying coal.

'A rare sight these days,' David commented and stopped to watch but Rachel had gone on ahead.

'There it is,' She cried out, 'let's see if we can get on board.' She tried the hatch door without success while David looked round the outside. The curtains were drawn so he couldn't see in. Everything looked in very good order and he felt a strange sort of excitement to be looking at the boat he had dreamt about so often.

Rachel called 'I've found the key.' She had discovered it under an empty gas container in an outside locker in the bow. She opened up and drew back the curtains.

'Do you know how to drive it, we could go for a spin?'

'No, I don't know anything about boat engines and it would be highly improper in any case,' he said primly.

'No more improper than nips of whisky.'

'And what's that supposed to mean? When you are as old as me you may find it helps to keep your circulation going.'

Rachel grinned. 'Don't get all shirty, it's none of my business. Even I know you don't buy booze from the chemist. I used to be a drug-addict you know. I've kicked it now.'

David was considerably rattled but tried not to show it. They decided to walk to the pub which they had already passed. David ordered a glass of white wine for Rachel and a pint of bitter for himself. David decided on steak and kidney pie and Rachel chose lasagne. Rachel went to the ladies. The bar was quiet and David quickly asked for a chaser and started talking to the landlord.

'Got a boat nearby, have you, or are you out with the guns?'

'No, but a friend of mine has. Did you know Charles Jefferson at all?'

'Terrible business that, really shocking. He occasionally came in here with his friend when they were down in these parts.'

'I've forgotten the name of that boating friend of his, can you remind me?'

'Don't think I ever knew his name. Keen fishing type. Another medical chappie I believe.'

David swallowed his chaser and hid his glass behind the menu as he saw Rachel coming back. They took their drinks to a table by the window.

Rachel saw him hide is whisky glass but decided not to say any more. 'Do you feel any safer with the dogs now you've got to know them a bit?'

'A little perhaps. Why?'

'They could do with a good run in the park after lunch and you can come with me if you like.'

'In the park? They'd be better off in the garden surely.'

'Not a parky park. I mean Blenheim Park. We're allowed to use it as long as we keep the dogs under control. There's a lake and things, I'm sure you'd like it. Aren't you interested in old houses and stuff? Americans flock to see Blenheim.'

David wasn't too enthusiastic but it was his turn to fit in with Rachel.

When they returned home Elizabeth and Kate were busy in the kitchen. Kate was making pastry and looking more herself again.

'We're taking the dogs for a run in the park unless we're needed for anything else. It's all part of David's dog training' Rachel added mischievously.

Elizabeth laughed 'You are having a time. Don't let my daughter bully you David, but the dogs would enjoy it. You'll like seeing Blenheim I feel sure.'

David said that he wanted to see the park having heard so much about it. Rachel fastened their leads and passed one to David. 'You take Jasper, he doesn't pull.'

David took hold of the lead and felt quite good about it. They walked up the hill and off the road in front of a row of picture book stone cottages and through a gate. It was starting to blow up with rain clouds as Rachel let both dogs loose.

'I hope it's not going to piss down now, it's a super walk down to the lake.' David was reminded of the last walk he'd had with Alex and realised he hadn't had any proper exercise since. He looked at his watch, it was only a couple of hours before Alex and Sam were due to arrive.

Elizabeth answered the 'phone to an excited sounding Alex. He apologised for a sudden change in arrangements. The two friends that he was expecting from Montpellier had already arrived, three days earlier than expected. There had been a real mix up of dates. So he wouldn't be able to come for the weekend after all. She assured him it was perfectly all right and there would be plenty more weekends. It was just a pity that he would miss his father who was already there. She put him on to Kate who explained about David. He told Kate, in confidence, that Sam had leant him the 'Oriole' for the weekend so he could have some time alone with Martine. They couldn't stay at the Oxford flat because a friend of Sam's was using it for the weekend.

'How romantic . . . it's really super. I know you'll have a fantastic time . . . why don't we fetch you over here tomorrow so you can see David . . . no, OK I won't say anything to anyone.'

Elizabeth couldn't help hearing Kate's end of conversation and wondered what Alex was up to. Kate ended by saying 'Give my love to Martine. Be good, have fun.'

Elizabeth said 'It's a pity Alex will miss seeing David but it can't be helped. He sounded very excited about the arrival of his friends.'

'We met Martine in Olargues. She lives there and Alex really fell for her. She is over with another French girl from the university in Montpellier. She should have arrived in Oxford on Monday.'

'I expect Sam knows all about it. Here comes Rachel and David. I expect they'd like some tea.'

David came first. Rachel re-filled the dog's water bowl.

'You've just missed Alex on the 'phone. Unfortunately he won't be coming after all. Some friends have arrived unexpectedly from France,' Elizabeth told him. Before he could answer Rachel said 'What shitty news. I was looking forward to meeting him.'

David said 'I suppose it can't be helped, these things happen.'

Kate looked surprised at his calm reaction. It was not like David to be so laid back. David's eyes were on Elizabeth who said 'We shall just have to make it up to you for being disappointed.'

David thought than an excellent idea but not quite the way she meant it. Actually he was rather pleased the more he thought of it. He would have a better chance of seducing Elizabeth without Alex around. Kate would be occupied with Sam, perhaps it was a pity Rachel hadn't got Alex though. Wild thoughts raced through David's mind. Elizabeth noticed his preoccupation and suggested tea by the sitting room fire.

Sam's car pulled up as they were finishing tea. Kate shot out of her chair saying 'I'll make a fresh pot for Sam shall I?' She didn't wait for an answer. They stayed in the kitchen for a while and by the time they joined the others Sam had already had tea. He and Kate looked very happy together. David had never seen Kate so radiant.

Sam greeted everyone and gave Alex's apologies to David and Elizabeth. This time it was Rachel who went to help her mother and David read the paper. Sam had his arm round Kate as they sat on the sofa in front of the fire.

Alex was in a frenzy. Although he was pleased to see Martine it could hardly have happened more awkwardly. She arrived at Hackforths with Hélène to the great interest of everyone in production. It was a busy, open plan office with no facility for social calls. Alex arranged for some coffee and left them sitting in reception.

Hélène was older than Martine and on her way to stay with friends in Bristol, so she soon had to leave to complete her journey. Martine watched the office comings and goings with interest. She was extremely pleased to see Alex but very disappointed that he was so preoccupied with work.

Sam finished earlier and came to talk to Martine. He explained that she could not stay at the flat as both he and Alex had leant their rooms to friends of his for the weekend. He described the 'Oriole' and assured her that it was warm even though there wasn't much space. He suggested she re-pack some of her things so that she only had one hold-all. He would leave her other luggage at the flat ready for her return on Sunday night. By the time Alex finished Sam had arranged a lift to Thrupp for them. He handed Alex the key to the boat, clean sleeping bags and two boxes of provisions.

For Alex this arrangement was heaven sent. He had wondered about the sleeping possibilities at the apartment, not wanting to upset or offend Martine. Now Sam had explained the boat situation to her, and she had agreed, he needn't worry about it.

Maggie, one of the typesetters, drove them to Thrupp. Martine said 'You never tell me about your interest in boats.'

'I've never actually seen this boat except on a painting. It belongs to Sam's family.'

'Is it so beautiful that it is on a painting.?'

'I don't really know. It's not very big and is on the Oxford canal.'

'I was 'oping to see Oxford not the canal,' Martine complained.

'You will next week. It's your own fault, Martine, making such a cock-up of the dates.'

'What is a cock-up, I don't understand?'

'The confusion, mix up, mistake about dates. Never mind, let's have a great weekend.'

Maggie knew Thrupp and where to find the boats. She lived just a mile farther on. They thanked her very much and off-loaded their kit. The wind howled and it started to rain.

'Oh Alex, what 'ave you done' wailed Martine, 'it is so cold 'ere.'

'It's bound to feel cold after the Midi but I'll soon have the stove lit.'

He opened the hatch and they clambered in hampered by all they were carrying. Martine looked around as Alex lit the lamps. It was well fitted but small and cold. He quickly lit the gas heater and checked the spare gas containers: one was full and another empty so there was plenty until tomorrow.

Martine sat huddled by the fire wrapped in a rug. Alex found a large tin of soup and heated it. As the boat heated up, and the soup warmed her inside, Martine started to come to life and look round. She found the shower and loo. 'Oh là là! C'est impossible! Regardez-vous.'

Alex looked and said 'We play loud music when we go in there so it is more private!' She looked doubtful. He, too, thought it embarrassingly intimate and not in the least romantic. He went on 'We'll go to the pub for a meal tonight, Martine, and then sort the cooking out tomorrow.'

She looked relieved. At least there would be a proper toilet at the pub.

Back at Woodstock, dinner was a lively meal full of witty conversation. David had primed himself well beforehand and enjoyed it enormously. His eyes hardly left Elizabeth who looked stunning in a sapphire blue close fitting dress. Sam noticed David's admiration for his mother with some amusement. Kate had warned him to keep the decanter well away from David but he seemed to be already tanked up. David wasn't bothered, he had his private supply safely in his room and in a pocket in the cloakroom. Elizabeth noticed how much like Alex he was as he became more animated. Kate knew that his bonhomie would soon give way to being maudlin. She was so happy to be with Sam that she couldn't worry about David. He was not her responsibility even in Alex's absence. Rachel was fascinated by his interest in her mother and wondered what she was thinking.

After dinner they watched a much acclaimed television play during which David made several visits to the cloakroom. Sam and Kate drifted off upstairs to listen to CDs and be on their own. Elizabeth, Rachel and David went to bed shortly before midnight.

David had a long soak in a scented bubble bath trying, vainly, to relax. He was impressed by the luxuriously appointed en suite bathroom and tried to work out what it must cost for the upkeep of a house like this. He gave up and visualised Elizabeth in the bath and then had to sublimate like mad as he dried himself. He prowled round the bedroom, wearing only a dry towel, deciding what to do.

He poured himself a large glass of Dutch courage. He would wait until one o'clock before going to Elizabeth's room. He opened his door and listened. There was no sound apart from feint music coming from Sam's room at the far end. He left the door slightly ajar and turned off all but the bathroom light so he could see without being seen. He found a towelling robe behind the bathroom door. It was a little on the small side but would do. He debated whether to put on his boxer shorts. As he was rather well endowed he thought perhaps he'd better. He didn't want to alarm her and it would look better if he encountered anyone else on the landing. He sat in an armchair out of sight of the light from the landing. He heard a board creak and then another. The hairs on the back of his neck rose as the door slowly opened. Could she be coming to him? The stealthy steps changed to action as Jasper bounded in. He was very pleased to have found his new friend and licked his bare legs. David told him to 'be quiet and go away' in a hissed whisper. Jasper wagged his tail and sat down. David stood up and Jasper jumped up catching David hard in his most vulnerable place with strong front paws. He doubled up in agony clutching his assets shouting 'Get down you great black mutt.'

Elizabeth appeared in the doorway of his room looking startled and sleepy. Even in his anguish David saw Elizabeth's nude figure clearly, the landing light shining through her filmy nightie like a spotlight. She looked achingly erotic.

She ordered Jasper out and he went obediently. Another door opened farther down the landing. Elizabeth stepped in and quickly closed David's. She stood with her back against it and a hushing finger to her lips.

There were steps along the landing and Jasper's tail outside the door went thump, thump, thump.

Rachel's voice whispered 'Are you all right David?'

Elizabeth shook her head to silence him from replying. Then Rachel tapped on the door and Jasper started to growl.

'Don't be stupid Jasper it's only me. You don't guard David, you only guard Ma.'

She called him quietly but he wouldn't move, just growled purposefully.

'Oh bugger you then and him as well. You'll just have to sort yourselves out.'

Elizabeth was trying not to laugh. By the time Rachel's door closed she was shaking with suppressed laughter. Her closeness and the shaking of her breasts were too much for David. He lunged forward and drew her on to the bed stroking her breasts with a terrible urgency. Elizabeth couldn't believe it. She struggled free and stood over David's prone form.

'I know you're drunk but this is my house and I will not have you touch me David. Is that clear?'

'I love you Elizabeth and I want you. I've wanted you since the moment I set eyes on you.'

She saw his concupiscent gaze and grabbed a towel to wrap round herself.

'By the morning I hope you will have forgotten all this. Either way I want you out of my house before anyone is up. I shall wake you early, David, and you will go. You're a disgusting drunk.'

'You've got a beautiful bottom, has anyone ever told you,' he went on. 'What a bottom!'

She hurried out of the door tripping over Jasper in her anxiety.

156

David's surprise at her reaction turned to anger directed both towards her and himself. He poured a large whisky spilling most of it. He was furious to have his plans foiled by a dog. He drank deeply. He was wide awake and felt alert, his fury mounting. The time had come for him to burn the boat. He dressed, grabbed the car keys and opened the door. Jasper and Oscar were lying outside Elizabeth's door. Their tails thumped as they saw David but they made no effort to follow him. He turned off the burglar alarms carefully as he had seen Elizabeth do it and let himself out of the house. The laser beams threw a brilliang light over him as he made his way to the car.

He could see a figure at a lighted window as he drove away flirting gravel in all directions. He could remember the way to Thrupp and he looked at his watch. It was a quarter past one. He always carried a can of petrol in the car and there were matches in the glove compartment. If he couldn't have Elizabeth at least he would get rid of that confounded boat once and for all. It would destroy his tormenting nightmare.

There was no one about when he reached Thrupp and only one house had a light burning. He left the car where he'd parked it earlier and picked up the petrol can, matches and a pile of old newspapers. He prayed there were no roaming dogs.

The meal at the pub wasn't cordon bleu but Alex and Martine were warm and full and had had a little too much to drink. They couldn't stop laughing as they tripped over mooring ropes finding their way back to the 'Oriole' just before midnight. The night was dark and they had no torch. Their earlier inhibitions were forgotten as they listened to cassettes and made love. They didn't get properly undressed and wrapped the sleeping bags round them and slept together happily. Alex slept heavily. Martine was awakened by the cold and unfamiliar sounds outside. The boat seemed to be moving, perhaps it was the wind.

David squatted on the tow path and soaked the newspapers in petrol. The fumes made him retch and feel sick. He looked for the key but couldn't find it, maybe Rachel forgot to put it back. He placed one ball of petrol soaked papers in the locker with the gas bottles and the other by the hatch door at the rear of the boat. The fumes made him retch again and his head was pounding.

He lit the back of the boat first and then the front. The bow caught alight right away. The stern took longer and he sprinkled the remaining petrol on to the doormat.

Martine could smell petrol. She got up carefully, so as not to disturb Alex, and went to the loo. She felt her way round the dark boat. She could definitely smell petrol and there was a sudden bright flare of light. She pulled back the curtain and saw flames. She could see the retreating figure of a tall man; it looked like Alex. She screamed and opened the door to a wall of flame shouting 'Alex come back, don't leave me 'ere.' The figure vanished and she realised Alex was behind her. He threw a blanket over her and pushed her through the door.

'Jump off, Martine, quickly.' He pushed her off the boat, she was paralysed with fear. He dived back inside to get the fire extinguisher off the wall. There was an explosion as the gas canaster blew up. Alex was thrown against the steps of the aft deck and lost consciousness.

Martine raced to the nearby cottage. A man rushed out saying 'You go inside.' Martine grabbed his arm crying hysterically, 'Alex, 'e is on the boat. 'elp 'im.'

A woman led her indoors and gave her some brandy and wrapped her in a rug. She dialled the emergency services and asked for all three of them. The man came back after dragging Alex onto the towpath. Two men stayed with him.

David couldn't believe his eyes when first a curtain moved and then a girl screamed and leapt through the flames. He ran as fast as he could and didn't stop until he was in the car. His heart was racing. He started it up and drove off. He had to stop to be violently sick. A signpost indicated he was driving towards Oxford. Who was that girl or had he imagined it? She sounded foreign and yelled to him to come back. Why had she called him Alex?

There couldn't really have been anyone there, it must be the whisky affecting his mind. She sounded French he thought. Martine was French. Where had Alex and Martine gone to? Panic seized him and he turned the car round feverishly, grazing a wall and just missing an ambulance, blue light flashing, as it sped round the corner. Oh my God, he thought, what have I done?

The woman was running the cold tap on the burns on her husband's hands and wrists. Then he ran out with blankets and they gently rolled Alex's inert body on to them and carried him to the cottage.

He was unconscious and badly burnt. Martine could hardly recognise him and fainted with the shock. The ambulance and fire engines arrived simultaneously. The men had nearly extinguished the fire with a hose from the watering point. The firemen made sure it was out with their powerful hoses as Alex and Martine were carried into the ambulance by the paramedic team. They were rushed to John Radcliffe Hospital Accident and Emergency Department. It was the police when they arrived who noticed David crying in the shadows. 'Where do you live Sir? I think it's time you went home. There's nothing more you can do unless you witnessed the fire.'

'I started it' David howled with anguish.

'You started it? Are you sure? What is your name sir? You seem to have been drinking, are you sure you started it?'

He led the constable to his car and handed him the petrol can and matches. He cried uncontrollably.

The constable used his radio and then took David to the cottage where the sergeant was questioning a small group of locals. He explained to the sergeant who looked doubtfully at David. The landlord of the pub recognised David and came over to him. The sergeant said 'Do you know this man?'

'Yes he came to the pub yesterday lunchtime. I think the young man from the boat might be related. They look very alike.'

David groaned and said 'Was it Alex?'

'That's right, it was Alex. I heard the French girl call him that when they had dinner earlier.'

The sergeant said 'If you knew your son was on the boat why did you set fire to it?'

'I didn't know. How could I know? There shouldn't have been anyone there' David sobbed. 'Will he be all right? Where have they taken him?'

'You'd better come with us to the station. We shall need a statement. What's your name?'

They took his particulars, locked his car and drove David to the police station where he was cautioned, breathalised and left in a cell to sober up. The constable said 'He's more than three times over the legal limit of alcohol and right out of his box.' The sergeant was ringing the hospital.

Alex's condition was critical. Martine was in deep shock and had sustained superficial burns. The ambulance men, the doctors and later the police could get no sense out of her. They presumed her language problem as well as her condition prevented her from answering their questions. One of the doctors addressed her in French and her response was better. He asked for her name and address, and she gave them her home address in Olargues. All she would say in English was 'Alex, 'ow is 'e?'

'He is being moved to a special burns unit where they can look after him better. We must have his name and address.'

Martine asked for pen and paper and still shaking pitifully she struggled to write his name, age and address in Oxford and Ludlow. The doctor asked her for her address in England and she said it was the Oxford one of Alex.

The police telephoned the Ludlow address. There was no reply. They could not find a number for Alex Green in Oxford and so sent a car round to the address. The two students who were staying there said the flat belonged to Sam Jefferson. They had never heard of Alex Green or Martine Bouvet.

The man from the pub had said the boat belonged to a Jefferson from Woodstock. The police rang Oriel Manor at 7.00am.

Elizabeth had been up most of the night worrying about David driving off in such a drunken state. His leaving had disturbed Rachel. She and Elizabeth had talked the night away drinking endless cups of tea. Eventually Rachel fell asleep in the chair and her mother covered her up with a duvet.

Elizabeth knew she should have informed the police. She tried to resolve the conflict between ratting on a friend and doing her public duty. As dawn broke she knew her lack of action was the wrong decision. She dozed off into a fitful sleep and was wakened by the telephone ringing.

'Hello, yes? . . . Hold on a minute and I'll wake him up for you.' Elizabeth looked at her watch. It was just gone seven and it was the Oxford police wanting to speak to Sam. Her heart sank. It must be serious to be ringing so early. She woke Sam and he took the call in her bedroom. She sat on the bed anxiously trying to glean what it was all about. She prayed David hadn't killed anyone. Sam was giving the police Alex and Martine's names. He looked very grim, all the colour had drained from his face. He put the 'phone down and turned to Elizabeth.

'There's been a serious fire on the 'Oriole'. It's completely gutted.'

'Oh thank goodness that's all. I was afraid David had had an accident.'

'David? Isn't he asleep in bed?'

'No. Never mind that. Tell me what the police wanted you for.'

'They were checking the ownership of the boat and also who was on it. Alex and Martine were on board Ma.'

Her hand went to her mouth as she asked 'Are they all right?'

'No, I'm afraid not. Alex is being transferred to the Burns Unit in Birmingham. He has not regained consciousness. Martine is suffering from shock in the John Radcliffe.'

'What can we do?' Elizabeth's eyes were round with horror.

'They want me to go and identify Alex as Martine is rather confused. Alex's condition is serious.'

'Would you like me to come with you?'

'No, I think Kate had better come. She's known Alex longer than any of us. Could you and Rachel go to see Martine?'

'Of course. Did they say how it happened?'

'No but they have someone helping them with their enquiries. It seems it wasn't an accident.'

'How depraved. Why would anyone want to do such a dreadful thing?'

'I'd better break it to Kate. She's very fond of Alex and I don't know how she will take it. We'll have to take David with us. It'll be a terrible shock for him. Could you tell him Ma?'

'No. I'm afraid he left in the early hours very drunk. He left by car. I should have informed the policy but I didn't.'

'You couldn't. He's our guest and Alex's father.'

'I should have done Sam.'

Sam rang the Ludlow number but there was no reply. He went upstairs to tell Kate.

Elizabeth made them have a little breakfast. Kate couldn't stop crying. Rachel came in saying 'I can smell coffee and toast. What about me? She looked at their grim faces and Kate's tears and asked 'Has he killed someone?'

'No, but there is bad news of Alex and Martine.' She listened with horror.

The telephone rang. Sam answered it.

'For you Ma. It's David.'

A very contrite David asked if she could verify what time he left Woodstock last night. He apologised for being drunk and hoped he hadn't given any offence. He said he was at Oxford Police Station. She asked him how Alex was but he didn't seem to know. He sounded subdued and rather disorientated. She told him that Sam and Kate were leaving to see Alex and he seemed grateful. She found it difficult to think of anything helpful to say to him. She told him she was coming into Oxford to see Martine at the Radcliffe but it didn't seem to register properly.

Sam and Kate left at eight thirty and she and Rachel shortly afterwards.

CHAPTER 13

A regular vigil was kept at Alex's bedside. It was a week later that he opened his eyes properly for the first time and it was Rachel sitting there. Ironically out of them all she was the only one that Alex didn't know.

She smiled and said gently 'Hello Alex. I'm Rachel. I'm Elizabeth's daughter, Sam's sister.'

'Where am I?'

'You're in hospital in the burns unit. You've been here for a week.'

'What day is it?' followed after a long pause.

'It's Saturday. Saturday the 20th of November.'

Alex tried to alter his position and winced with pain as he attempted to move.

'Shall I get someone?'

'No thanks, just a bit sore. So you're Rachel Jefferson. Not a bit like I expected, but you do look a lot like Elizabeth.'

'Shall I ring for Martine to come? She was here this morning.'

'No. Martine . . .' and there was another silence. 'Is she OK?'

'Yes. She's staying at Oriel with us, she's fine.'

'What happened?' Alex kept moistening his dry lips with his tongue. Rachel poured him a glass of water.

'There was a terrible fire on the boat. You helped Martine off and lost consciousness yourself. You fell, do you remember Alex?'

'No. I can remember seeing Martine in the doorway and flames. Nothing else.'

'Probably shock or the fumes.' Rachel was beginning to feel out of her depth. 'We've been quite worried about you' she said in a bright tone.

'Sorry about that.' Alex was looking in horror at the burns on his arms and hands.

Rachel managed to press the bell without him seeing. Staff nurse hurried to the bed. Rachel said 'I thought you'd like to meet Alex now he's awake.'

The nurse spoke reassuringly and felt his pulse.

'Will you leave us for a minute, Rachel, please.' She drew the curtains and checked his drips and catheter. She told him what they were for and asked if he needed more pain relief. He tried to nod but it was too painful. He wondered if there was any part of him unaffected.

The nurse spoke to Rachel and she returned to the bedside.

'I won't stay and tire you too much. Martine and David will want to see you. I'll let them know you're awake. Is there anything I can do for you?'

'No thanks. Come again some time if you can.'

'Cheers. I'd like to. See you soon Alex.'

His eyelids were drooping, the injection was taking effect.

David was relieved beyond measure to learn that Alex had regained consciousness and was lucid apart from a small memory loss. He dreaded going to see him but made himself go that afternoon.

Alex was sleeping when he arrived and he sat by the bed as he had done for the past few days. The difference was that before he'd prayed fervently for Alex's recovery and now he found he was praying for strength for himself. He had never been a religious man. He suddenly became aware of Alex's open eyes and smile, a slight and painful smile because of the tautness of the healing skin around his mouth.

'Hello Dad.'

'Hello son. How are you feeling?'

'Sore but I shall be OK. They say it will take time.'

'Of course.' David was shocked by his calm acceptance and choked back tears. He hadn't realised until these anxious days the strength and depth of his love for his son. It was torturous to see him in such pain and disfigurement and know that he was the cause of it all.

'You OK?' Alex asked.

'Yes thank you, at least I shall be when you are feeling better. You'll never know how sorry I am. It's the cross I shall bear for the rest of my life.'

Alex was puzzled by this but hadn't the strength to pursue it at present.

'It must have been a shock for you.'

'It was. A terrible shock, a tragedy.'

Again Alex was mystified, not like his father to be so emotional and dramatic. He imagined that David had received the news of the fire in Ludlow. David thought Alex knew what had happened and so they were both at cross purposes.

Alex licked his swollen lips. 'What d'you think of Martine?'

'She won't speak to me and who can blame the poor girl after all she's been through.'

'She's OK. Rachel told me. I'm sure you're imagining things.' Alex closed his eyes exhausted by the effort of talking.

David sat quietly making himself look at the burns and agony he had caused.

He went to see Sister who said they were pleased with his progress today but there was a long way to go. The important thing was to keep his morale up and let him come to terms with the situation in his own time. David said to Alex he would be coming again tomorrow.

Martine found visiting Alex excruciatingly painful. Elizabeth had taken her home to Oriel Manor from the hospital in Oxford and looked after her. She knew Kate and Sam slightly from Olargues and Rachel was kind and friendly. If she had been asked a week ago she might have said she was in love with Alex. Now she realised how little they knew one another. She felt unable to provide the support she knew he would need and knew that Kate was closer to him than she was. They had a lifetime's friendship behind them.

The fire had come between Martine and Alex rather than drawing them closer. They had nothing important to say to each other and both found it a strain trying to talk. Martine needed to talk about the fire and her fear but knew this wouldn't help Alex's recovery. They couldn't speak freely and share the experience.

She could not understand the English reaction to such an emotive and dastardly act as David's being so low-key. He had nearly killed them and yet all the Jefferson family spoke of David as 'poor David'. In Martine's eyes he was un scélérat – a villain. It made little difference to her why he set fire to the boat. She knew he had done it deliberately and that was enough for her wrath. Elizabeth had asked her not to tell Alex how it happened until he asked. Martine thought she should give vent to her anger and resentment. Elizabeth said David was being punished every time he looked at Alex. This was, she supposed, the British disease that she'd heard about, the stiff upper lip. She could not see the point of it.

She found living in opulence rather daunting. The entire family made her most welcome but she longed for her close knit home life in Olargues. She wanted to feel the comfort of the sun on her back and hear the hollow chime of the tower bell and the rough and tumble of life with her young brothers and sister. She was counting the days until her return. Meantime she would try to avoid meeting David at the hospital. There was only one word for him, he was dingue – mad.

Rachel was very helpful and seemed to understand her best. She kept telling Martine to 'let it all hang out' and get it out of her system. She told her that David had a problem of alcohol dependence and needed treatment. At least her attitude made the whole situation a little more understandable and manageable.

Rachel arranged to meet David after he had visited Alex the second day after he regained consciousness. She gave him a real piece of her mind and asked him why he had persuaded her to take him to the 'Oriole'. He told her about his nightmares and how he had believed them. She listened attentively and without interruption as the the truth of David's confession poured out in torrents. He had been obsessed by the idea of Faith and Charles having an affair on the 'Oriole'.

'Why didn't you have more faith in Faith?'

'I don't know Rachel, I just don't know. It all seemed so real to me at the time.'

'You were jealous and wanted someone to blame for your misery. When did you start to hit the bottle?'

'That's not really a problem it just . . .'

'Hang on a minute David, it's a very big part of the problem. You didn't have the confidence in yourself to believe in Faith's innocence. Using a mind altering drug distorted your thinking.'

'Perhaps I was drinking too much. I certainly was out of my right mind when I set fire to the 'Oriole'.'

'Yes but you planned it and used me in the process. I really resent that.'

'I wouldn't put it quite like that.'

'I would. How much have you downed today?'

'I haven't had anything yet.'

'Why aren't you shaking then? Come on, you can't fool me, don't bull-shit around.'

'You have no right to talk to me like that Rachel.'

'True, but it won't stop me. Do you want to get over your addiction or are you choosing to become an old soak? Alex doesn't want a lush for a father, think of your self esteem.'

David couldn't believe his ears but felt as if a trap was closing on him. He mustered as much dignity as he could, 'I shall address myself to controlling carefully what I drink in the future.'

Rachel laughed scornfully. 'Then you are more of a fool or more addicted than I thought. What a dick head!'

'There's no need to be abusive. Let us consider the matter closed.'

'Oh no. Alex is going to need your support. I want to help you David. Will you let Jethro come to stay with you for a bit?'

'Who is Jethro?'

'Me and Jethro lived together in London. He got me off drugs. He's out of work so you'd have to pay him.'

'Why should I pay him if I was giving him a place to stay?'

'Because he'd be your therapist. When Alex discovers exactly what you did he will be glad to know you are getting help. You'd feel better if you faced up to yourself and started to cope.'

'I couldn't possibly afford to pay this Jethro person.'

'Course you could. Think what you'd be saving on whisky. You could pay him and feed both of you on the whisky money.'

David couldn't bear all this talk of whisky money. Rachel went on 'It's no use looking all po-faced, you're an addict the same as I was. With Jethro's help I recovered. I didn't want the whole bit at the time, it was effing torture.'

David shuddered and said 'I'll give your friend a trial if he wants to come.'

'He'll come. He sees it as vocational. When then?'

'I don't quite know, it depends on his commitments I suppose.'

'Tomorrow then. I'll get him to ring you tonight. Is there a station in Ludlow?'

'Yes, but tomorrow's a bit soon.'

'I'll ring him from here. Won't be a minute,' and she disappeared.

David was in need of a drink and went to the gents. Rachel came back to find him sitting at the table smelling strongly of peppermint. She didn't comment.

'Jethro will give you a bell tonight and see you tomorrow.'

David felt threatened and said 'I'm sure all this is not necessary. I've got Alex to think about first.'

'The best thing you can do for Alex is to make yourself a responsible person. Think about it.'

'Why are you going to so much trouble on my account, Rachel, when you clearly disapprove of me.'

'I'm being a friend when you need one. It's called tough love. I've been through it. I've cheated myself and everyone else but I've recovered. You can, but you've got to learn to want to. It was Jethro who made me want to.'

David viewed the prospect with nothing but trepidation. 'Thank you for your interest Rachel. I know you mean well. Give my very best wishes to your mother.'

Jethro's impact on David's life was torpedic. He was like a shadow who never left him for a minute. The only privacy he had was in the bathroom and there was no possibility of buying booze. Jethro watched him like a hawk. David asked him 'What exactly is your brief?'

'To dry you out and get you thinking honestly and positively.'

David tried to pull rank, using his years, but it was utterly lost on Jethro. He had now recovered from the worst of the shakes but had terrible panic attacks and cravings. He learnt not to try to cheat Jethro as the result was humiliating.

David brought up the subject of social drinking and how to make soft drinks look like proper ones. He was told to avoid pretend drinks and just order coke or tomato juice.

'Are you allergic to any food David?'

'Yes, I can't eat shell fish. I come out in a rash and feel really ill.'

'So you don't eat shell fish. What do you do if it's in sandwiches when you're out.

'I avoid them. People understand if you have to explain.'

'Do you often have to explain?'

'No, hardly ever.'

'It's the same with drink. If you order a tonic no one says don't you want gin or vodka in it. They ask whether you want ice or lemon. Don't create a rigmarole man.'

'What about trays of drinks at functions when all the drinks are alcoholic?'

'What would you do if it was shell fish?'

'That's different. I'd just apologise and say I can't eat shell fish.'

'Same with booze mate. You can't drink alcohol as you're allergic to it. Simple.'

'But I'm not.'

'Really? Where d'you get that idea. The minute you're on the drink you're a bum. One drunk's much like another. Boring and devious.'

'I'll learn to control it.'

'Learn to control eating shell fish at the same time.'

'Don't be stupid, you know I can't.'

'Same difference, although shell fish isn't a M.A.D., a mind altering drug. Remember a drunk doesn't only risk killing himself but other people too. You could have killed a bus quene of children driving round as you were doing.'

'But I didn't, did I?'

'No. You only managed to burn your own son and frighten his girl friend to death. No thanks to you that they weren't killed.'

'Don't remind me. I want to forget that.'

'No chance mate, until you've got your act together. You've been given a second chance, Alex is recovering. But you've got to keep sober for yourself otherwise it won't last.'

David couldn't coherently argue with Jethro, nor could he find ways to outwit him either.

'How is it you're so sure of yourself Jethro?'

'I've been there. I used to do drugs. Lucky to be alive really. I've learnt to live one day at a time, it's the only way.'

'Do you drink?'

'Occasionally, but not a lot. I can take it or leave it. I am responsible for myself. Every day I remind myself of that.'

Twice David found hidden half bottles and drank them. He felt so guilty and went through withdrawal horrors again. Jethro merely said 'Proves the point doesn't it. No chance of giving up drinking until you've cracked your thinking.'

These words went round and round in David's head. His nightmares about Faith had stopped, he hardly seemed to dream at all. Instead each day seemed like a living nightmare as he battled with Jethro.

Martine went back to France after saying a tearful au revoir to Alex. He was improving each day apart from minor set backs and short bouts of depression. He was not upset when she left as he found it was Rachel's visits that he looked forward to most.

Life returned to normal at Oriel Manor apart from regular visits to see Alex. The hospital was concerned that Alex still did not know that David started the fire. His memory was unreliable and he seemed to have forgotten his bedside interviews with the police. It fell to Rachel to tell David to put this right on a day when Alex was well enough to cope with it.

David had never had to confront anything so difficult. He hadn't had a drink for nearly three weeks and was thinking clearly. He told Alex what he had done and why. It was a relief to get it over but he could hardly bear to maintain eye contact with his son as he spoke. He made himself do it.

Alex reached for his hand and said simply 'I guessed, Dad, in the end. The only thing I can't grasp is how you could think so badly of Mum.'

'I don't know myself now that I'm in my right mind. I'm so sorry Alex and I can't expect you to forgive me. What I've done is despicable.'

'I do forgive you but it's a sad business. We must make something good come out of if somehow.' Simple spoken words numinous with meaning.

A warm tear dropped on Alex's scarred hand from his father's drooped head.

'I don't know what to say son.'

'Don't say anything, there's no need.'

A nurse brought them tea and told Alex the plastic surgeon was doing his rounds later on. David asked if he could see the consultant afterwards and was told to go to Sister's office when Alex was being examined.

Elizabeth arrived unexpectedly with Charlotte. David and Charlotte shook hands and she was introduced to Alex.

'So you are the young man my grandson has such high hopes of in publishing.'

Alex's face lit up with pleasure. He thought what a handsome old lady she was and could see why they all liked her so much.

'How are you coping David?' she asked.

'I am coping, thank you, but feel a terrible sense of failure.'

'This is no time for self pity. Remember no man's life is entirely wasted, it can always serve as a bad example.'

Elizabeth and Alex took deep breaths and watched David.

'That's quite a relief, Mrs Jefferson, to think that something worthwhile may come out of all this misery. Thanks for being so honest.'

They breathed again with relief. Charlotte's harsh words seemed to help David as she knew they would. She went on to regale them with hilarious stories of life at Cherwell Close. With Christmas approaching there were dinners and parties looming daily.

'You should see what those old people can eat.! The funny thing is that those who have trouble with their stomachs seem to put away the most. Quite disgusting greed but some of the poor old things have nothing more interesting than food to think about.'

'Do you have meals on wheels?' David asked.

'There is muck in a truck daily I believe, but I don't have it.' Charlotte was stopped in full flow as Elizabeth intervened.

'That's not fair Charlotte. I used to deliver meals on wheels and they were very good.'

'These are different, they're produced by a private company and so we are perfectly entitled to have an opinion. The customer is always right my dear, remember?'

Alex was most amused and Charlotte spied a ready audience. She winked at him wickedly. 'You should see some of the washing when it's pegged out, unbelievable. Drawers the size of marquees. Hectic pink Celanese knickers with strong elastic below the knee; talk about all being safely gathered in, it takes on a whole new meaning.'

The consultant heard the end of Charlotte's tale and apologised for eavesdropping. He was laughing too.

As they left the ward Charlotte asked David 'How are you getting on with your minder?'

'It isn't easy but I have to admire his dedication and pertinacity.'

'Real terrier-like qualities, hasn't he? He's done a lot for Rachel. Quite restored her to being a useful member of society. Oh hello Jethro, I didn't see you there.'

'I was just waiting for David, Mrs Jefferson.'

She turned to David again. 'This is the young man who wants us all euthanased in old age. Probably despatch us all at sixty if he had his way.'

'Hardly seems worthwhile bothering to get better then, does it?' David quipped.

'Well done David! A sense of humour at last. It's an essential part of our survival kit' Jethro said.

'I never seem to have a problem with it myself, but it isn't always appreciated' Charlotte added.

'I can imagine that' and David smiled broadly.

'Christmas is only around the corner and they don't like you dying at Christmas when everyone is on holiday and services have closed down. So we must keep going until it's more convenient. The crematorium queue is as long as your arm after the Christmas break. Not that I want to be burnt like a heathen.'

Jethro opened his mouth to interject but Charlotte stopped him with 'I know there isn't room for us all to be buried. It's more natural though. What do dogs do with old bones, bury them! If every person could be buried and a tree planted on the top it would be ideal. We should provide the food for the trees and improve the landscape at the same time. Much better than grave stones. Save on flowers too. 'Charlotte's doing well this year, they'd say."

'It's a great theory, Mrs Jefferson, but it wouldn't work in practice.'

'No, I'm sure you're right. In any case at my age one is required to enjoy Christmas at any cost. It doesn't matter if you expire in the process as long as you had a good time, covered in tinsel and a silly hat, and over-indulge until you're sick.'

'I see the hospital are putting their decorations up. I can't believe Christmas is so close' Elizabeth observed. She went on 'When Alex is well enough to leave here he will need convalescent care. I should be delighted to have him at Oriel and he would have plenty of young company as well as rest.' David shot her a grateful glance. 'That would be ideal Elizabeth. I'm sure he'd like that.'

David stayed behind to see the consultant and Jethro went to introduce himself to Alex.

*****

Alex had plenty of time to think whilst he recovered from skin grafts. If he didn't ask the right questions he found there were things he wasn't told. Rachel was good at giving straight answers and he talked his worries out with her. As they indirectly affected a parent of each of them, whether alive or dead, they found their discussions mutually therapeutic. Rachel addressed the death of her father head on for the first time. Her anger and guilt and now her sorrow overflowed. Alex helped her through it and in the process dealt with many of his own emotions concerned with his mother's death. He told Rachel about his father's fantasies about Faith and Charles, and talked David's crazy ideas out with her. Rachel told him how they had been out to the 'Oriole' the day before the fire. How he was still on bail and had to report regularly to the police. Alex was thoughtful.

'Does Elizabeth know Dad's reason for setting fire to the boat?'

'She does now but she seems OK about it. Puts it all down to the booze. He fancies her you know.'

'Are you sure? He's so against emotional display and anything to do with sex.'

'Yeah I'm sure. I've seen the way he watches her. There was something going on the night of the fire.'

'What sort of thing?'

'Dunno. An upstairs sort of something. After he freaked out and vanished Ma and I were talking most of the night. She was livid about something.'

'How odd. She's always so together.'

'She wasn't that night. Really rattled. I think David's quite sexy though.'

Alex didn't pursue that line, instead he asked 'What will happen with the police? I told them I don't want any of it to go to court or anything. Sam isn't pursuing it and it's his boat.'

'What about Martine?'

'I suppose she must have talked to them when I was pretty out of it.'

'Funny girl Martine. She seemed to have burnt her brains and kept her bra, really mixed up.'

'She was great in France. Very attractive you must admit and really got style.'

'Les vacances mon ami, makes all the difference! How well did you know her there?'

'Not very. We kept in touch after and it seemed to get hot. I really fancied her.'

'Do you miss her now?'

'Not really. I think I was relieved when she left. She was wiped out by it all, poor girl.'

'What d'you think of Jethro?'

'Weird but OK. He's certainly got Dad sussed. Never thought anyone could deal with him like Jethro does.'

'I'd back Jethro against anyone. He's real steel when he's onto you. Hope it works out.'

'Christmas will be a tricky time, so much booze about.'

'Don't worry. Jethro's invited himself to stay for Christmas. He'll charge double time!'

'The old man won't like that.'

Rachel shrugged her shoulders. 'He pays, he has to. Does it bother you Alex?'

'No. I just hope it works.'

Rachel left him with plenty of crossword puzzles and a change of cassettes. She always brought flowers. Alex had never been given flowers before and they brightened up his locker. All the nurses teased him about Rachel.

Unknown to him she went to see his consultant and asked whether he would be out by Christmas. She was told he would certainly be able to go home but would have to come back for more skin grafts. He was recovering very well and his positive attitude and determination helped. She asked whether he would be permanently disfigured. He wouldn't commit himself but was optimistic that there wouldn't be extensive scarring. His face had healed up splendidly and the colour would fade with time. He could always grow a beard if not.

The surgeon's parting shot was 'Keep up the good work Rachel. You can do more for him now that we can.'

She wondered if it was true. One thing she was sure about, she was falling in love with Alex and wanted to help nurse him back to full health. It was not just feeling sorry for him. He was on her mind all the time. She had started to take more of an interest in her appearance because she wanted to appeal to him. She longed for the day when he came to stay at Oriel for his convalesence and romanced about how it would be.

Elizabeth noticed her daughter's heightened interest in Alex and her devotion to regular visiting. She also observed with great pleasure Rachel blossoming into a beautiful, feminine young woman. She never went to see Alex in old jeans and grunge. She was experimenting with new styles of clothes which were much less way out and trendy. Apart from complimenting her from time to time Elizabeth had the sense not to comment. Best of all was the contented expression on her face which transformed and animated her. She sang around the house and was a joy to behold.

Together they changed the morning room into a bedsitting room for Alex's use. Rachel's excitement was mounting almost unbearably. Elizabeth wished that Charles had lived to see his daughter grow into womanhood. Rachel's long absence and destructive life style had cause them years of worry and sadness. So many good things were happening now and she longed to share them with Charles. The last six months had seen so many changes, all of which were triggered by Charles' death. Faith's death was also affecting their lives profoundly as the young family members wove the two families closer together. Sam and Kate's engagement and Rachel's interest in Alex had all come about through Charles' and Faith's death.

CHAPTER 14

During Alex's hospitalisation Kate helped out at the production office at Hackforths. Her library experience was useful for some of the office work and she learned how to paste up layouts with Maggie. She enjoyed being employed again and Sam liked to see her at work. Afterwards he drove them back to Woodstock and they had dinner with Elizabeth and Rachel. When Sam worked late Elizabeth picked Kate up, often with Rachel at the wheel. She was becoming a proficient driver and couldn't wait to take her test.

Sam usually slept at his flat during the week but was looking out for a home for him and Kate. Their weekends were spent looking at houses and cottages and visiting Alex. This weekend they looked at a small cottage in Thrupp and a more splendid one in Nuneham Courtney by the Thames. Kate preferred Thrupp but wondered whether the association with the 'Oriole' fire would affect Sam. He assured her that it would not. Although 'Oriole' was extensively damaged he had decided to have her restored in due course when the insurance company had finished their assessment.

It was beautiful by the Thames in Nuneham Courtney but the river attracted weekend visitors. The cottage was quite a large house and Kate said it was far too big and perfect for them to start off in. She much preferred the idea of renovating the canalside cottage in Thrupp. It would be a challenge and interest for them and was in no way pretentious. The financial difference was an attraction too, although Sam thought the Nuneham Courtney house a good investment.

They were very excited by the idea of Willow Cottage which has its own little canal mooring. The owners were a dear old couple who were moving to Worcester to be nearer their daughter. The old lady had had both hips operated on and could no longer manage the steep staircase. They had hoped to move before the winter weather but the sale had fallen through because of a breakdown in the housing chain. Vacant possession would be on completion and they could move out immediately. They were delighted that Sam and Kate were first time buyers.

Sam arranged to have a survey made and said he would be in touch shortly. It was reasonably priced and he could see no problems with a mortgage. Kate was so excited when they arrived at Oriel that she raced into the house ahead of Sam while he was putting the car away. Elizabeth was writing letters and put her correspondence on one side to listen to their enthusiastic talk about the cottage.

'It sounds charming and rather a good buy. The owners must have liked it to live there for forty years. A sound reason for leaving too. I hope it works out.'

'I shall die if it doesn't, Kate said, 'it's exactly what we want.'

Sam smiled and added, 'We'll take you with us next time, Ma, if you like.'

'That would be lovely dear.'

'I'm wondering whether I should give notice on my flat and save some money meantime. Would it be OK if I moved back here? It wouldn't be for long.'

'A sensible idea. Have you decided on a wedding date then?'

'No, but we're thinking about April or May.' Sam said.

'A spring wedding, how lovely. Where will you be married?'

'I was wondering about that.' Kate said. 'It should be Ludlow but it's a great big church. We don't want a huge wedding, do we Sam? Then there's my parents,' and she sighed.

'It's high time I met your parents Kate. You can't keep us apart forever you know.'

'Yes I know Elizabeth, but . . .'

'Why don't I ask them for lunch on Sunday and see whether they can come?'

'What do you think Kate?' Sam added, knowing how worried she was about it.

'We could ask them I suppose. Dad would be intimidated here with a bit of luck.'

Elizabeth laughed and said 'I wonder what you say about me when I'm not about. I shall ring them up and ask them if that's all right.' Kate agreed.

'I'd like to be married here in Woodstock and Sam would of course. Would it be awkward d'you think?'

'We must talk it over with your parents Kate, it's only fair on them. They may have their own plans for you.' Kate nodded gloomily and gave Elizabeth the telephone number on a piece of paper.

She rang right away. Kate chewed anxiously at the side of her thumb nail. 'Hello . . . It's Elizabeth Jefferson here, Sam's mother . . . How are you? . . . and Mr Evans? . . . oh good. Kate and I have been talking and she wants me to meet you. I wondered whether you and Mrs Evans would like to come for lunch next Sunday . . . yes, I'll hold on . . . Yes? Oh hello Mr Evans . . . how are you? . . . We're hoping you will bring your wife to lunch here next Sunday . . . That will be lovely. About 12 o'clock suit you and then we'll have lunch at one . . . Here's Kate to have a word with you, just a minute . . .'

Kate was shaking her head vigorously but Elizabeth put the receiver firmly into her hand. 'Hello Dad . . . yes . . . no, it's not that far . . . I'll get Sam to write out the route and post it to you . . . No, I won't forget . . . see you on Sunday then . . . Cheerio.'

She pretended to faint on the nearest chair.

'He sounded fine to me Kate. Don't let's say any more about it. I look forward to meeting them on Sunday, it'll be all right, you'll see.'

Kate did not share her optimism. Suddenly she bounced out of her chair and said 'Could we ask Charlotte, please Elizabeth?'

'Well we could but don't you think she might be rather daunting for them?'

'Yes she would and Dad wouldn't dare be awful with her.'

'You naughty girl! Charlotte would love it of course and maybe she is the best one for building bridges. She can be very diplomatic at times.' Elizabeth looked thoughtful and then went on, 'Yes, I'll ask Charlotte, if you will drive her over Sam.'

'OK Ma, whatever you women say,' and he went back to the newspaper property columns.

The Evans' visit to Woodstock went off well to the surprise of all concerned. Both Kate and her mother had a restless night beforehand and Mr Evans was thoroughly ill at ease as they drove through the gates.

'Are you sure this is it Mother? It's a proper mansion.'

'It is a manor house dear. Kate said it was a big place.'

'Never thought our Kate would be a go-getter. I hope they aren't too lad-di-dah.'

Mrs Evans smoothed the creases out of her skirt and patted her newly set hair.

Jasper and Oscar ran up to the car barking. The Evans' liked dogs, especially George Evans. He called 'Come on boy, come here boy,' and patted their heads. The dogs were quick to recognise potential friends and chased round to greet Gwyneth Evans who was torn between stroking them and keeping her best clothes clean. She didn't want to let Kate down.

Kate and Sam came out to meet them. George was looking uncomfortable in his good suit, Sam had never seen him looking so spruce.

'Two grand black Labs, what are their names?'

'That's Oscar with the red collar and Jasper with the brown one,' Kate said proudly kissing her mother.

'Are they good with the guns?' George asked.

Sam said, 'They don't get a chance much I'm afraid. You interested in dogs then Mr Evans?'

'I like proper dogs like these not pampered pooches. I was a gamekeeper at one time, years ago, and trained a few dogs.'

'Of course, I'd forgotten. You must miss the life.'

'I do. Nice place you've got here. Where's Mother gone?'

'She went in with Kate. Come and meet my family.'

Elizabeth was in the hall helping Gwyneth off with her coat. Sam introduced George and he and Elizabeth shook hands. Kate hovered round anxiously but Elizabeth was perfectly at ease.

'Come along in and meet my mother-in-law. Charlotte may I introduce Kate's parents, Mr and Mrs Evans. This is Charlotte Jefferson, Sam's grandmother.'

'Excuse my not getting up but I'm feeling my age rather today.' Charlotte gave them a welcoming smile.

They all sat down and Sam brought the dogs in and told them to lie down. Elizabeth looked at him enquiringly and Sam said, 'Mr Evans likes dogs Ma. He used to be a gamekeeper.'

'I'm fond of dogs too,' added Mrs Evans quietly.

Charlotte sat forward in her chair. This sounded promising, she had never met a gamekeeper before. Sam busied himself with drinks and Kate handed round nuts and dried fruit.

'Now tell me Mr Evans, do you think it's entirely fair to raise pheasants by hand and then shoot them for sport?'

'Yes Ma'am I do. They are well looked after and most of them have a good life and a swift end.'

'Hardly sporting though is it?'

'Not like it used to be in the old days. People aren't what they were either. All sorts shoot nowadays, some as common as muck and other riff-raff besides the gentry.'

Mrs Evans shuddered and hoped he'd mind his language. She said, 'I looked after any injured birds Mrs Jefferson. We've reared all sorts in our time haven't we Katy?'

Kate agreed and smiled at her parents, relieved at the way they were coping so far.

'Proper soft with birds and animals these women but good at nursing the really sick ones.'

Rachel came in from the kitchen and was introduced. Mr Evans turned to Kate and said, 'You never mentioned Rachel. We thought Sam was an only one like you.'

'I didn't meet Rachel until a few weeks ago.'

'I'm the black sheep of the family, Mr Evans, so they keep pretty quiet about me,' Rachel grinned.

'Take no notice of her,' Charlotte said, 'we've forgiven her for abandoning us all and going off to London. She's been away some years.'

Mrs Evans sipped her sweet sherry and said, 'Never fancied London myself. All rush and bustle and so expensive. No one seems to care about anybody else.'

'I quite agree with you,' Charlotte said and leant forward to engage Mr Evans' attention again. 'Are there many badgers round the Ludlow area?'

'Shropshire has a large population of badgers when they're left in peace. They like the sandy soil and there's plenty for them to eat. But we've been plagued with badger baiters in recent years. They come from out of the county to try to dig them out. Cause a lot of suffering to the badgers and their dratted dogs.'

'Terrible business, I've read about it in the papers. I believe some have been prosecuted.'

'Not enough. We've got badger watches now.'

'And what about the increase in rabbits?' Charlotte asked.

'They're on the multiply again, pesking the farmers. But we like a nice rabbit pie, don't we Mother?'

'Yes we do. Katy makes a good rabbit pie. Get her to do you one, she's a nice little cook.'

'Sam's a lucky man all round. I know Kate cooks and bakes beautifully. She helps me in the kitchen sometimes,' Elizabeth said.

'I haven't tasted rabbit pie for years. Not since that dreadful myxomatosis epidemic in the fifties,' Charlotte said.

'You need to mind where you get them, Ma'am, and be sure they're Myxy-free. The rabbits get over it now you know.'

'So I believe, nature is amazingly clever. What do you think about your daughter marrying an Oxfordshire man?'

'We miss her at home but I'm sure she'll make Sam a good little wife,' Mr Evans said proudly.

Elizabeth intervened to say lunch was ready and Sam helped Charlotte out of her chair and took her arm. Elizabeth went with Mrs Evans and Kate linked her father's arm. He said audibly, 'Nice to see a young chap looking after his granny. I think you've chosen well, Katy, after all.'

Rachel came through carrying a steaming soup tureen. Kate began to relax and enjoy herself. Mr Evans tucked his napkin into his collar, struggling because he wasn't used to wearing a tie. Charlotte immediately tucked hers under her chin, to Rachel and Sam's amusement.

Kate said, 'We think we've found our future home. It's a lovely cottage, north of Oxford, in a village called Thrupp.'

'Isn't that the place where Alex had his accident?'

'Yes, he was in a boat that caught fire on the Oxford canal there. Terrible business.'

'How is the poor boy? We do miss him coming round and his dear mother. We always had a soft spot for Alex.'

'He's going on fine. I'm going to look after him when he's well enough to come out of hospital,' said Rachel.

Charlotte was interested to hear this, in fact she found the whole occasion today quite fascinating. 'I expect you'd know Faith Green quite well and David of course,' she said.

'Mother and Faith were friendly. Always hoped Katy and Alex would make a go of it one day. Mr Green's a dull sort of man, isn't he Mother?'

'I wouldn't say that exactly.'

'You often do say it,' Mr Evans persisted.

'He's had a bad time poor man,' Mrs Evans said

'It has been a hard year for his family and ours which is how we have all come to know each other,' Elizabeth said diplomatically.

Sam who had offered very little during lunch, said 'We are wondering how you feel about a late spring wedding. April or May if we can secure the cottage.'

Mrs Evans looked all flustered and her husband inscrutable.

'We want a small wedding. I wondered whether we could be married at Woodstock. Ludlow church is lovely but so big,' Kate added.

Mr Evans said he was glad they were thinking of a church wedding. He didn't hold with registry offices. He talked to his wife for a minute and then said, 'I suppose you could get wed here if the Vicar agreed. Be a bit more awkward to arrange a reception away from home.'

Elizabeth chose her words carefully. 'It depends on what kind of occasion you have in mind, but you are welcome to use this house if you think it would be suitable.'

'Very kind of you I'm sure, but we wouldn't want to put you to that trouble,' Mrs Evans said.

'It would be a pleasure. I don't expect I shall stay on here much longer. It's too big for Rachel and I and she will want her own place before long I expect. It would be lovely to celebrate their wedding here.'

'What do Sam and Katy think?' Mr Evans asked.

'We haven't discussed it,' Elizabeth said firmly. 'I needed to have your opinion first before asking them.'

Mr Evans looked pleased. 'If they want it here, Mother, I don't think we should get in their way.'

Sam said, 'Kate and I would like that very much but I'm equally happy to be married in Ludlow.'

Mr Evans beamed at Sam. 'There speaks a gentleman. No use Mother and I pretending we could match this though. As you know ours is a simple but loving home.' Kate nearly choked on her roast potato remembering the endless rows.

Charlotte said, 'It will be good to have a wedding to look forward to after such a trying year. We are very fond of Kate as I am sure you can see.'

'Where do you live Ma'am, here at the house?'

'No. I used to live in an apartment in Oxford and have recently moved into a sheltered retirement scheme on the outskirts.'

'How do you find the old people?'

'Very dreary and tiresome.'

'I should hate to be cooped up in one of those places. Have you got a busybody running it?' Mr Evans asked.

Charlotte's day was made. She entertained them all through pudding with tales of the goings on at Cherwell Close. They were all laughing by the end of it and Charlotte was flushed with success. Elizabeth thought Kate was absolutely right to have invited Charlotte.

'More apple pie for anyone?'

Mr Evans proffered his plate. 'It's nice to have proper custard Mrs Jefferson.'

'Do call me Elizabeth please. I like custard too, but the young people seem to prefer cream.'

'Can I have the skin please?'

Elizabeth gave it to him. 'I like the skin on milk puddings too. Don't you?' He nodded.

'It's a nice pie Mrs er . . . Elizabeth. I like the mixture of ginger and cinnamon. Nice light pastry too,' Mrs Evans said. Sam had another helping to keep Mr Evans company.

Rachel excused herself to go to see Alex with a friend. They took coffee in the sitting room by the fire. Tobermory was sitting in front of it toasting himself, his tail wrapped round his paws.

'That's a big cat Mrs Jefferson. What sort is it?'

'I don't really know. He looks part Persian, with that thick coat, and part tabby I think. We've had him from a kitten and he grew and grew.'

'Dreadful superior creature, grinning all the time,' Charlotte complained.

'I take it you don't like cats Ma'am.'

'Not overmuch and definitely not that one.'

Tobermory gave Charlotte a disdainful look and jumped on to the back of Elizabeth's chair.

Oscar sat with his head on Mr Evans' knee and enjoyed the rhythmic stroking and patting he received. If it stopped a strong black paw attracted his attention effectively.

'Do push Oscar away if he's a nuisance,' Sam said.

'You're all right old fellow, aren't you?' and Oscar's tail thumped appreciatively.

Mrs Evans offered to help Elizabeth with the washing up. Kate said she and Sam wanted to do it, but thanked her very much.

'It will be exciting to have a wedding in the family,' ventured Mrs Evans, 'and I hope you will find Kate a help to you while she's here.'

Kate told her mother she was working at Hackforths to help out while Alex was in hospital. Sam was showing Mr Evans a book about Bladon. It seemed he was very interested in Winston Churchill and the Marlboroughs. So Sam lent him the book and said he would take him there the next time he came.

'Time we were going Mother. You've done us proud, Mrs Jefferson, and I think Sam and our Katy will get along nicely. It was a great pleasure meeting you Ma'am.' He was positively genial and effusive.

After they had gone Charlotte observed thoughtfully, 'I think we all passed muster and they seemed to enjoy themselves.'

'Why did he call you Ma'am Charlotte?'

'I expect he once knew an old lady who was titled or aristocratic.'

'He did,' Kate said, 'Lady Anders. She's dead now. Dad worked for her at one time.'

'Why didn't you stop him Charlotte?' Sam persisted.

'Why should I? It made him feel more at home and I enjoyed it. I'm sick of being called 'dear' and 'lovey' at Cherwell Close. So remember in the future you can call me Madam!'

CHAPTER 15

David opened the post as he and Jethro finished breakfast. There was the usual junk mail, the telephone bill and a large envelope with a local postmark addressed to Faith. He opened this first and was shocked when an airmail envelope addressed by Faith fell out. It was to Jennifer in Melbourne but had obviously never been posted. He felt very shaken looking at Faith's strong, clear, familiar hand writing. There was a covering letter in the large envelope from the local library explaining that 'the enclosed was found by a reader in one of our books and returned to us. We regret any inconvenience caused and felt we should return it to you immediately rather than post it to Australia.' There was no stamp on the envelope but Faith had written her name and address on the reverse side. David opened it with trembling hands and a folded newspaper cutting fell out of the letter inside.

Jethro watching him said, 'You all right mate? Who's rattled your cage?'

'Bit of a shock that's all. I could do with some more coffee.'

Jethro went to make it, wondering what the letter could be about. It couldn't be from the police as it looked like foreign air mail. He put the kettle on.

David read the letter which was dated the 8th June – the day before Faith died. At first he skimmed through it quickly and then read it slowly and carefully.

My dear Jennifer, 8th *June*

Many thanks for your letter and the enclosed photos. I can't get over how Angela has grown up. She's very like you were at that age. It's a good one of you and I really like your dress. Did you make it or don't you have time nowadays? Your new hair-do is trés chic and makes you look years younger. Shall have to think what I can do with mine. I still can't believe you've got two grand-children.

I wonder what sort of winter you're having. Our summer is rather cool and grey so far. The grey skies seem to sit on your head somehow and are depressing. They don't stop me painting though.

I'm still working at The Hospice Shop one morning a week and fill in when people are away and off sick. It's interesting and rewarding and well worthwhile as we want to open some more beds. Most people are incredibly generous and give us a wide range of items besides clothes – books, bric-a-brac, curtains, furniture, records, etc. I've bought a warm winter skirt for £4. It's a size 10 and I'm a 14 but there's plenty of material. I've taken off the tiny waistband and put on a new elasticated one. It's fully lined and hangs beautifully in unpressed pleats. It's black, white and grey with feint over-checks and a soft tweedy wool material. Should be ideal for winter - like wearing a blanket!

David is well and expecting promotion any day now. We've booked to go to Menorca for a fortnight in September. I can't wait! We haven't been abroad since our honeymoon and you know how long ago that is!!

Alex is getting on fine at Keele but finds the work hard. Another year go to after this and then his degree. I just hope the job situation will be better by then. He has a lively social life and is living off the campus now.

9th June – Sorry about the gap. It came on to rain and I had to rescue two lines of washing yesterday. Anyway, I'm glad I had to stop because the enclosed cutting was in this morning's paper. I've decided to go to the funeral. I don't know the deceased, never heard of him until today, but it's a tragic story isn't it? Makes you think too, he's the same age as us. He looks so kind and nice it seems so unfair when he had so much going for him. Anyway I've always wanted to see Blenheim Palace and Woodstock Church. I had a bet with myself about it concerning two bees in our conservatory. I was reviving them on sugar lumps and decided if they both recovered and flew off I'd go, if they didn't, I wouldn't. (One bee wouldn't do!!) They did! So I shall go next week. Crazy aren't I? Just like we used to be years ago. Daren't tell David as he'll think I've gone around the bend. I can get there and back between dropping him at the station and picking him up as usual in the evening. My only suit is black and white so I'll wear it for the funeral service and Blenheim. Very rarely give it an outing these days *as I don't often have a reason to dress up. I'm quite looking forward to a day out.*

Have started painting individual flowers, detailed coloured drawings really. I can work indoors when the weather's cold instead of freezing on the river bank. Must be getting old!

All for now. I'll send you some pics with my next letter. Take care meantime.

My love to you all, Faith x

David looked at the newspaper cutting. There was a photograph of Charles Jefferson and a long obituary account from The Telegraph.

His horror at the whole sorry mess sent his mind reeling.

'Oh my God. Forgive me Faith, please forgive me. Why did you have to do something so bizarre? Why, oh why?' He was speaking aloud, his head in his hands in an attitude of despair.

'Drink your coffee while it's hot. Looks as if you need it.' Jethro's tone was gentle.

David didn't even notice him, just drank the coffee automatically. The awful realisation dawned. So Faith did not even know Charles, they never met, and it was on a whim that she had gone to his funeral. She didn't even know that it was his boat she'd painted some years before – it was sheer coincidence. And now he couldn't apologise for thinking so badly of her, to try to explain. She was on the other side of silence.

He thought of all his actions and reactions, his nightmares and, worst of all, Alex's brush with death. What a god-damned mess he had created out of jealousy and vengeance. How could he ever face Alex and tell him about this letter? The one thing he knew for sure that he would have to and do it today. He craved for a drink. He knew it would not solve anything but yearned for that oblivion to take away his pain. He looked up to see Jethro looking thoughtfully at him.

'More coffee David?'

'Yes please. I need a drink badly. Help me Jethro.' David was sweating profusely.

Jethro poured him some coffee and hugged him tightly. 'Can you tell me what's happened?'

David passed the letters and cutting across the table and Jethro read them through. He asked David to tell him the whole story so that they could talk it over properly. David recounted the whole sorry business from the day Faith died until he opened the letter. By the end he felt drained but the craving had passed. He was beginning to have insight into both obsession and addiction and see how one became the excuse for the other.

Jethro grasped the opportunity to talk seriously with David about dependence and excuses. He was forthright, clear and helpful. 'You can make anything an excuse – my work is too difficult, my wife doesn't understand me, my children are delinquent or a butterfly kicked me on the head. They are all equally valid. But not one of those excuses ever really drove anyone to drink or drugs. It is our own inadequacy to cope with the situations which is the catalyst. Judgement is impaired and 'bingo' off we go down the slippery slope. Remember your shell fish allergy. It's the first mouthfuls that do it, nothing to do with the amount. You and me are more susceptible than some people, probably in our genes.'

'What can I do Jethro?' I feel lower than nothing.

'You can go to AA. I've checked out the local meetings in my directory and the nearest one tonight is Hereford. I shall come with you.

He handed David a list of days, times and places and contact telephone numbers.

'What a lot of meetings. Do people go to them much?'

'You can go to an AA meeting somewhere every day. I've been to them all over the place and always felt welcome. We only use first names and hold each other's confidences. You can ring AA contacts day or night.'

'I don't like the idea at all. It's not going to sort out this mess.'

'Most people don't until they've been. You'll find people very friendly and understanding and positive in their thinking.'

David felt very threatened and dubious but resolved that he would have a go.

Jethro went upstairs and came back with several leaflets for him to read and a card called 'Just for Today.'

David found the AA meeting strange but interesting. A small group of respectable looking men and women of mixed ages from varied backgrounds. Most of them knew one another well but he and Jethro were made very welcome. The air in the room was thick and unpleasant as many of them smoked incessantly. They chatted over cups of tea and coffee until 7.30 when the meeting started. It opened with a sort of prayer of welcome.

The man who took the meeting was about sixty and called Harold. He went round the group, sitting in a semi-circle, asking members to tell their story. Each one started with 'My name is so and so and I am an alcoholic.' David didn't like this idea at all. Some of the stories were horrific and others incoherent and dull. Jethro's was mind boggling. David couldn't believe that this young fellow whom he'd come to know so well had been a thief, a burglar and in prison for acts of violence. No one in the group looked particularly surprised, they were evidently used to colourful stories. Harold said, 'Thank you for sharing that with us Jethro. Good to have you with us tonight.'

It was David's turn next and he turned pleading eyes towards Jethro hoping he'd protect him. He just smiled encouragingly. David took a deep breath and said 'I am David and I suppose I must be an alcoholic. This is my first meeting and I would like to just listen rather than speak this time please.'

'Well done David, in your own time. But if you feel like sharing later on please do.' He passed on to Gerald who was a doctor with a horrendous story recounted calmly.

They drank many cups of tea and the smoky haze grew thicker. David noticed that two of the group smelled of drink and were rather maudlin and full of self pity. He asked Jethro about this on the way home.

'We make everyone welcome and although we don't want to encourage active drinkers to dominate meetings we must try to help them. The message may get through in their more sober moments. It can be a salutary reminder to those of us who are sober to see how dishonest alcoholics are with themselves as well as other people. We are all in different states of recovery. Harold hasn't had a drink for eleven years.'

'Why does he keep coming then?'

'Because he is truly working the programme and gives hope to those who are struggling at the same time.'

'I was surprised that doctor had the nerve to come. Risky for his professional life.'

'Not half as risky as staying on the drink merry-go-round. Remember what Harold said about trust. All the confidences remain in that meeting room and are not to be discussed with anyone else. It is essential to be able to trust one another.'

'You've had quite a criminal career. I'm glad I didn't know some of it when you first came, I'd never have dared go to sleep at nights.'

'I've never set fire to anyone. I could never be as much of a problem to you as you have been to yourself David. What did you think of the meeting?'

'I don't know. Some nice people there and intelligent too. They wouldn't keep on going if there was nothing to it. I hate the idea of talking about myself and my family, it seems so disloyal somehow. It was embarrassing at first. I was surprised none of them looked like alcoholics.'

'What about the spiritual side?'

'Not too struck on that either in company, but I find I'm thinking along those lines more since the fire.'

'How long do you want me to stay? Now that you've dried out and have started on AA, it may be time for me to move on.'

'Oh dear, I've got quite used to you being around and don't fancy being on my own again.'

'Well I can't stay much longer and you've got to learn to be responsible for your own sobriety. Do you want me to see you through Christmas and New Year?'

'Yes, if you would. I'm dreading Christmas. Faith used to make it lovely and Alex always came home. Don't know how I'm going to face it this year.'

'Just take one day at a time. We could see if the Sally Army or old people's home need helpers. What about the place where your Mum lives? I bet she'd like to have you there or we could have her at home for a change?'

'I'll have to think about it Jethro. Can I take it that you will definitely be here until the New Year?'

'OK mate if it'll help. Probably help me through it too.'

David hadn't thought about that, too preoccupied with himself. He resolved to buy Jethro a good Christmas present.

David took Faith's letter to the hospital. Alex was sitting in a chair wearing a loose sort of cotton dressing gown watching television. He looked better apart from the drawn expression round his eyes. They moved into a quiet area away from other patients. Once David ascertained Alex was on a good day he explained about the letter and showed it to him. He was startled and upset to see Faith's writing but collected himself and read the letter and the cutting slowly. Then he read the letter again.

'Did you let Jennifer know about Mum's death?'

'Yes I did. You can imagine how dreadful I feel reading the innocent contents of Mum's letter.'

'I can't understand why you had all those crazy ideas in the first place. Can only think it was the booze affecting your brain.'

'I can't understand it now either but it was terribly real at the time. I was tormented by nightmares Alex. You will be pleased to know I've been to my first AA meeting and shall go to another tonight.'

'How did it go? You certainly look better since Jethro took you over. The whites of your eyes were all bloodshot when you drank and you've stopped shaking.'

'I didn't notice.'

'No you wouldn't. Well I'm glad. Keep it up Dad. Rachel's been to see the consultant and he says I can go to 'Oriel' for a fortnight at Christmas all being well.'

'You'll need looking after son.'

'Rachel has volunteered for the job.'

'That's good, she's an intelligent girl, attractive like her mother.'

'She comes every day and doesn't get fazed by any of the awful sights here.'

'Alex, will you ever be able to forgive me for what I've done to you and your mother's memory?'

'I told you Dad I do forgive you for me. It's entirely up to you how you square it with Mum. Only you can do that. You'll think of a way.'

'I shall do everything in my power Alex, I promise you.' David couldn't think how though.

'It's not long until Christmas. What are you and Jethro doing? I expect you could come to Woodstock for Christmas dinner. Shall I ask Rachel?'

'No, don't do that. Jethro has suggested we make ourselves useful somewhere. Perhaps at the home where Gran lives if they want some help.'

'Does she know about me?'

'No, she gets very confused these days and I didn't think it fair to upset her.'

'Good. Poor Gran. She's so lonely without Mum and me.'

That settled David. He would spend Christmas with his mother however much he hated the place.

'By the way, Alex, Tabitha has moved back in.'

'Good. I think she was frightened of you when you were out of your tree. The Evans' have been over to 'Oriel'. Can't imagine old man Evans there, can you? Seems he went down quite well, especially with Charlotte!'

'I'm glad for Kate's sake. She's had such trouble with her parents. Not that I can talk or point fingers of course,' David added wryly and ran his hand through his hair. 'Is there anything you're needing? I shall be in again soon.'

'I want some Christmas presents but shall have to make a list. Will you get them for me?'

'Yes. If I get in a mess Jethro will help me choose things.'

'I can't afford much but I thought some talc or soap for Kate and Elizabeth. Special tea for Charlotte. A book for Sam and I can't think what for Rachel. Jethro might find some earrings or a bracelet that Rachel would like. He knows the sort of thing.'

'Hang on a minute and I'll make a note of these. The time soon goes.' David wrote out a list in a notebook. 'What was it for Charlotte?'

'Earl Grey tea or Orange Pekoe or something like that.'

'I hate that smoked water sort of tea,' David said.

'So do I, but Elizabeth and Charlotte like it.'

'What about something for the nurses? Shall I get a nice big box of biscuits?'

'Good idea. There are so many of them.'

'I'll get wrapping paper and then I'll help you wrap them up here.'

'Thank's Dad. My left hand's pretty useless.'

David could have cried at the matter of fact way he said it.

'I'll get Gran a bottle of port from both of us.' Their eyes met, Alex not thinking this such a good idea. 'I've got to learn to go into a wine shop without lapsing haven't I?'

'Of course. Good idea.'

'See you tomorrow or the day after Alex. Keep up the good progress.'

'And you Dad. Cheers.'

David decided to take some flowers to Faith's grave before Christmas. He had only been there once since the headstone was erected. There was nothing flowering in the garden apart from the yellow winter jasmine growing against a sheltered wall. David cut several sprigs and wondered what to buy to go with it. He went to the florist and looked at the limited choice of flowers that would stand up to the biting east wind and night frosts. The assistants were busy making up Christmas wreaths and there were pots full of brilliant poinsettias, cyclamen and orange trees. One of them came over to help him and suggested spray chyrsanthemums and carnations in yellow and white would go with his jasmine.

The wind whistled round in the cemetery but David hardly noticed it. He filled the flower container with water and cut the flowers short to withstand the icy blast. The gold and white flowers looked fragile and beautiful and gave a lift to the dark, stark stone. Faith would have loved them he thought. As he tidied round the grave, pulling up weeds and clearing dead leaves he saw an insect crawling about on one of the flowers. He flicked it off with his fingers but it didn't go, it clung to the back of his right hand. He looked closely. It looked like a bee but how was that possible in December? It hardly moved and seemed half asleep but it was alive.

David wished Faith could see it, she loved bees. How could a bee be around on the shortest day of the year? His neck went all prickly, could Faith have sent him a message, a sign of forgiveness, an emissary in the form of a bee?

He knew no one could believe him, they would think he'd been at the whisky again. He didn't need to tell anyone except, perhaps, Alex one day. He was filled with a sense of well being and peace. Faith, dear Faith, had sent him a message from the other side of silence. It was bees that killed Charles, two bees that sent Faith to Woodstock and a phantom-like Christmas bee that crept from her grave to free him from a life of guilt. The bee's inert form fell to the ground, its successful mission completed.

David felt elated and humbled simultaneously. As he turned up his collar to walk home he put his mind to thoughts of Christmas presents. As he passed one of the craft shops he saw two of Faith's riverscapes in the window. He went inside and asked if they had any more paintings by Faith Green. A surge of pride rushed through him as he asked. They had five altogether, the other three were not framed.

'How much are they?' he asked.

'The framed pair are £25 each and the mounted scenes £12.'

David thought quickly and decided to buy them all.

'How quickly could you get the other three framed?'

'Not until after Christmas. It's a very busy time. I do them myself.'

'If I tell you how very important it might be for my son's recovery to have his late mother's paintings for his Christmas present . . . I'm prepared to pay more.'

The young man's expression changed and he put his hand comfortingly on David's arm. 'I've just realised you are Alex's father. Say no more. I'll do them tonight, no sweat. You come in tomorrow Mr Green and I'll have them ready for you.'

'I'll take the two now. How much shall I owe you altogether?'

'We'll sort that out tomorrow, no problem. By all means take the framed pair now.' He wrote something in a book and placed the pictures in plastic bubble wrap before tying them up in brown paper.

David was thrilled. He couldn't think of anything that would please Alex more. He was so ashamed of his destruction of Faith's work and so thankful to find a small way of atoning for it. He decided to keep two paintings for himself.

When he arrived home he went straight to a drawer in the bureau where he'd put Faith's sketch book and loose paintings after he'd sorted out her things. They were mostly drawings and pastels of flowers and on each one there was a bee. He examined the two paintings he'd just bought from the shop and on each one he found a tiny bee.

David ran his fingers through his thick hair as he thought about the bee factor. The events of the last seven months had been caused by bees and now, it seemed, also resolved by them. He knew the connection between bees and the soul was once generally maintained and hence Mohammed admits bees to Paradise. He wondered how God felt about bees. He wondered, too, how it was that he had spent years surrounded by paintings that he had seen but never looked at with interest.

It was time to celebrate this discovery and he put the kettle on. Jethro would be back soon and they planned to decorate their Christmas tree this afternoon. He hummed to himself contentedly.

ABOUT THE AUTHOR

This is Ann Hulme's first novel after many years of writing poetry, radio scripts and commissioned articles and features. She has written personal diaries since the age of six.